Sharon hated his guts,

Fergus suspected. So much so that she hadn't even asked for him at first when she was arrested for murder.

When she found out they would be joined at the hip for the duration of her trial, she'd be outraged. It could only lead to more heartbreak. And Fergus had had about all that he could stand.

Sharon would never forgive him for what she saw as his betrayal while they were married. So the kindest thing he could do for her now would be to stay out of her personal life. To protect her from the murder charge—and from himself.

He just hoped to God he was strong enough to resist his overpowering need to hold her.

To cherish her.

And to plead with her for a second chance....

Dear Reader,

Welcome to Silhouette **Special Edition**...welcome to romance. This month of May promises to be one of our best yet!

We begin with this month's THAT SPECIAL WOMAN! title, *A Man for Mom,* by Gina Ferris Wilkins. We're delighted that Gina will be writing under her real name, Gina Wilkins, from now on. And what a way to celebrate— with the first book in her new series, THE FAMILY WAY! Don't miss this emotional, poignant story of family connections and discovery of true love. Also coming your way in May is Andrea Edwards's third book of her series, **This Time Forever.** In *A Secret and a Bridal Pledge* two people afraid of taking chances risk it all for everlasting love.

An orphaned young woman discovers herself, and the love of a lifetime, in Tracy Sinclair's latest, *Does Anybody Know Who Allison Is?* For heart-pounding tension, look no further than Phyllis Halldorson's newest story about a husband and wife whose feelings show them they're still *Truly Married.* In *A Stranger in the Family* by Patricia McLinn, unexpected romance awaits a man who discovers that he's a single father. And rounding out the month is the debut title from new author Caroline Peak, *A Perfect Surprise.*

I hope you enjoy all these wonderful stories from Silhouette **Special Edition,** and have a wonderful month!

Sincerely,

Tara Gavin
Senior Editor

Please address questions and book requests to:
Silhouette Reader Service
U.S.: 3010 Walden Ave., P.O. Box 1325, Buffalo, NY 14269
Canadian: P.O. Box 609, Fort Erie, Ont. L2A 5X3

PHYLLIS
HALLDORSON
TRULY MARRIED

Published by Silhouette Books
America's Publisher of Contemporary Romance

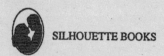 SILHOUETTE BOOKS

ISBN 0-373-09958-4

TRULY MARRIED

Books by Phyllis Halldorson

PHYLLIS HALLDORSON

at age sixteen, met her real-life Prince Charming. She married him a year later, and they settled down to raise a family. A compulsive reader, Phyllis dreamed of someday finding the time to write stories of her own. That time came when her two youngest children reached adolescence. When she was introduced to romance novels, she knew she had found her long-delayed vocation. After all, how could she write anything else after living all those years with her very own Silhouette hero?

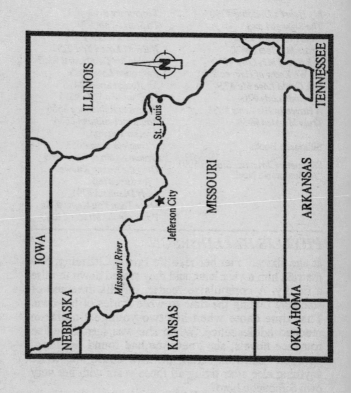

Chapter One

Sharon Lachlan shivered and pulled her quilted parka snugly around her as she huddled behind the steering wheel of her new red Corvette. The car had been a present from her husband, Fergus, on the occasion of her twenty-third birthday last August.

Was it a gift of love? Or of guilt?

She shook her head as though to dislodge the unwelcome but persistent suspicion that had nagged at her since morning, when she'd received the third anonymous note.

Although it was only a little past six on this cold November evening, the darkness was total, broken by neither moon nor stars in the heavy cloud-covered sky. The only illumination came from an insufficient number of street lamps and the light that spilled out the windows of the neat older homes nestled behind rows of huge elm trees lining the curbs of this staid middle-class neighborhood on the outskirts of Chicago.

She was thankful for the dark. It sheltered both her and her car from the prying glances of passersby. Or, more precisely, from Fergus Lachlan, who most certainly would recognize her.

Sharon shivered again and rubbed her arms with her gloved hands. The waiting seemed interminable. Dare she start the engine so she could turn on the heater?

If she did it would call attention to the fact that the car was parked at the curb, occupied.

She decided against it, and focused on the second house up the street from her. No lights brightened its windows, but surely its occupant, Ms. Elaine Odbert, attorney-at-law, would arrive home soon. That is, if the note Sharon had received in the mail this morning could be believed.

But why should she believe it, any more than she'd believed the other two she'd received earlier?

In spite of her resolution not to dwell on them, her mind dredged up the first one as clearly as if she had it in front of her. It had arrived at the apartment on a sunny Tuesday in mid-September. She remembered the day because she was leaving the building to go to the hospital where she did volunteer work every Tuesday afternoon.

As she'd passed the bank of mailboxes she'd stopped to check theirs, and found it filled with envelopes. As usual, most of them had been bills, pleas for money from various charities and advertisements, but as she'd sorted through them one had caught her eye because it was different. A plain white envelope addressed to Mrs. Fergus Lachlan, but with no return address.

Curious, she'd ripped it open and found a folded piece of typing paper. There was no greeting, closure, or signature, and the one line message was typed in capitals. "YOU'D BETTER CHECK OUT THE RELATIONSHIP BETWEEN YOUR HUSBAND AND ELAINE ODBERT."

Sharon had been more startled than shaken. Fergus and another woman? Impossible! No! Fergus loved her, and she adored him. Of course, their marriage had had its ups and downs. Fergus acted more like a father than a husband toward her. He tended to be bossy and overprotective, and she often got fed up and overreacted. She knew she should do a better job of controlling her temper, but she was just getting her wings, so to speak, as an independent woman and his habit of making decisions without consulting her was maddening.

Sharon knew that Elaine Odbert was the newest member of Newberry, Everingham and Jessup, the law firm where Fergus was making a name for himself as a rising young defense attorney. She'd even greeted Ms. Odbert a couple of times when she'd gone to the office to meet Fergus for lunch. The woman was thirtysomething and nice looking but not the seductive type.

Sharon had torn up the offending missive and scattered it in the nearest trash can as she'd walked out the door. She wasn't going to upset him with that kind of garbage. She couldn't deny that she and Fergus quarreled a lot, but the making up was sheer ecstasy.

Now her reverie was broken by headlights coming slowly down the street toward her, and she snapped to attention. Maybe this was Elaine. In spite of her determination to give no credence to those poison-pen notes her stomach muscles knotted. Damn! So much for her faith in her husband.

She should have destroyed the third note the same as she had the other two and ignored it, but her self-confidence in her own judgment, and even her trust in Fergus's integrity, had been whittled away by the repeated insinuations. If she ever got her hands on the creep who wrote them she'd throttle him.

Somehow she always thought of the troublemaker as a man. Someone who worked at the firm and was jealous of Fergus's success. A rival hoping to extract a petty revenge for being left behind in the competitive climb to the top.

Sharon drew a deep breath as the headlights neared Elaine's driveway, then let it out as the car drove on past and turned in at a house at the other end of the block.

Her relief was maddening. She should have been disappointed that it wasn't Elaine coming home unaccompanied so that Sharon could prove to herself that her husband wasn't carrying on with the woman.

A rush of self-disgust nearly overwhelmed her. She shouldn't have to prove that Fergus was an honorable man. She'd never doubted it until those insidious notes kept coming.

The second one had arrived in October. If it had been packaged the same way as the first had been she probably would have burned it unopened, but this one came in a beige square envelope postmarked from Oak Park, Illinois, the suburb of Chicago where Sharon had been born and raised.

Although her parents were dead, and she had no brothers or sisters, she still had friends there. She'd assumed the envelope was from one of them.

It hadn't been. Inside she'd found a note card with a reproduction of a Homer Winslow painting on the front and a message again typed in capitals.

She couldn't remember exactly how it was worded, but it had been one paragraph informing her that because she'd ignored the first note, her husband and Ms. Odbert were now lovers.

Sharon had fought off a chill of foreboding. Why was someone tormenting her this way? Could there possibly be any truth in these vicious missives? No, she couldn't, wouldn't believe that! She'd set a match to it in the fireplace and watched it burn, but the feeling of apprehension continued.

She would have told Fergus about it, but he was in Washington that week pleading a case before the Supreme Court and she hadn't wanted to discuss it on the phone. By the time he'd arrived back home she'd calmed down and realized that by destroying both notes she had no evidence to back up her story.

Not that he wouldn't have taken her word for it, but she couldn't bring herself to confront him. She'd tried to deny the doubts that made her so cowardly, but finally decided to wait and see if the writer would continue his insidious campaign before she took any action.

Still, the nagging doubts had persisted, and she'd found herself questioning Fergus when he would call to say he would be working late, or when he had to go into the office on a weekend.

But she'd taken herself firmly in hand after she'd picked up the phone one Sunday afternoon and actually dialed his office number to see if he'd answer. Fortunately she'd caught herself in time and slammed the phone down before it rang at the other end.

She'd been ashamed for letting an anonymous tipster cause her to doubt her husband, and had firmly put it out of her mind.

Sharon shifted uncomfortably. It was really cold now. She could see her breath, and it was clouding up the windshield. She was either going to have to roll down the window or turn on the heater so she could see out.

It was really no contest. No way was she going to open the window and let the cold wind off the lake blow in on her.

She turned on the engine and the heater and again settled back to wait. This was getting more ridiculous by the minute. If something didn't happen in the next quarter hour she was going home. That's where she should have stayed in the first place!

The third note had been delivered by messenger just a few hours ago. It was encased in a white business envelope, an exact duplicate of the first one she'd received. Obviously the sender had been confident that he'd planted enough suspicion in her mind to assure her opening it even though she knew it was more of the same vicious lie. She'd played right into his hand.

Reaching for her purse on the seat beside her she rummaged through it in the dark until she came up with the envelope and a penlight she always carried. Quickly extracting the piece of typing paper, she unfolded it and reread the typed message by the dim light of the tiny flashlight.

I TRIED TO HELP YOU, BUT YOU IGNORED MY WARNINGS. NOW YOU'RE GOING TO PAY FOR YOUR ARROGANCE. ELAINE ODBERT AND FERGUS LACHLAN HAVE RESIGNED FROM THE FIRM AND ARE MAKING PLANS TO ELOPE THIS EVENING. IF YOU WANT TO SAY GOODBYE TO YOUR HUSBAND YOU'D BETTER BE AT THE ODBERT HOME WHEN ELAINE AND FERGUS RETURN THERE FROM WORK. SURELY YOU AREN'T GOING TO HIDE YOUR HEAD IN THE SAND AND LET THAT BASTARD TREAT YOU SO SHABBILY. THE ADDRESS IS—

Sharon didn't have to reread the address. It was branded into her brain.

The writer had assumed right. The earlier warnings had planted the malignant seed of doubt in her mind, and by the time the last one arrived she'd been compelled to read it.

Neither could she blithely discount this letter as she had the others, though God knows she'd tried. She'd told herself that Fergus would never be unfaithful to her. He loved her, but even if he hadn't he was too moral a man to take a mistress when he had a wife.

But that line of thinking led her into a truth she'd preferred not to face. The inescapable fact that she had been the aggressor in their courtship, and in their decision to marry.

She'd seduced him, although he hadn't put up much of a fight. He had been upset, though, when he discovered, too late to stop, that she was a virgin.

She'd been raised with moral standards, too, but she'd fallen in love with Fergus Lachlan, brilliant young attorney, the first day she'd met him. He'd also been attracted to her then. He'd told her as much.

Had she trapped him into a marriage he hadn't really wanted because he felt guilty about taking a nineteen-year-old girl's virginity?

No! She couldn't believe that. Although he was ten years older and possibly thought he should have exerted more control, she was the one who'd come on to him, and she hadn't told him ahead of time that it would be her first sexual experience.

If there was blame it was hers, but what could be so wrong about two consenting adults making love?

Besides, in the three years they'd been married he'd never indicated that he was really unhappy. Oh sure, they quarreled a lot, but it was only because she objected to him taking charge of her life and not giving her space to grow and make her own decisions, or mistakes if that was the case. And there'd always been those passionate reunions when they'd both said they were sorry just before they rocketed to the stars.

Most of the time they were still lovers in every sense of the word. They laughed together, played together, sometimes even cried together, and in bed they were sheer magic.

Another set of headlights appeared at the far end of the street in front of her, and this time the front of the garage at the house she was watching lit up and the door opened as the car swung into the driveway. Although she was too far away to identify the driver, Sharon could see that it was a woman and she was alone before the vehicle glided into the garage and the door closed behind it.

This time the relief Sharon felt was joyously welcome. She sank back against the seat and let out the breath she'd been holding. The self-appointed informant had been wrong! Fergus wasn't with Ms. Odbert. He really did have to work late as he'd told Sharon on the phone when he'd called her earlier in the day.

It was that message from him, seeming to confirm the letter's evil accusation, that had toppled her off the fence she'd been straddling and frightened her into checking up on him. *How could she have had so little faith in a man she loved as much as she loved her husband?*

The lights went on in the Odbert house, and Sharon couldn't wait to get away from there. Although she doubted that she could bring herself to tell Fergus about this episode, she could try to make up for it by being especially loving when he did get home.

She looked down to shift into Drive, but when she raised her head again there was another set of headlights coming toward her. A shudder of apprehension ran through her as the car swung into Elaine's driveway and the sensor light came on, illuminating the satiny black BMW.

Fergus's car!

As she watched, frozen with shock, the door opened and her husband stepped out. Possibly she could have been mistaken about the car, but even if he hadn't been wearing the same tan Burberry overcoat he'd worn to work that morning she'd recognize his collar-length brown hair, and his tall, loose-jointed frame anywhere. He was as much a part of her as her own image.

Quickly he closed the door and strode around the car and across the front of the house to the porch, where another sensor light came on, illuminating that area. Within seconds the door opened and he stepped inside and closed it behind him.

Sharon was stunned, unable either to move or to cry out her anguished disbelief. This couldn't be happening! It was all a nightmare, and she'd wake up any moment.

But she didn't, and as the minutes ticked by she knew this was no dream. She wasn't going to wake up warm and safe in their luxurious king-size bed with Fergus's long, lean, hard-muscled body wrapped around her, spoon fashion, his hands cupping her breasts even as he slept.

So what was she going to do now? Was she going to condemn her husband just because he'd followed a fellow lawyer home from work? That didn't mean he was going to run away with her. There could be any number of innocent reasons why he would do that. Couldn't there?

She could at least give him the benefit of the doubt.

Quickly she turned off the engine, opened the door and got out. She'd go up to the house and confront them, tell them about the anonymous notes, confess that she was spying on him and lay this thing to rest for good. They'd probably insist on taking legal action against the slimy creature who sent libelous letters through the mail if they could find out who it was.

Slamming the door behind her, she hunched her shoulders against the cold wind that buffeted her and blew her long medium-brown hair across her face. She'd forgotten to wear one of her wool knit tams that would have kept her head warm and her hair from blowing.

As she walked across the lawn the porch light came on again, and she felt somehow exposed, as if she had no business being there. Which was probably true, but now that she'd succumbed to the doubts raised by the notes she had to see her course of action through.

At the door she was looking for the doorbell, when she noticed that the metal blinds on the big window to her right were open. Not fully, yet slanted enough so that she could see in but anyone inside probably wouldn't see her.

Even as her conscience screamed protests she moved toward the glass. She couldn't stop herself. Although she knew she could be seen peeping by anyone passing by, she had to know what was going on between her husband and that woman in what they thought was the total privacy of Elaine's living room.

The sheer white curtains covering the blinds from the inside obscured her vision slightly, but she could see the whole room. It was tastefully decorated and furnished and looked warm and comfortable, making Sharon aware that she was shivering outside in the cold.

The room was unoccupied, and she was wondering where Elaine and Fergus were, when Elaine walked through the open archway at one end. She was dressed in a dark-gray suit and a white tailored blouse. A Gucci purse swung from her shoulder, and she carried a brown leather suitcase in one hand and a large matching cosmetic kit in the other.

Sharon gasped, then stared in horror, as Fergus came in behind Elaine, carrying two large Pullman cases!

Dear God, they really were going away together.

Dazed, she watched as they stacked the luggage on the floor next to the end of the sofa, then straightened and turned to face each other. Fergus had his back to the window, but Sharon could see Elaine's upturned face clearly.

It wasn't a beautiful face. The nose was too large, the lips too thin, and the hazel eyes were set a little too close together, but even through metal blinds and a curtain Sharon could see the love that radiated from Elaine's plain features and made her glow when she looked up at Fergus.

Sharon hunched forward and hugged her arms around her waist, trying to deflect the awful pain as Fergus reached out and took the other woman in a lover's embrace. He lowered his head and covered her mouth with his own in a long, passionate kiss.

Sharon's vision blurred, and for a moment she felt lightheaded and dizzy. She clutched at the window casing to steady herself as the tears that had welled in her eyes spilled down her cheeks and were replaced by more in a continuous cycle over which she had no control.

It was like trying to see through a waterfall. The image shimmered surrealistically, and she couldn't discern details. Still, there was no doubt but that she was watching a man and woman making love, even though they weren't having sex.

In those few minutes she discovered that it was possible for the human heart to break.

Her breath came in tearing gasps, and the pain in her chest was almost unbearable as she wrenched her gaze away from the two entwined figures and stumbled the few steps back to the door. In her crazed state she couldn't think, she could only react, and she had to be sure that what she'd just seen was real and not a hallucination.

This time her finger found the doorbell, and she pushed the button and held it in until the door was pulled open and Elaine Odbert stood facing her.

Elaine's lips were slightly smeared and swollen from Fergus's kisses, and her once neatly styled blond hair was disheveled. She blinked in confusion as her gaze fell on Sharon, but before she could speak Sharon did.

"I'm Sharon Lachlan," she said in a voice too raspy to be her own, "and I want to see my husband."

Before the other woman could speak or move Sharon pushed past her and entered a foyer. At first she thought she was looking at a picture on the wall directly in front of her. A distorted portrait of a woman in torment, her hair windblown and wild, her face white and ravaged with tears and the features twisted in a grimace of anguish.

But it was the eyes that startled her most. They were wide open, the blue irises dark and distended, and the torment that looked out of them was frantic in its intensity.

It was only then that she realized it wasn't a picture she was gazing at but a mirror, and it was her own tempestuous image that she saw.

The shock was like a slap in the face, but it brought her back to her senses. Mindless hysteria would get her nowhere. She had to pull herself together. If need be, she could fall apart later, alone and in private.

She swiped at her eyes and face with the back of her hand as Fergus's voice broke the electrifying silence.

"Elaine, who is it? Is anything wrong?"

Sharon swung around to look at him as he came through the archway from the living room. He stopped in midstride and stared at her as astonishment replaced the inquisitiveness in his expression.

The blood drained from his face. "Sharon!" It was a cry of surprise and...fear? "Dear God, what's the matter? Have you been mugged? Why are you here?"

He started forward, his arms reaching out to her, but she stepped back and put up her hand. "No!" It was almost a shout, and she made an effort to lower her voice. "Don't touch me. I've been watching you through the window."

He gasped, but she hurried on. "I haven't been mugged— I've been violated. Betrayed in a most intimate and degrading way by my own husband."

Fergus's face went even whiter, and the agony that crept into his eyes as understanding dawned almost made her forget her own.

"Oh dear Lord," he moaned, as he sagged against the wall.

She'd momentarily forgotten that Elaine was there, as well. Although it seemed to Sharon that the events since she'd forced her way into the foyer had been acted out in slow motion, actually everything had happened so quickly that Elaine was just now recovering her composure.

She looked from Sharon to Fergus and straightened her shoulders. "We'd better go into the living room, where we can talk," she said firmly. "You're welcome to stay as long as you want to, but I'll have to leave in twenty minutes. I have a plane to catch."

She had a plane to catch? Didn't she mean *they?*

Elaine led the way into the other room and Sharon and Fergus followed. "Please sit down," she invited, and settled herself in a chair, then turned to look at Sharon. "I'm sure you have things to say to me, too." Her voice quivered, betraying her emotional upheaval.

Sharon's knees were trembling so, she practically fell into the nearest chair, but Fergus remained standing.

Now that Sharon had confronted them her mind went blank. She hadn't considered how she'd handle the situation because she'd been so sure there was no situation to handle. Had it all been wishful thinking? Her way of hiding from an unbearable truth?

As Sharon floundered Fergus spoke. "How did you know I was here, Sharon?" His voice was tight with strain.

Wordlessly she opened her purse, pulled out the envelope and handed it to him.

His eyes widened with shock as his gaze flew over the message. "Where did you get this?"

"It was delivered by messenger earlier today," she answered in little more than a whisper.

"And what's this reference to trying to help you and having the warnings ignored?" he asked grimly as he handed the note to Elaine.

Sharon didn't answer immediately, but watched while Elaine's face turned red as her mind absorbed the message she was reading. Then Sharon took a deep breath and told them about the other two malicious notes she'd received previously.

"Why in hell didn't you tell me?" Fergus raged.

"Because I didn't for a minute believe them." Her lips trembled and her teeth worried the lower one. "I only investigated this one because I wanted to prove him wrong."

Fergus's eyebrows lifted. "'Him?'"

She shrugged. "I always think of the writer as 'him,' but it could as easily be a woman."

Again the scalding tears poured down her cheeks. "I was so sure that you loved me, that you'd never be unfaithful—"

A shuddering sob shook her, and she dropped her face in her hands.

Fergus groaned and walked over to her chair, but again she cringed from him and he stopped short of touching her.

"Sharon, I do love you," he said raggedly, "and I haven't been unfaithful to you."

His words tore at her like a knife in her chest, and she sprang out of the chair. "Dammit, Fergus, don't lie to me," she yelled. "Not any more than you already have. Don't forget, I saw you and Elaine making love just minutes ago."

"We weren't making love—we were just kissing," he insisted.

The anger that had been curiously missing in the myriad of emotions she'd been feeling finally surfaced, and she whirled around to face him. "Don't play word games with me." Her tone was low and grating. "I'm not stupid, and I belatedly lost my innocence when I saw you take that woman in your arms. You weren't just kissing—you were making love, and don't deny it."

Fergus clenched the back of the chair she'd just vacated, as if trying to steady himself. Elaine hadn't moved, nor did she speak, but her expression mirrored both guilt and despair.

"Sharon, you must believe me," he pleaded. "No matter how it looked to you, Elaine and I have not committed adultery."

Sharon's eyes widened with disbelief, and the only thing she could think of to say was "Why?"

Elaine gasped, but Fergus seemed to understand what she was asking. "Because I'm married to you. I love you, and I couldn't betray you in that way."

The pain of knowing he thought she was simpleminded enough to believe his lies was almost more than she could bear. "I told you not to lie to me," she said angrily. "How can you say you love me, when you and Elaine have resigned from the firm and are running away together tonight?"

She swallowed a sob that tore at her throat. "Why haven't you been honest with me? Why didn't you come to me and tell me you wanted out of our marriage? I'd have given you a quiet divorce if you really wanted it. You didn't have to scheme to run off in the middle of the night with another woman and make me an object of pity and gossip."

A spasm of pain twisted Fergus's face as he ignored her wish not to be touched and clasped her by the shoulders. "Honey, I know this is going to be hard to believe after the notes you've received and what you've seen here, but whoever wrote those letters has only given you half-truths and vicious speculations. I haven't resigned from the firm, and I'm not going anywhere, but Elaine has accepted a position in a law office in California and is flying out there tonight."

He sighed and released her. "I . . . I admit that there is an . . . an attraction between Elaine and me, but neither of us wants to break up my marriage. I've always loved you, Sharon, and I didn't take our marriage vows lightly. I don't want a divorce. The kiss you saw was one of goodbye, not a prelude to making love."

He turned away from her and put a few steps between them. "I was going to take Elaine to the airport and then go home to you. I'm sorry that we were indiscreet enough that someone picked up on the attraction and used it to poison your mind with their venom."

Even in her numbing grief, Sharon realized that she should be relieved. Fergus really didn't want a divorce.

So he'd gotten involved with another woman. Well, that happened a lot in marriages. He was sending the other woman away, and Sharon tended to believe him when he said they hadn't had sex. She'd never known him to be anything but honorable in his dealings with people.

Surely that meant he loved her more than he loved Elaine. Or did it?

Sharon fought against her doubts, but couldn't put them to rest. As he said, she was his wife, and he took the vows of marriage seriously. It would be just like him to abide by them, even if it meant giving up the woman he really wanted.

With great effort she resisted the urge to break down and sob, to do whatever it took to bind him to her. Instead she again dried her wet face with her hands and pulled in a deep breath to choke back the sobs that shook her.

When she had herself under reasonable control she turned to Elaine, whose cheeks were also wet with tears. "Don't you have something to say about this?"

Elaine looked Sharon straight in the eye without flinching. "Nothing except to assure you that Fergus has told the truth. We haven't been intimate, although I've let him know that I'd be willing, and I've always known that he'd never divorce you."

She was being searingly honest, and Sharon almost felt sorry for her. This triangle had the elements of a Greek tragedy. It could ruin all three of their lives.

Still holding Elaine's gaze, Sharon asked, "Are you in love with him?"

The woman didn't even blink. "Yes."

Sharon winced, then turned to face Fergus. He appeared so tormented, as if he'd been caught in a nightmare and couldn't wake up.

Her whole being cried out to her to let well enough alone. To accept the situation and let Fergus and Elaine play it out as they'd planned. Sharon would keep her husband, and the other woman would be gone for good. They could all get on with their lives and pretend that none of this had ever happened.

But could they? She wouldn't know unless she asked Fergus the same question she'd asked Elaine, and she wasn't sure she had the courage to do that.

She closed her eyes for a brief moment, then opened them and put her future on the line.

"Fergus, are you in love with Elaine?"

He opened his mouth to answer, but she hurried on. "I've always thought of you as an honorable man, and now I'm appealing to that honor. I don't want to hear about your duty to me. All I want is the truth. Please. You owe me that much."

He closed his mouth and shook his head. "Sharon, I... You don't understand...."

"The truth, Fergus." She sounded like an attorney cross-examining a witness, but she had to know.

His gaze searched hers, and he must have seen how important this was to her. Slowly he looked from Sharon to Elaine, then back again. "Elaine and I have a close relationship. I care deeply for her, but you're my wife—"

In spite of the scalding anguish his words caused, Sharon felt a calm dignity as she let out the breath she'd been holding. "That's not good enough. I'm selfish. I want all or nothing."

Her voice broke, and she took a deep breath. "There won't be any need for Elaine to go to California. I'm sorry, but I can't live with you knowing you're not totally committed to me. I'll file for divorce in the morning."

She held her head high and managed to walk steadily across the room and out of the house even though she was blinded by tears of grief.

Chapter Two

Five years later

Spring was late arriving this year in St. Louis, Missouri, after a long, cold winter. Sharon had about given up on it, when, almost overnight, it blazoned across the land in a riot of color and bright warming sunshine. Red tulips, yellow daffodils, purple pansies, and peonies in a variety of hues turned the drab landscape into the glory of new life once more affirmed.

New life reaffirmed. The phrase caught Sharon's fancy, and she turned it over in her mind and examined it as she stood gazing out the window of the staff conference room on the fifteenth floor of the luxurious Starlight St. Louis Hotel. The view overlooked rambling Jefferson Barracks Park along the Mississippi River; the spectacular Gateway Arch, the tallest man-made national monument in the nation; and the majestic riverboats still plying their trade on the treacherous river that had spilled over its banks and caused such catastrophic damage to the towns and farmland of five states during the floods of '93.

Her thoughts returned to that surprising phrase that had popped into her mind unannounced, and she realized it was true. Five years ago when her marriage to Fergus Lachlan had shattered around her she'd thought that the fullness of her life was over, that she was destined to a colorless existence devoid of love and laughter and happiness.

For a long time it had been that way, although she'd managed to camouflage it well. Even then her pride hadn't allowed her to be an object of pity, and few suspected that she was merely going through the motions.

But gradually she'd begun to heal, and the color, very pale pastel at first, had crept back into her life until now she was once more blooming. Not as brightly as she had during that first blush of youth, but by age twenty-eight she'd gained the courage to really live again. Like the tulip bulbs that lay brown and dormant in the ground for months until, in a miracle of life, they once more burst from the earth in full, glorious blossom.

Not that she'd been reborn unscathed. She hadn't. She had deep-seated scars that would be with her always, the most damaging of which was her inability to feel sexual desire. She had numerous men friends, and for the past couple of years she even dated frequently, but when they came on to her romantically she froze up inside.

Her soul apparently knew what her mind rejected—that she would never love again with the passionate intensity she'd loved Fergus.

That was no small defect. She didn't relish spending the rest of her years alone without the companionship of one special man, and a select few of the ones she'd dated had actually met most of her requirements for a lifetime relationship.

On the other hand, there were others who seemed nice at the start, but turned out to be jerks—

"Sharon, snap out of your trance and come sit down. The meeting's about to start."

The male voice immediately behind her made her jump. Speak of the devil! Her boss, Floyd Vancleave, was rapidly gaining the title of King of the Jerks.

He put his hand at her waist, but she shied away and turned to face him. He was a spritely looking man in his forties, medium height, with a receding hairline and an evolving paunch. He was also a little too loud, a little too jovial and a whole lot too free with his hands around women he fancied.

"Sorry, Floyd." Her tone was polite, but cool. "I was woolgathering and didn't realize that everyone was here."

She quickly walked away, hoping to find a single seat at the conference table, but he caught up with her and took her arm to lead her to a space with two chairs. She sighed and sat down while he took the place beside her. There was nothing else she could do without making a scene, and unfortunately, he was her immediate supervisor.

When Sharon had fled Chicago after the divorce she'd come to St. Louis, where her grandparents had lived when she was growing up. She'd spent part of her summers here as a child, and although her grandparents had died by the time she'd come to stay she knew the city well and felt at home in the area.

She'd taken a job at the registration desk at the Starlight St. Louis and two years ago had been promoted to assistant to the front-office manager, Floyd Vancleave, who was in charge of the booking office, front desk, bell staff, night auditor and night manager.

At first she'd worked the night shift and hadn't seen much of Floyd, but a year ago she was transferred to days, which put her in direct contact with him. She'd heard rumors about his being a chauvinist, and at that time she'd experienced it firsthand.

He referred to the women who worked under him as "girls" or "doll" or "honey," and asked them to run personal errands for him in such a way that they knew it was an order. Most of the female employees, Sharon among them, put up with the irritation, rather than complain and take a chance on being fired.

Lately, though, she'd become aware that he was also a lecher. She'd heard rumors that he solicited sexual favors from some of his younger and prettier "girls," but again no one had come to her with a complaint, so Sharon hadn't pursued the gossip. After all, he was married, and his wife was the shy, clinging type who seemed devoted to her husband.

It wasn't until he started coming on to Sharon that she was forced to face the fact that he was a womanizer, and now he was after her.

The staff meeting was called to order by the hotel's general manager, and Sharon focused on the business at hand. Not for long, though. Midway through the meeting, when everyone's attention was on a potentially volatile situation in the housekeeping department, she was startled when Floyd reached under the table and put his hand on her knee.

She moved her leg, hoping to discourage him, but he just patted her knee and kept his hand there. She reached down and brushed it aside, but it landed on her thigh and she heard his low chuckle.

Damn him! He was enjoying her discomfort and was counting on her being too well-bred and embarrassed to make a scene.

The loud discussion around them went on, and he moved his fingers to caress her thigh. Again she reached down to dislodge his hand, but all he did was move it to her knee again.

This time she leaned over and spoke softly into his ear. "Take your goddamn hand off my leg or the next time I'll tell you loud and clear for everyone to hear!"

The words were spoken before she realized she'd used a profanity. That had not been her intention. It had just slipped out in the heat of anger, but his face lit up with a big smile and he squeezed her knee as he turned his head to answer.

"Come, now, that's no way for a lady to talk," he admonished her cheerfully, but in an equally low tone. "I'm surprised. You're probably the type who likes to talk dirty in bed. We'll discuss that later."

He squeezed her knee again, but then put his hand back on the table.

Sharon was furious, and she was still irate when she got home that evening.

Home was a two-story brick Tudor-style house that she shared with two other women in the Forest Park district of the city. The shady streets were lined with huge old trees, and the yards were green and abloom with spring flowers and blossoming bushes.

A red sports car and a blue compact sedan, both fairly new and belonging to her housemates, were parked in the driveway, so Sharon pulled up at the curb and stopped. Obviously both Anna and Tracey had beaten her home, and Anna was coming up the walk toward her, being pulled along by her playful golden retriever, Viking.

Sharon watched as the cool Nordic beauty walked briskly behind the dog. Anna had changed out of her business suit and into snug-fitting blue jeans and an oatmeal-colored ribbed turtleneck sweater. Her long blond hair had been released from its usual daytime chignon, and swung, unbound and shining, to her shoulder blades.

Sharon sighed enviously and waved as she got out of her black sedan and slammed the door shut behind her. Anna Grieg could easily pass for a high-fashion model!

The two women greeted each other, while the dog stood by, wagging his tail and eagerly waiting for Sharon to pet him.

"I see Viking's taking you for a walk," Sharon said as she crouched down and nuzzled the impatient pet.

"You got that right," Anna said with a laugh. "The paperboy apparently missed us this morning, so Viking and I galloped down to the supermarket to pick up a paper."

She wrapped the dog's leash around her wrist and took the newspaper from under her arm. "Have you heard that your ex-husband won an acquittal for Sonny Alberts? It made the front page." She held the paper out to Sharon, who reached for it.

"You mean the athlete who was charged with killing his girlfriend?" she asked as she opened it.

Sure enough, there in the middle of the page was a color picture of the famous, blond, muscular basketball forward and his tall, slender, dark-haired attorney, standing on the steps of the courthouse in Chicago. The headline read Alberts Not Guilty.

"I'm not surprised," she murmured around the lump in her throat. "Fergus is a brilliant lawyer. He's been getting a lot of high-profile cases lately."

Sharon hadn't seen or talked to Fergus since the divorce, but they had mutual friends in Chicago who considered it their duty to keep her informed on what he was doing. It was one of them who had sent her the clipping from the paper when Fergus and Elaine were married, and another one who had called two years ago with the sad news that Elaine had died suddenly of an aneurysm.

In spite of herself, Sharon's gaze was drawn back to the picture. Fergus didn't seem to have changed much. His dark-brown hair was clipped a little shorter, but it was very becoming.

Quickly she refolded the paper and handed it back to Anna. She didn't want to be reminded of Fergus Lachlan. She'd spent five years trying to forget him!

"Sorry to be late when it's my night to cook dinner," she said, switching to another subject. "I'll change my clothes and get right on it."

"No need," Anna said cheerfully. "Tracey volunteered to switch nights with you." Anna made a face. "She said she didn't mind at all fixing hamburgers and French fries."

Both women shuddered, and Sharon straightened up. "It serves me right for being late," she said with a laugh. "I don't think that kid will ever understand the concept of nutrition and well-balanced meals."

Anna was thirty and Sharon twenty-eight, and both were well established in their chosen careers, hotel management for Sharon and real estate for Anna. On the other hand, Tracey Weisner, the newest addition to the house-sharing plan, was a young twenty-three, one year out of college and struggling to get the hang of investment counseling at the bank where she was interning.

Inside the house, Anna stopped to take off Viking's leash while Sharon hurried through the dining room on her left and on to the kitchen behind it. Little redheaded, freckle-faced Tracey, five-one and ninety-eight pounds, stood at the sink with her back to Sharon, peeling potatoes. She, too, had changed clothes, and was wearing stone-washed jeans and her familiar ragged white sweatshirt with St. Louis University splashed across the front, a comfortable souvenir from her college days.

"Hi, Sharon," she said cheerfully, without turning her head to look behind her. "I figured you wouldn't mind if I went ahead and fixed dinner, since you were late and I have a date tonight."

"How did you know it was me?" Sharon asked. There were times when she'd bet the farm that Tracey Weisner was either a "good" witch or a descendant of one. It was positively spooky the way she seemed to read other people's minds.

Tracey laughed. "No, I don't read minds, but I have sensitive olfactory nerves. That's what the doctor calls it, anyway. I smelled your perfume. You always have the fragrance of flowers around you. Like an English garden bouquet. If it had been Anna I'd have smelled spices."

Sharon shook her head in wonder. "I haven't added a drop of fragrance since I left the house this morning. I don't see how there could possibly be any scent left," she said. "You know, you really should have joined the canine corps of the police force. You'd probably be better than the dogs at sniffing out drugs. Do you need some help in here?"

"Nope. Now that you're home, I'll fry the potatoes and hamburger. It won't take more than twenty minutes."

Sharon accepted the dismissal gratefully and went upstairs to change her clothes.

Later, when they were finishing their meal, the subject of how their day had gone came up and Sharon's outrage at being so rudely treated returned. She told them about her experience with her boss. "Sure it's against the law," she admitted, "and I was seriously tempted to yell at him so everyone in the room would know what he was doing, instead of whispering, but I was married to a lawyer long enough to grasp that you have to prove an accusation like that. No one could see what was going on. It was all happening under the table. It would have been just my word against his, and he's the boss."

She sighed and made an effort to calm down. "Thank God, he's being transferred to the Starlight Honolulu in a few weeks. If I can stay out of his way until then he'll be gone and I'll move up into his job. I'd like nothing better than to expose him for the creep he is, but I really can't afford to make waves now. You can be sure he'd do something to jinx my promotion if I did."

"I understand he has a lot of seniority with the company," Anna said. "Do you suppose the management at your hotel has received complaints against him and is having him transferred rather than firing him?"

Sharon didn't answer immediately, but took time to think about Anna's question. It was a possibility, but... "No, I don't think so," she said. "The Starlight hotel chain is a big one. It wouldn't make sense for them to transfer a known troublemaker from one of their facilities to another.

"Also, this guy is going to go too far one of these days and pick on some woman who's in a position to fight back. The company would be courting a multimillion-dollar lawsuit if it could be proven that they knew Floyd was sexually harassing women employees and hadn't dealt with it."

Tracey joined the conversation. "But, Sharon, if you don't report him he'll just harass the women he works with in Hawaii."

Tracey had zeroed in on the load of guilt that weighted Sharon's conscience, and she reacted angrily. "Dammit, Tracey, don't you think I know that? I have no proof that he's making sexual advances to some of the women who work under him. If none of them have come forward by now to assert their rights you can bet they're not going to just to save my job. With the unemployment rate soaring, none of them can afford to take a chance on being fired."

She ignored Tracey's shocked protest that she wasn't blaming her and continued. "If I file unsubstantiated charges against one of the hotel managers I'll be branded a troublemaker and lose everything I've worked so hard for the past five years. Besides which, my hopes for a career in the hotel business would be blown away."

"Sharon, I'm sorry," Tracey cried plaintively. "I didn't mean... that is, I meant... Oh damn, I don't know what I meant! I always speak before I think and then say the wrong thing."

She jumped up, knocking over her chair, and ran out of the room, but not before Sharon saw tears running down her face.

Sharon knew she'd overreacted, and muttered an unladylike expletive as she dropped her face in her hands.

It was Anna's cool reason that defused the situation. She stood and came around the table to put her arm across Sharon's hunched shoulders. "No one's criticizing you or blaming you for anything, Sharon," she said gently. "You're absolutely right. There's nothing you can do without proof and lots of it. When Tracey grows up a little more, she'll learn that we women have to fight our own skirmishes in our battle for equal rights and not expect a mother figure to do it for us."

Sharon raised her head and patted Anna's hand that rested on her shoulder. "I know. It's just that I'm torn between doing what's right for me and my responsibilities to the women who look to me for guidance."

She straightened up in her chair, and Anna moved away and started stacking dirty dishes.

"You can't help those women unless they come to you and file a complaint," Anna said. "Now, why don't you go upstairs and convince Tracey that you don't hate her while I load the dishwasher."

On the following day, Floyd left for a conference at corporate headquarters in Los Angeles, leaving Sharon to shoulder his duties as well as her own. Not that she minded. It was a relief not to have to confront him again, and she used the time to acquaint herself with the finer details of the position she was in line to move up to when he left for Hawaii.

She was excited and happy about the promotion. She hadn't been officially notified yet that the job was hers, but she expected the confirmation any day now. It would be most unusual if she didn't get it. She was the best qualified, and her record was spotless.

When Vancleave returned on Monday, the first week in June, he summoned her to his office. Since hers was just down the hall from his, she arrived at his reception room in only a couple of minutes. His secretary, Beverly Maitland, was young and pretty, just the way he liked his "girls." She smiled at Sharon and motioned toward the inner door. "Go on in. He's waiting for you."

Floyd stood when Sharon entered. She'd always envied him this office. It was so cheerful, with its sliding-glass door that looked out over the outdoor swimming pool and cabana, and she felt a thrill as she realized that in a few short weeks it would be hers.

"Good morning," he said pleasantly. "I hope you weren't overworked while I was gone. Have a seat."

Sharon returned the greeting and sat down. He looked tan and rested. Obviously not all his time in L.A. had been spent in stuffy conference rooms.

He settled himself comfortably in his executive chair and smiled, only Floyd's smile always seemed to Sharon like more of a leer.

"I've got good news for you, love," he said.

She was immediately on guard.

"If you play your cards right there's a good chance I can take you with me to the Starlight Honolulu as my assistant."

He leaned back and beamed, and she wondered if he really thought he was God's gift to women, or if his self-esteem was so low that he had to make himself believe it. She suspected it was the latter. If so, she should feel sorry for him, but unfortunately she couldn't bring herself to be that charitable.

Still, she'd play his game for a little while just to be sure she wasn't misreading him.

She, too, settled back. "Oh?" She raised her eyebrows slightly. "And just what cards do I have to play?"

He made a steeple of his fingers and settled his chin on it. "Why, the king and the queen, of course. We can have a great time cavorting among all that tropical flora and fauna. In some places it's so thick we wouldn't even have to wear clothes."

Just the thought of Floyd Vancleave in the nude was repulsive to her, but she fought to control her temper. "And what about your wife?" she asked, far more coolly than she felt.

He brightened and sat up straight. "You want a *ménage à trois?*" he said eagerly. "That can be arranged, but not with my wife. She's far too straight—"

Sharon had had enough! She clutched the arms of her chair and leaned forward. "Mr. Vancleave," she said tightly, making his name sound like an obscenity. "There's no way I'd go to Hawaii or any place else with you. I don't sleep my way to the top."

She stood and had started for the door, when his voice, cold and filled with rage, froze her.

"Stop right there, you arrogant bitch. Don't forget, I hold your future right here in my hands."

She turned around as he cupped his palms together in front of him.

"If you want my job when I'm gone you're gonna have to be nice to me, get it? Extra nice! You need good references from me to get that promotion. I can fix it so you won't even be able to get a job as dishwasher in the hotel industry."

Never before had Sharon felt such fury. The pressure of it was so hot she could almost feel smoke coming out her ears.

How dared that overbearing bastard threaten her. She'd been wrong not to file a formal complaint about his harassment earlier, but she was going to rectify it.

She glared at him, hoping the disgust she felt showed in her expression. "I have just one thing to say about that," she rasped. "If I don't get the promotion I'm entitled to I'll file a complaint of sexual harassment against you with everybody from the general manager of this hotel to the federal bureau that handles such things. Believe it. That's not a threat, it's a promise."

Floyd's face twisted in a sneer. "Who in hell do you think you're kidding? Don't pull that outraged-virgin bit on me. A hot little hussy like you can never get enough. Besides, nobody would believe you. It's your word against mine, and we in management protect our own."

Without even trying to answer, Sharon turned and stormed out of the office, slamming the door behind her.

For the next week the atmosphere between Sharon and Vancleave figuratively dripped frost. They communicated only through written memos or a third party, usually his secretary.

Then, on Wednesday, Sharon received a letter from the general manager, expressing regret that she hadn't been chosen to succeed Floyd Vancleave as front-desk manager and notifying her that the position had been filled by a more qualified person from the chain's Starlight Denver.

Sharon was stunned. Her knees gave way and she sank into the chair behind her desk. She'd been passed over! They were bringing in an outsider to fill the position. Something the Starlight Corporation almost never did!

There could only be one reason. Floyd Vancleave had carried out his threat to block her promotion!

Although her whole body was trembling with shock, her mind was clear and her self-preservation instinct powerful. He wasn't going to get away with this!

She jumped up out of her chair, picked up her purse and hurried down the hall to Floyd's office. When she opened the door she was aware that there were several people waiting in the reception room, but she strode straight through and had her hand on the knob of the inner door when Beverly called to her.

"Sharon, wait, you can't go in there!"

Sharon paid no attention, but pushed open the door and walked in. Floyd was sitting behind his desk, facing her, and it crossed her mind that she must look pretty wild, because his eyes widened with alarm as he stood.

"You rotten bastard!" she shouted before he could open his mouth. "I'm going to make you sorry you ever tried to coerce me into playing musical beds with you!"

She pushed the door shut and paced toward the desk, her smoldering gaze locked with Floyd's alarmed one.

"What in hell...! he rasped. "You can't walk in here like this and call me names—"

She'd caught him off guard, and could see that he was rattled. "I just did, didn't I?" she said as she stopped squarely in front of his desk. "And I'm far from finished with you. I'm going to do exactly what I told you I'd do if you carried out your threat to derail my promotion unless I submitted to your disgusting sexual advances. When I get through filing suits and complaints everyone in the hotel industry is going to know what a pathetic lowlife you are."

He backed away slightly, as if her fury were a physical presence. "Now, hold on a minute," he said shrilly. "I didn't—"

"Oh yes you did," she shouted. "I just received this." She tossed the letter she still held crumpled in her fist on the desk. "There's only one reason I'd be passed over for that promotion, and that's because you told the general manager lies about me."

Floyd looked around nervously. "Sharon, for God's sake lower your voice. Everyone in the building will hear you."

"Good!" Sharon shouted even louder. "That's exactly what I want. I'm sorry I didn't leave the door open. You've humiliated the women who work under you long enough, with your groping hands and your dirty innuendos—"

"Christ, woman, will you shut up and get out of here!"
This time it was Floyd who was shouting. He was also gesturing frantically. "We'll talk about this later, somewhere
else, when you've calmed down...."

"Oh no, we won't," she told him. "I'm through talking
to you. From now on you can speak to me through my attorney."

Sharon saw the blood drain from his florid face as she
stalked past the desk, out the sliding-glass door and across
the pool area.

She was shaking so badly that she could hardly walk, and
she knew she had to get away from there! Go someplace
where she could get a grip on her runaway temper and cool
off a little.

She'd never been so flat-out furious in her whole life.
Even when she'd found out that her husband was in love
with another woman she hadn't been so much angry as hurt.
Fergus hadn't deliberately set out to break up their marriage, but Vancleave had maliciously and willfully taken the
necessary steps to derail her promotion for his personal satisfaction, just to exercise his power and show her that he
could do it!

The screech of tires and the blare of a horn jolted Sharon's wandering attention, and she realized that she'd started
across the street at the end of the block and had almost been
hit by a car. The driver was busily cursing her out even as he
drove on.

Sheepishly, she turned back and headed for the front of
the hotel and the entrance to the attached parking garage.
She'd better keep her wits about her until she got home or
she was apt to end up either in the hospital or in jail.

She was all the way up to the top floor of the garage where
the employees parked, when she realized that she didn't have
her purse. She'd taken it with her because she'd known she
wouldn't stay around after her confrontation with Floyd,
but then she'd left it in his office!

Obviously this was not her day, and everything that could happen would. She had to have her keys and her driver's license, so there was nothing she could do but go back to the office and get the purse.

But how was she going to face Floyd after that grand exit she'd made so dramatically? Damn! Damn! Damn!

Dejectedly, she returned to the street level and decided to go back the way she'd left, through the glass door, so she wouldn't have to face all the people in the waiting room. Maybe Floyd would be gone and she could retrieve the handbag without confronting him again.

For the first time that day she was in luck. The door hadn't been locked again after she'd left, and although her eyes were slow to adjust from the bright sunlight to the darker interior, she could see that the office was empty.

Then she noticed that the desk lamp was overturned on the floor. That was odd. It had been in place when she'd walked out.

Glancing around the room, she spotted her purse on the floor beside the door, where she vaguely remembered it sliding off her shoulder when she'd come in the first time. She started toward it, eager to get out of there before Floyd came back and found her.

It wasn't until she'd taken several steps that she saw the large bundle on the floor in front of the desk.

Only it wasn't just a bundle.

She blinked rapidly to adjust her eyesight to the dimness of the richly paneled office, then gasped. *Oh dear God, it was a man!* She knelt down beside him and saw that it was Floyd Vancleave curled up on his side on the thick tan carpet, with his knees drawn up to his waist and his hands clutching his chest.

"Floyd!" Sharon cried, and put her hand on his shoulder. He rolled limply onto his back, and it was only then that she saw the blood on his shirt and the silver handle protruding from the left side of his chest.

This couldn't be! When she'd left just a few minutes ago he'd been standing behind the desk, breathing fire and smoke, furious with her and apprehensive, too. Now he was lying on the floor with a knife in his chest, and he didn't seem to be breathing at all.

She leaned over him and put her fingers at the pulse point of his neck. It took a few seconds, but she finally felt the pulse, weak and thready.

She had to do something! If he wasn't dead already he would be very soon with that knife penetrating so close to his heart. She needed help immediately, but first . . .

Without fully comprehending what she was doing, she wrapped her fingers around the handle and tugged. It didn't move, and she tugged again, this time harder.

The weapon pulled free, and when it did blood gushed onto the bodice of her dress.

It was then that the door to the outer office opened and Beverly entered, followed by another woman. "Mr. Vancleave," she said, "Mrs. Mitchel has been waiting—"

Sharon lifted her head and saw the look of alarm on Beverly's face as her gaze fastened on Sharon, her dress spattered with blood, as she crouched on the floor over a body, holding a bloody knife in her raised hand.

The secretary's shrill scream rent the silence, and was quickly joined by Sharon's shriek in a crescendo of horror.

Chapter Three

Fergus Lachlan heard the phone ringing inside his high rise apartment on Chicago's Lake Shore Drive as he inserted the key in the lock, but he didn't hurry. If he got to it in time to pick it up he would; if not, so much the better.

Fergus refused to have an answering machine in his home. A few key people had his beeper and unlisted phone numbers, but anyone else who wanted him could contact him at the office. His home was off-limits to anyone except those he invited in.

However, he'd recently won an acquittal for a well-known and roundly disliked basketball star accused of killing his girlfriend, and the general public as well as the news media were outraged. It didn't seem to matter that the man had been found innocent of that crime; he was an egomaniac and a bully, and people wanted to see him punished.

Ever since the verdict was announced Fergus had been plagued by reporters and photographers wanting to interview him. A few had even managed to get his private numbers. This was probably another one of those, but it was after nine o'clock and he'd been on the go since eight that morning, including a working lunch. He'd missed dinner altogether, and was in no mood to take abuse from a stranger wanting to cash in on another person's misery.

The ringing stopped just after he stepped into the foyer and shut the door behind him. Breathing a sigh of relief, he went to the bar in the living room and mixed himself a whiskey and soda. Ordinarily he didn't drink alone. He'd known too many men who tried to drown their loneliness in alcohol, only to succumb to its addiction without solving any of their problems.

Fergus had no desire to join their ranks, but tonight he was too weary and depressed to face the emptiness of his expensive apartment, with its impersonal, decorator-selected furnishings.

He missed Elaine, which was only natural. Her sudden death two years ago had come as such a mind-boggling shock. One minute she'd been happily making plans to re-model the kitchen of the elegant old home they'd bought in the Oak Park community, and the next she'd crumpled to the floor and died in his arms before help could arrive.

An aneurysm, the doctors had said. A weak spot that she didn't know she had in the wall of the aorta had ruptured and killed her within seconds.

His bright, vivacious wife dead at age thirty-five.

He couldn't live in the house after that. He'd sold it and moved into this upscale bachelor apartment, with its three large rooms and an extensive view of Lincoln Park and Lake Michigan far below.

But Fergus was not a swinging bachelor. He was a griev-ing widower, and he'd have been far more content in the old, slightly rundown neighborhood where he'd grown up, but that address wasn't prestigious enough to pass muster with the partners of his law firm, Newberry, Everingham and Jessup. Their lawyers were expected to live up to the image of the highly successful attorney who wore thousand-dollar suits, lived in the most impressive sections of town and supported all the politically correct charities. Fergus hadn't cared enough at the time of this last move to fight for his independence.

It really didn't matter where he lived; he was seldom there anyway. In his grief and loneliness he'd taken on more and more cases, until he was putting in twelve-hour days six days a week and sleeping most of Sunday.

It kept him busy, but it didn't ease his pain.

He leaned back on the sofa and closed his eyes. He should stick a TV dinner in the microwave, but couldn't bring himself to make the effort. Besides, he could hardly stomach the damn things. He and Sharon had eaten so many of them during most of their marriage when she was going to college and he was intent on becoming a partner in record time—

Sharon. His eyes flew open as he quickly sat up. *Dear God, he didn't want to think about Sharon!* He'd been trying for five years to get her out of his mind, but she was always there, in his subconscious, waiting for him to let down his guard so she could creep in and torment him.

Only it wasn't Sharon's doing, it was his. Why couldn't he let her go? It had been his fault that their marriage had broken up. She'd no doubt forgotten all about him by now. Why did it hurt so much for him to remember her?

He'd truly loved Elaine, was shattered when she died, so why did he still feel this aching need for Sharon? Not necessarily a sexual need, but a certainty that he had lost an essential and irreplaceable part of himself.

Abruptly he stood up and headed for the bathroom. He was going to take a warm relaxing shower and go to bed.

Twenty minutes later Fergus turned off the water spray and heard the phone ringing. Not again, he thought impatiently as he quickly wrapped a towel around his hips and knotted it at the side. He'd better answer it or whoever it was would probably continue calling at intervals all night.

Stepping out of the shower stall, he headed for the phone in the bedroom and wrenched it from its cradle. "Lachlan," he said, making no effort to screen out the annoyance in his tone.

"Mr. Lachlan, this is Anna Grieg," said a woman's voice from the other end. "I'm sorry to bother you so late and at home, but you have an unlisted number and it's taken me hours to track you down—"

"Ms. Grieg, if you're a reporter I don't appreciate you bothering me at home in the middle of the night—"

"No, Mr. Lachlan," gasped the woman. "I'm not a reporter. I'm a friend of Sharon Sawyer's, and I'm calling from St. Louis."

Fergus wasn't buying it. Some of these people would go to any length to get an interview with him. He was good copy.

"Then call my office tomorrow and set up an appointment," he said angrily, "and just who is Sharon Sawyer—"

It wasn't until he said it that the name clicked, and when it did it knocked the breath out of him. "Sharon Sawyer!" he yelped. "Are you talking about my wife...um...ex-wife, Sharon Sawyer Lachlan?"

He'd forgotten that Sharon had taken back her maiden name after the divorce.

"Yes," Anna Grieg confirmed. "But she's known as Sharon Sawyer now."

Fergus attempted to pull himself together. He knew Sharon would never contact him unless something awful had happened.

"What about Sharon?" he asked anxiously. "Is she all right? Good Lord, woman, speak up. Has anything happened to her?"

His stomach muscles clenched, and the hand that held the phone shook. *No, not Sharon. He couldn't lose Sharon, too!*

"She... she's in jail," Anna blurted.

Fergus nearly dropped the phone. *"She's what?"*

This had to be a crank call. Somebody had found out about his ex-wife and where she lived and was playing a monstrous hoax. Lawyers were an easy target, and there were a lot of people out there who would like to see him squirm.

"I'm warning you, lady, if this is your idea of a joke it's not funny." Fergus was deadly serious. "I can and will have you arrested for harassment...."

"No! Mr. Lachlan. Believe me, it's no joke. Sharon's been arrested on a charge of murder!"

Fergus could distinguish the edge of desperation in the woman's voice, and his fear escalated. Taking a deep breath, he made a supreme effort to calm down and think straight. "Tell me about it."

"I don't know very much," Anna said. "The police won't talk to me, and Sharon's lawyer isn't having much better luck. All I know is that sometime this afternoon she quarreled with her supervisor, and a few minutes later was found leaning over his body, with a bloody letter opener in her hand. He was dead of a stab wound in the chest."

Fergus muttered an obscenity. Sharon was the kindest, most compassionate woman he'd ever known. She couldn't even kill an insect. There was no way she could murder a man no matter what he'd done to her.

That last thought set him off again. "What did the bastard do to her?" he growled, then listened as Anna told him how his sweet, trusting Sharon had been sexually harassed by the vermin who was the victim.

"Where is she now?" was all he could trust himself to say.

"The police arrested her and took her to the St. Louis City Jail, where she's being held—"

"What do you mean she's being held?" he demanded, and silently chided himself to stop acting like an outraged husband and start thinking like an attorney. "Doesn't she have enough money to post bail? I'll wire it—"

"No, you don't understand," Anna admonished. "Sharon's attorney couldn't get the judge to release her on bail. The district attorney thinks she's dangerous."

Son-of-a-bitch! Fergus thought, but managed not to say. "Did Sharon ask you to call me?"

"No." He heard the sob in her voice. "She didn't even mention you. She used her one phone call to ring me and ask me to get her a lawyer. I did, but he couldn't persuade the judge to set bail. Mr. Lachlan, I've got to get her out of there. I thought maybe you—"

Fergus's heart was hammering, and it was all he could do not to shout. "Ms. Grieg... Anna... listen to me. I'll leave here as soon as I can arrange for use of the company plane. I should be there in a few hours. Give me your address and phone number and I'll be in touch with you as soon as I arrive."

Sharon sat huddled on the lower bunk of her jail cell and shuddered as the sound of another inmate retching violently made her own stomach churn. Would this night ever end? It seemed that she'd been in this hellhole forever, but a glance at her watch told her it was only a little past midnight.

In another part of the vast lockup an intermittent moan became a continuous wail, a mournful keening that set Sharon's nerves on edge. Even so, it was better than the screams that had bounced off the walls an hour earlier. That prisoner had finally been taken away. Sharon hoped it was to the dispensary and not an isolation cell.

Sharon had thought nothing could be worse than the degrading body search she'd been subjected to when she was booked, but now she knew there were more horrors in a jail than she'd ever imagined.

How many of the people in there besides her were innocent? She'd never really thought about that before, even when she was married to a defense attorney. Fergus had seldom discussed his cases with her, but she'd just assumed that all his clients were free on bail.

A sudden shout made her jump. It was followed by a maniacal laugh that went on and on, until she covered her ears with her hands and burrowed her face against the wall in an effort to shut out the spine-chilling sound.

Dear God, was she going to have to stay there until her trial was over and she'd finally proven that she hadn't killed Floyd? But that could take months! Maybe even years. And she'd be stark raving mad by then.

Her efforts to shut out the sound didn't dim the crazy laughter much, but it did keep her from hearing the guard until he'd unlocked the door to her cell, then come in and touched her on the shoulder.

She let out a frightened shriek and dropped her hands as she turned around to find him standing over her, a big burly man.

"Sorry, lady," he said gruffly. "I didn't mean to scare you. Are you okay?"

She swallowed and nodded. "Is it... Is it always this noisy in here?" Her voice shook with the fright he'd given her.

He grinned. "This is tame," he said. "Wait a few more hours, when the druggies start coming down off their highs. That's when it gets rowdy."

She groaned, but he continued talking.

"You are Sharon Sawyer, aren't you?"

She nodded. "Yes."

"Come with me," he said. "Your lawyer's here and wants to talk to you."

Ray Quinlan? What was he doing here in the middle of the night? She'd talked to him twice earlier, during the first interview and again at the hearing to set bail, which had been denied.

Still, she wasn't going to argue. She'd do anything to get out of this place, even if only for a few minutes.

In one of the private rooms where attorneys conferred with their clients Fergus paced restlessly as he waited for Sharon to be brought to him.

Brought to him. She'd hate that phrase. The last time he'd seen her she'd been coolly polite, but had let him know that she wanted absolutely nothing from him. Not his love, not his money, not even the community property she was entitled to, although her lawyer had finally insisted that she accept what the law mandated.

Not that he could blame her. He'd not only hurt her badly, but had shattered her trust and respect for him. He couldn't expect her to understand how he could still love and want her when he'd admitted that he had strong feelings for Elaine, too.

His short marriage to Sharon had been a turbulent one. She'd been young and immature, and she'd accused him of being too bossy and overbearing. She was probably right, but he hadn't been able to stand by and let her make obvious mistakes that he could prevent because of his more mature outlook.

They'd always seemed to be either quarreling or making love. There'd been no real depth to their union, and he'd worked closely with Elaine during that time. She'd been so levelheaded and easy to please. Such a pleasure to work with. The exact opposite of Sharon.

It had been a potentially dangerous situation, but he hadn't realized it until it was too late. When their lives had been unalterably changed.

That had been five years ago, and he hadn't seen or heard from her since, although he'd kept track of her through mutual friends. He'd known of the important changes in her life since then as soon as they happened: when she moved to St. Louis, when she took the position with the hotel, when she was promoted to assistant manager, but if she was involved with another man no one was willing to tell him.

It was just as well.

A knock on the door interrupted his thoughts, and he whirled around to face it as it opened. A uniformed guard entered leading a young woman dressed in regulation jail coveralls.

Sharon! He'd know her anywhere, but the fear and anguish that were clearly visible in her expression and demeanor was almost more than he could bear. The long brown hair that he used to love to run his fingers through had been cut to just above her shoulders, and wispy bangs teased her forehead. Even in its disheveled state it was becoming, but her beautiful face was pale and pinched, and the despair that looked out of her deep blue eyes made him long to do something, anything, to make it go away.

Although he'd been studying her, she hadn't yet noticed him. Her gaze was cast downward, and she seemed to be in a state bordering on shock.

Before he could thaw his frozen vocal cords and say something, the guard spoke.

"Here's your client, Mr. Lachlan."

"Lachlan?" Sharon's head snapped up and her gaze locked with his.

"Fergus!"

It was a cry of shocked disbelief. He watched the blood drain from her face as she wavered, then staggered. Closing the distance between them in two strides, he caught her in his arms before she could fall.

"Bring me a glass of water," he ordered the guard as he wrapped her in his embrace and cradled her against him.

She was trembling violently, and he silently cursed himself for an unthinking fool. When he'd called her friend Anna from the airport as soon as he'd landed in St. Louis

he should have asked her to meet him here and let her prepare Sharon for this.

The problem was that he was still thinking like a distraught husband instead of a coolly analytical attorney.

But, dammit, he *was* a distraught husband. Or at least ex-
husband. How could he help her if all he could think to do
was carry her off somewhere private where he could comfort her, take care of her, protect her.

A sob shook her slender frame. "Oh, Fergus, I didn't kill
Floyd. Get me out of here!" she wailed against his chest just
before a series of smaller sobs broke through her tenuous
control and she cried in his arms.

He lowered his head and rubbed his face in her soft thick
hair as he gently caressed her back. "I will, sweetheart," he
murmured. "With God as my witness I won't let you down
again."

The guard came back with a glass of water, and Fergus
half led, half carried Sharon to the table in the middle of the
small room and sat her in one of the straight-backed chairs.
"Lean down and rest your head on your knees for a few
minutes," he told her. "It should make the dizziness go
away."

Sharon did as he said. The shock of seeing him had left
her too confused and disoriented to think for herself. But
what was he doing here? How had he known she was in
trouble?

"Feeling a little less rocky now?"

He'd asked the question close to her ear, and she realized
that he was hunkered down beside her. The sound of his familiar voice was like a dream. Something she'd never expected to hear again.

"Yes," she answered, and sat back up.

He put the glass of water in her shaking hands and helped
her hold it. "Here, take a few swallows of this," he said,
and guided the glass to her mouth.

As she sipped the water his face was on a level with hers. He'd changed very little. He still parted his dark-brown hair on the left side, and he still had the shadow of a heavy beard on his handsome face, even though he was clean-shaven.

But he looked tired. There were dark smudges under his green eyes, and he was pale and drawn. She saw the anxiety in his expression that she'd also heard in his voice.

Anxiety for her? How like Fergus. Although they'd been divorced for years, he still felt responsible for her. Right now she was grateful for that, even though she'd hate it later. She wasn't functioning well at all in this crisis.

She hiccuped and swiped at the tears that continued to cascade down her cheeks. "I'm sorry," she said on a sob. "I don't mean to be such a crybaby, but I . . . I can't go back to that cell. It's like a nightmare—"

Another sob cut her off, and Fergus handed her a handkerchief. "I know," he said softly, "and I'm going to do something about that right now. That is, if you're willing to retain me as your attorney."

Sharon felt the panic rising again. "But I already have an attorney. I can't afford both of you."

Fergus winced, and a brief flash of pain flitted across his face. "We'll work something out, Sharon," he said brusquely, "but if you want me to represent you you'd better give me a couple of dollars to make it legal."

"I . . . I don't have my purse. I don't think I even brought it to jail with me."

How ironic. If she hadn't gone back to Floyd's office to retrieve that purse she wouldn't have been anywhere near there when his body was found, and now, after all the trouble it had caused, she still didn't have it.

Fergus stood and reached for his billfold. He took a five-dollar bill out and handed it to her. "Here," he said. "I'm loaning this to you. Now, give it back to me."

Without fully comprehending what she was doing, Sharon held it out to him. "I'll pay you back," she promised, "but what about Ray Quinlan?"

"I talked to Ray on the phone, and he's agreed to be co-counsel with me. I'll need him to file papers, et cetera, since I'm not licensed to practice in the state of Missouri, so there's no problem."

Sharon's mind was too muddled to sort it out, but if Fergus said it was all right, then it was. She'd go over it with him again later when she wasn't so frightened and confused.

He reached out his hand to her. "Now," he said, "if you feel up to it, let's go see about getting you released so I can take you home."

She'd never heard sweeter words in her entire life.

Night court was a dreary place. Most of the prisoners were pretty unsavory types—drug pushers, drunks, muggers and the like—but Sharon considered it a haven compared with the jail. Especially with Fergus at her side, exuding confidence and determination.

When it was his turn to plead her case he stood. "Your Honor," he said respectfully, "I'm acting as co-counsel with Raymond Quinlan in the defense of Sharon Sawyer. I understand that Ms. Sawyer was denied bail earlier tonight, but I just arrived from Chicago and would like to plead on her behalf."

The judge looked annoyed. "Mr. Lachlan, I'm well aware of your reputation, but since the issue of bail has already been resolved for the time being I see no reason to reopen it."

"I understand, Your Honor," Fergus said, "but this is a special circumstance. I have knowledge of the prisoner that neither Mr. Quinlan nor the district attorney are aware of. Ms. Sawyer is my ex-wife. We were married for three years, and I probably know her better than anyone else, since she has no other family. I assure you that she is neither a danger to society nor a flight risk. Actually, she's in a state of shock, and should have been held in the dispensary instead of a jail cell. When I arrived about an hour ago she was hysterical. The guard will testify to that."

Sharon watched Fergus. He didn't move around or gesture, but stood quietly and looked straight at the judge, while speaking in a low, respectful tone. She'd never seen him in action before. Most of the time when they were married she'd been in college and had classes during the day when court was in session.

He was dressed in a superbly tailored gray suit, with a green tie that highlighted his deep-set green eyes. He looked elegant and every inch the professional. She still couldn't believe that he was there, at her side, defending her in a court of law!

The judge spoke, interrupting her thoughts.

"I wasn't made aware that the prisoner needed medical attention."

The lawyer from the district attorney's office stood. "She didn't, Your Honor. When we brought her in she was upset but rational. If need be we can have her held in a hospital ward, but we still object to having her freed on bail. Our case is almost airtight. She was caught leaning over the body of a stabbing victim with a bloody letter opener in her hand."

"I should think that would be enough in itself to send her into shock," Fergus drawled acidly. "Sharon has a spotless record. She's never even had a parking ticket. While we were married she wouldn't go fishing with me because she couldn't stand to see the fish hooked and killed."

His voice throbbed with emotion as he continued. "This woman has absolutely nothing in her background to suggest that she would kill anybody or anything. In fact, I'm willing to stake my career on her innocence. I'll take full responsibility for her if you'll release her in my custody."

That snapped Sharon out of her apathy and she gasped. Even the judge looked startled.

"Mr. Lachlan," he said, "are either of you married to anyone else at this time?"

Fergus shook his head. "No, Your Honor, we're both single. There won't be any problem with prior commitments."

The assistant district attorney muttered a halfhearted protest, but the judge reversed his previous decision and granted Sharon freedom on bail. Her relief was short-lived. Bail was set at two hundred thousand dollars, and she couldn't raise anywhere near that amount.

"Don't worry," Fergus said, helping her to stand. "I'll take care of it. Come on, we've got one more stop to make and then we can go home."

Sharon wanted to protest. To refuse his much-too-generous offer. But the thought of being locked up again in that dungeon was one she couldn't face. She'd pay him back somehow, but for now she had to accept his charity. All she wanted was to get out of there.

It didn't take long to have her released, but when they brought her the bag containing the clothes and personal possessions that had been taken from her when she was booked there was one essential item missing. Her dress!

"Sorry," she was told when she pointed out the oversight, "but it's being held as evidence. There's quite a lot of the victim's blood on the front of it."

Again panic froze her. Was she going to have to spend the night there after all? "But I don't have anything to wear home," she cried.

The man behind the counter shrugged, but Fergus swore and reached for his wallet. Extracting a bill, he tossed it on the counter. "Here, I'll buy the damn coveralls she's wearing," he snapped, and took her arm to guide her through the building and outside into the cool, sweet night air.

* * *

Fergus had been fortunate to find a parking space within half a block of the jail, and he breathed a sigh of relief as he seated Sharon in the white Cadillac he'd rented at the airport. Getting her released had been easier than he'd expected, but now what was he going to do with her?

He shut her door, then walked around and slid into the driver's side. What had possessed him to volunteer to be responsible for her? That meant he had to act as baby-sitter, bodyguard and parole officer for her, and she was going to object to that when she realized the extent of his commitment.

Neither of them spoke as he started the engine and pulled out into the street. Anna Grieg had given him her address. *Their* address. Apparently she and Sharon shared a house with another woman named Tracey, but he had no idea how to get there.

He turned his head to ask her for directions, but the words died in his throat. She was crumpled against the seat with her eyes closed, and she looked beaten and exhausted. That settled it. If he was going to be responsible for her then he was also going to make some of her decisions until she was better able to make them herself.

He turned at the next corner and headed for the riverfront.

Fergus was well aware that Sharon hated his guts. So much so that she hadn't even asked for him when she was arrested for murder. When she found out they were going to be joined at the hip for the duration of this case she'd be outraged.

He couldn't blame her. It wasn't going to be a picnic for him, either. As a matter of self-preservation he didn't want to spend a lot of time with her. It could only lead to more heartbreak, and he'd had about all that he could stand.

She'd never forgive him for what she saw as his betrayal while they were married. There was no reason why she should. He'd have felt the same way if he'd caught her in the embrace of another man. The kindest thing he could do for her now would be to stay out of her personal life. To protect her from himself as well as from a false charge of murder.

He just hoped to God he was strong enough to do that and not give in to his overpowering need to hold her, cherish her and plead with her for a second chance.

Sharon felt wrung out, both emotionally and physically. As the car sped down the nearly deserted city streets her eyes felt glued shut, and her mind had shut down completely. There were a million questions she wanted to ask Fergus, but right now she couldn't think of one of them. Either he was as done in as she was or he was being sensitive and understanding, because he must have as many questions as she did, but he wasn't badgering her with them.

He'd gotten her out of jail and she felt safe with him. For now that was enough. Tomorrow she'd fight for her freedom, but tonight she just wanted to surrender to more of the tender, loving care he'd lavished on her while they were married.

He had loved her once—she was almost sure of that. So what had happened? She'd adored him, and was unstinting in letting him know how she felt. So why had he stopped loving her? What had Elaine offered him that she hadn't? She'd asked herself these questions time and again over the years and had found no answers.

She must have dozed, because the car was stopped and two big hands cupped her head and repositioned it gently as Fergus's voice murmured gently but distinctly, "Wake up, honey. We're home."

She opened her eyes and sat up. A quick look around convinced her they were parked at the curb of one of the downtown city streets.

"This isn't home," she said. "Fergus, where are we?"

There was enough street light for her to see his small smile.

"We're in the valet parking area of the Adams Mark Hotel. You're going to spend the rest of the night here with me."

Chapter Four

Sharon woke up by degrees. Like a diver surfacing from the deep, she drifted through several layers of diminishing darkness until she gained enough control over her muscles to open her eyes. She found herself in an upscale hotel room, but not one of the Starlight's.

Then the events of the previous day came back to her, and she groaned as she curled up in a ball and pulled the sheet over her head. Floyd Vancleave was dead, and she'd been arrested for murdering him!

Not that she hadn't been mad enough to do the dastardly deed, but fortunately the idea hadn't occurred to her. Instead, she'd walked out and left him furious with her, but alive and healthy.

Then Fergus had come to her rescue.

Just the memory of the shock she received when she walked into that interview room and saw him there made her heart pound and sent a tremor through her whole body.

He said Anna had called and told him she'd been arrested. She should be mad at her housemate for contacting Fergus without her permission, but after spending several hours in that jail cell, Sharon felt nothing but gratitude toward Anna for doing what Sharon had been too proud and stubborn to do.

So where was Fergus now? She shoved back the sheet and sat up, then saw her image reflected in the mirror of the dresser against the opposite wall. She was wearing only her panties and a man's white T-shirt.

Dear heaven, where had that shirt come from? It must be Fergus's, but she didn't remember putting it on. Had he undressed her...?

No. No, of course not. Now it was coming back to her. She'd insisted on taking a shower before going to bed. After being in that jail cell she'd felt dirty all the way to her soul. Fergus had loaned her a shirt to sleep in.

A glance at the bedside clock told her it was 11:43 a.m. Her memory of what had taken place last night after Fergus had arrived was pretty jumbled. Apparently he'd been right about her being in shock, but she did remember that he'd brought her to his hotel instead of taking her home after she was released.

At first she'd objected, but then he'd told her he'd reserved a suite—a bedroom, and a living room with a pull-out bed. She could have the bedroom complete with her own bath.

A wave of sadness washed over her. She should have known he had no intention of seducing her. He'd stopped wanting her a long time ago. Why else had he gotten involved with another woman? Even so, he'd been protective of her. A half smile tilted the corners of her mouth upward as she remembered how he'd even taken off his suit coat and put it around her when they'd entered the hotel so she wouldn't be conspicuous walking through the lobby in her jail clothes.

Enough of this malingering, she thought, as she crawled out of bed and headed for the bathroom. She had to wake up and face Fergus and the mess she'd found herself in. He didn't deserve to be kept waiting around all day.

Her ex-husband was a busy man, but still he'd apparently dropped everything to come all the way to St. Louis to try to pull her chestnuts out of the fire. The least she could do was stop feeling sorry for herself and cooperate.

After splashing her face with cold water to banish the last of the drowsiness from her deep slumber, she brushed her teeth with the complimentary toothbrush and paste in her bathroom, then put on a white terry-cloth robe supplied by the hotel and went looking for Fergus.

She found him in the living room, working at a desk. She vaguely remembered his saying there was a fold-down bed in there, but if he'd slept on it, it had already been put back into the wall, because it was nowhere in sight.

"Well, hello there, sleepyhead," he said with a smile as he looked up. "I was just about to check on you again to make sure you were okay."

Her eyes widened. "Again?"

He got up and walked over to her. He was wearing jeans, with a dark-green polo shirt open at the throat, and he looked relaxed and incredibly sexy.

"Yes," he admitted. "I looked in on you before I went to bed, and again when I woke up this morning. I'm sorry if I invaded your privacy, but I was worried. You were in such a state last night...."

"I don't mind," she quickly replied. "That was thoughtful of you. I'm just sorry it took me so long to wake up. I don't think I've ever slept so soundly before."

"That's not unusual for someone who's been shocked as deeply as you have." His warm, caring gaze roamed over her. "You're looking much better this morning. Do you feel up to answering some questions after we've had something to eat?"

"Sure, I'll tell you anything you want to know," she said, "but I can't go out for lunch without any clothes."

"No problem." He walked across the room and picked up some parcels from the floor on the other side of his desk. "Your friend Anna stopped by on her way to work and brought you the things you'll need."

Sharon was startled. "Anna did? But how did she know...?" Then her unreliable memory cleared again. "Oh yes, that's right, we called her when we got here." Sharon shook her head impatiently. "I seem to be having trouble remembering all the things that happened after I found Floyd..."

Her voice wavered and she fought back a surge of horror at the memory of Floyd collapsed in a heap on the floor, with a letter opener sticking out of his chest.

"You're doing just fine," Fergus assured her, and walked across the room. "I'll put these things in the bedroom. I had coffee sent up earlier. It's there on the bar, if you'd like a cup before you get dressed. There's orange juice, too."

At the mention of food Sharon realized that she was starved. "Yes, I would," she said as she headed for the large bar area in one corner of the room. "I don't think I've had anything to eat since breakfast yesterday morning."

Fergus muttered an oath. "Didn't they feed you in jail?"

She poured steaming coffee out of the carafe into a china cup. "I was just about to go for lunch, when the letter came," she said thoughtfully. "Then the police questioned me all afternoon. I seem to remember a tray being brought to me in my cell later, but I was too sick and upset to eat."

She took a swallow of the hot brew and savored it as it trickled down her throat.

"Drink a big glass of the orange juice there, too," he said as he disappeared into the bedroom before he could see the face she made at him. He hadn't changed a bit. He was still bossing her around, but somehow it didn't bother her now.

Sharon was curled up in the corner of the black vinyl couch when Fergus returned, and his breath caught in his throat when he looked at her. She was sitting with her legs under her and the skirt of the terry robe draped over them, but the garment was too big and the bodice tended to gape when she relaxed her shoulders, revealing the top slope of her full breasts.

She had both hands wrapped around the coffee cup as she held it, and her blue eyes were unfocused while she gazed off into space. Her face was still a little puffy from sleep, and her lips were relaxed and slightly parted, as if waiting to be kissed. His stomach muscles clenched with the desire to oblige her. In all the years they'd been married he'd never seen her look sexier, and she was totally unaware of what she was doing to him!

What kind of hell was he subjecting himself to now?

He swallowed back a groan and switched his glance, and his direction, to the coffeepot on the bar.

After filling a cup for himself, he went over and sat down on the couch, too, but was careful to leave plenty of space between them. She smiled at him, and her face softened and lost the haunted look that had been so evident last night.

He tightened his grip on his cup, as if that could somehow prevent him from reaching out and taking her in his arms. His hands itched to slip inside that gaping robe and cup the firm round breasts he knew so well. He remembered the weight of them in his palms, the smoothness of her skin and the hardness of her nipples when he'd brush them with his thumbs—

The sound of her voice snapped him out of his erotic fantasizing. "How are your mom and dad, Fergus? Is your dad still practicing?"

Fergus's father, Ian Lachlan, was a physician.

Fergus took a deep breath and tried to focus his attention on her question. "Well, yes and no. He sold his practice in Evanston several years ago, and he and Mom moved back to that small village in Scotland where his family came from. He'd planned to retire, but when he got there he discovered there was no medical care for miles around, so he opened a clinic. Now he's busier than he was in Evanston, and he's never been happier."

"I'm glad," Sharon said. "I always loved your parents. I've missed them."

And what about me, Sharon? Did you ever miss me, as well?

Fergus clamped his mouth shut to keep the words from spilling out. He had no right to hope she'd been lonely for him.

"They loved you, too," he said, instead. "Although it was too awkward to continue a close relationship with you after our divorce, they never really accepted Elaine as a daughter-in-law."

Sharon frowned, and twisted on the couch to straighten up and put her feet on the floor. "I'm sorry about that," she said, as she faced him. "And, Fergus, I'm so very sorry about Elaine's death."

Her unexpected sympathy took his breath away, and it was a moment before he could respond. "That... that's amazingly generous of you—" he stammered before his voice broke and once more he had to fight for control.

"Not at all," she replied softly. "I never wished either of you harm. Oh, I was hurt and angry, but I was never vengeful."

Her voice shook, and he could tell that this was as difficult for her as it was for him. "Honey, I know that, but—"

She set her empty cup on the coffee table in front of them, then reached out and put her fingers across his mouth. The compassion in her eyes and voice was his undoing, and, no longer able to resist, he shifted closer to her so that their legs were touching.

"Please," she murmured. "Let me finish."

He nodded his consent, then put his hand over hers to hold it in place as he kissed her fingers.

She looked surprised, and her voice shook as she continued. "When I heard about Elaine's sudden death I knew you must be devastated. I wrote you a letter, but then I realized it would probably not be appropriate for me to intrude on you at such a time, so I tore it up."

Dear God, in spite of the anguish he'd caused her she still wanted to comfort him and help him bear his loss. It was incredible that she could be so forgiving!

Fergus was aware of the pressure of tears building up behind his eyes, and he blinked with the effort to keep them from falling. Dammit, he wasn't going to bawl like a baby and make her feel even sorrier for him. Pity wasn't what he wanted from Sharon. But it was hard to resist when he knew it was all he was going to get.

He wrapped his hand around hers and repositioned it to cup his cheek. It felt warm and soft against his skin, and he held it there while he fought to speak around the lump in his throat.

"I'm sorry you thought I wouldn't welcome your condolences," he said. "Actually, hearing from you would have gone a long way toward helping me to deal with a very dark and agonizing time in my life."

Sharon was close to tears, and she could see that she was upsetting Fergus, too. Why was it that she couldn't do anything right in her dealings with him? She'd only wanted him to know that she sympathized with him over the death of his wife, but all she'd done was reopen the wound and make him hurt again. She should never have started this. She couldn't handle his pain as well as her own.

"Then I'm sorry I didn't send the letter," she said, and quickly changed the subject. "Now, if you'll excuse me, I'll get dressed so we can go to lunch." She got up and went into the bedroom, closing the door behind her.

Fergus had put her overnight suitcase on the floor and laid the long dress bag across the unmade bed. She opened them and found a dress and a tailored pantsuit in the bag, and several changes of underwear, makeup, shoes, a pair of jeans and a knit shirt, and a nightgown and robe in the overnighter.

Good heavens, Anna must have thought she expected to stay there with Fergus for a while! Whatever made her think that? While it was more convenient last night, and Sharon appreciated his concern in giving up his bedroom to her, she was going to be sleeping in her own bed tonight.

That scene just now in the living room had scared her witless. When Fergus had kissed her fingers she'd wanted to melt into his arms, and when he'd cupped his cheek with her palm she'd had to restrain herself to keep from caressing it with her fingertips.

Obviously she was still highly susceptible to her ex-husband, and that would never do. It had taken her too long to get over him; she wasn't going to give him another chance to reject her.

If only he wasn't so damn nice!

She dressed quickly in the peach raw-silk pantsuit, then applied a touch of makeup and combed her hair. Her image in the mirror told her that she'd regained her natural rose color and lost the look of utter desolation that had been stamped on her face the night before.

That was good, because she had no intention of letting this experience beat her down. No matter what it cost her emotionally, she was going to accept Fergus's offer to defend her, and do everything she could to help him.

They had lunch in the hotel restaurant, and although Fergus did ask Sharon questions, he steered clear of the subject of the murder and asked instead about her friends and co-workers.

"Now, tell me about your other lawyer, Ray Quinlan," he said, after they'd exhausted the subject of her house-mates, Anna and Tracey.

Sharon swallowed a mouthful of quiche and washed it down with a sip of hot tea. "Ray's the son of our next-door neighbors. He doesn't live with his parents, so I don't know him very well. He just happened to be the only lawyer Anna and I knew at all, so I asked her to call him."

Fergus frowned. "That's not a very smart way to select an attorney who will be defending you on a murder charge," he said grimly. "Where did he go to school, and how long has he been practicing?"

"He's a native of St. Louis, and got his bachelor's and his law degree from Washington University right here in town," she said. "I met him when I moved next door to his parents four years ago. Ray was in his second year of law school then, and he graduated last year."

Fergus's expression was thunderous. "Are you telling me that you were willing to place your life in the hands of an attorney just out of law school? My God, Sharon, didn't you learn anything about the law while you were married to me?"

"Very little," she snapped as her temper escalated. "If you'll remember, you didn't want to talk about your work when you came home at night. When I'd ask you about it you always said we had more exciting things to do, and carried me off to bed."

She hadn't known what she was going to say until it was said, and then it was too late. The words hung in the air between them, and she felt the blood rush to her face while she watched it drain from his.

Embarrassment suffused her and left her immobilized, unable to speak or move. Dear Lord, what had she been thinking of?

But that was the problem—she hadn't been thinking pe-riod. How could she have blurted out something so intimate to Fergus, who was not only no longer her husband, but apparently didn't even remember how erotic and all-encompassing their lovemaking had been at one time?

For a long moment they sat in silence, neither of them able to pick up the conversation. Sharon couldn't bring herself to look directly at Fergus, but she'd seen the shocked expression on his face, and in his unblinking eyes, before she'd glanced away.

She felt like a tacky, insensitive clod. How was she ever going to apologize and make him understand that she hadn't deliberately planned to be so crude?

Before she could marshal her thoughts, Fergus spoke.

"You're right, Sharon." His tone was low and vibrant. "I did have better things to do than talk shop while I was married to you. Much better. So much better, in fact, that if I let myself think about those times now I won't be able to concentrate on anything else, and that's dangerous. For both your defense and my sanity."

His words freed her from the clutch of humiliation that had held her mute and still, and she took an unsteady breath. "Oh, Fergus, I'm so sorry. I swear I didn't mean to say that. I wasn't even thinking it."

He shook his head. "It's all right. I deserved it. I had no right to flare up at you the way I did. You and Anna did what most people would have done—you called on an attorney who was also a friend. Since I selfishly thought only of my own needs, when I should have taken the time to teach you about your rights under the law, you couldn't have known all the intricacies of selecting the right lawyer to handle the charges against you."

He took his napkin from his lap and tossed it on the table, then signaled the waiter for the check. "If you're finished eating we'd better go back upstairs. I have a lot more questions to ask you."

* * *

Back in the suite they settled themselves comfortably, Sharon on the couch and Fergus in the upholstered chair. They were still self-conscious because of her gaffe, but the embarrassment melted away as the interrogation progressed.

"Tell me all there is to know about your relationship with Floyd Vancleave, from the day you met until the time you were found bending over his body," he said. "Don't leave out anything, no matter how insignificant you may think it is."

It took her a long time, and when she was finished they went over it again, then again, until Sharon was tired, upset and becoming angrier by the minute.

"Now, tell me again about the advances Vancleave made toward you," he said for the second or third time. "Are you sure you didn't encourage him?"

"Encourage him!" she shouted. "Damn it, Fergus, are you deaf? How many times do I have to tell you? The man was a chauvinist pig, and I'm getting tired of you insinuating that I was flirting with him. I don't lead men on to tease them, and your insistence that I did that to Floyd is insulting."

"Then you'd better get used to being insulted," Fergus said grimly, "because if you're indicted and go to trial the district attorney is going to use every trick he can think of to make the jury believe that's exactly what you were doing.

"Now, let's go over this again. I don't want any nasty surprises when you get on the witness stand."

So they continued all afternoon. Fergus probed, insinuated, even accused her of withholding information, while Sharon reached deeper into her memory and seethed at his callous disregard for her feelings.

Fergus hated what he was doing to her. Every time she winced or cried out in indignation at his offensive questions it was like a knife in his heart, but he couldn't let up. He had to extract every bit of information she had, even what was buried deep in her subconscious.

The police would question her again before the arraignment, and although he'd be there this time to protect her as much as the law allowed, it could still get brutally savage. Also, he needed to test her breaking point. To see how far she could be pushed before she started fighting back and making herself more prone to errors in judgment as well as memory.

Fergus sincerely doubted that Sharon had ever had an enemy. She was sweet and kind, and liked by everyone she met. Unless he gave her a preview of what she would be subjected to by the D.A. in a court trial, she'd never hold up over the long run.

Damn that bastard Vancleave! It enraged Fergus just to think about him putting his slimy hands on Sharon and making vulgar propositions to her. Fergus silently vowed that if the police ever caught up with whoever had killed the man, he, Fergus, would defend the guilty party without charge and aim for an acquittal. Or at least the lightest possible sentence.

Sharon's endurance finally snapped late in the afternoon when he sank to a new low and asked her how many male employees of the hotel she'd slept with. He doubted the judge would allow her to answer a question like that, but that didn't mean the D.A. wouldn't ask it.

She came totally unglued. He happened to be standing at the time, and with a howl of indignation and rage, she sprang off the couch and hurled herself at him, arms swinging and feet kicking. She took him by surprise and landed several hard blows, all the time yelling denials and calling him names that questioned his parentage and his honor, before he managed to overpower her and pin her arms to her sides.

"Calm down, sweetheart," he shouted over the noise she was making while she continued to struggle in his restraining embrace. "I don't expect you to answer that question, but I had to ask it to see how you'd react."

She stopped struggling and stiffened as she gaped at him, eyes wide. "How I'd react? How'd you think I'd react? No, don't answer that. I'll show you. You're fired! You might as well pack up and go back to Chicago, because I wouldn't let you defend me if you were the last lawyer on earth. I'd get the gas chamber for sure."

Once more she started twisting and turning in his arms. "Let go of me, dammit!"

"I will," Fergus assured her. "Just as soon as you cool down enough to listen to me. I had to know how you'd react under stress to that question when you weren't expecting it, because in one form or another it's going to be asked of you."

Again she stopped squirming, and glared at him. "You wouldn't," she gasped.

"No, I wouldn't, but the prosecution will," he said through clenched teeth. "They have a strong case. You were seen going into the office in a huff, everyone in the waiting room heard you and Vancleave quarreling and just minutes later you were found bending over the body with the murder weapon in your hand."

She slumped against him, and he released her and put a few feet of space between them. "All they need for a conviction is to show that you were capable of killing your boss in a fit of rage, and you did a good job of convincing a jury of that by the way you attacked me just now. If you react that way in court the prosecution sure as hell won't let me get away with portraying you as a naively innocent young woman who was being unlawfully sexually harassed by this creep. Not without a fight, and believe me it will turn dirty."

His harsh words hit Sharon like blows. How was it possible to be innocent and yet look so indisputably guilty?

"But, Fergus, I wasn't there," she said for what must have been the hundredth time. "I was gone for at least five minutes."

He ran his fingers through his already disheveled dark hair. "I believe you, honey, but so far they haven't turned up anyone who saw you while you were gone. If only you'd left through the outer office . . ."

She sighed. "I know, but I was so mad, and the nearest exit was out the glass doors. There were people out there by the pool. Surely one of them must have seen me."

Fergus's smile wasn't very convincing as he said, "Someone did, that's for sure. We'll just keep looking till we find him or her. But meanwhile, you have to be prepared for some downright nasty questions from the D.A.—"

A sharp knock on the door interrupted him, and he looked at his watch. "That'll be Ray Quinlan now. I asked him to come over this afternoon so we could get together on our strategy before the arraignment tomorrow."

Fergus opened the door and greeted Sharon's other attorney. He was a nice-looking man, about Sharon's age, medium height and weight, with straw-colored hair and brown eyes. He wore a navy blue suit and had obviously just come from the office where he and a partner shared a fledgling law practice.

Ray spotted Sharon and walked across the room to put his arms around her. "Hi, angel," he said huskily. "I'm so glad to see you out of that jailhouse. I'm just sorry I couldn't get the judge to release you."

She hugged him. "I know, Ray. You did the best you could."

He grimaced. "Yeah, but it wasn't good enough. I'm glad Anna had enough of her wits about her to call Fergus. Man! I understand he walked into that courtroom and had you released within minutes."

"It wasn't quite that easy," Fergus said from behind them. "I had to give something to get something. Don't forget, Sharon is in my custody now."

She pulled out of Ray's embrace and looked at Fergus. "Just what does that mean?" she asked. "Did you obligate yourself for something?"

He grinned. "Yeah, I sure did. From now on you and I are going to be *very* close, if you know what I mean."

She felt both a thrill and a chill. Now what had she gotten herself into?

"No. I don't know what you mean," she said uncertainly. "Suppose you tell me."

"I mean that I'm responsible for seeing to it that you don't get into any more trouble, and that you show up for your court appearances."

He winked suggestively. "That means I'm going to keep you close beside me from now until the trial is over."

Chapter Five

This seemed to be Sharon's day for emotional highs and lows. She was both elated and dismayed. Elated that Fergus was going to be with her for the next few weeks, but dismayed at the thought of the damage that could do to her already battered heart.

There was no future for Fergus and her. They were a part of the past, and he hadn't loved her enough. Sharon couldn't forget that, nor could she ever trust him with her deepest, most sensitive feelings again.

She'd resigned herself to the fact that he'd always be the love of her life, but she could live without that kind of love. It would be extremely difficult, though, if they were together for long periods of time. There must be another way.

"Fergus," she said haltingly. "I can't tell you how much I appreciate your coming to my defense in this terrible mess, and I'd never do anything to get you in trouble, but I can't live here with you. I don't think that would even be ethical.

Surely you can trust me if I give you my word. Have I ever lied to you?''

Fergus's expression changed from good-natured, to startled, to regretful. "Of course I trust you, Sharon," he said quickly. "I'm sorry, I was mostly teasing. I didn't mean you had to live with me, although considering our past relationship that would not be unethical, but I am responsible for your court appearances and I intend to keep you safe. Someone killed Vancleave, and I'm going to make sure whoever it was doesn't come after you, too."

Sharon was more surprised than alarmed. "Do you think that's a possibility?"

He moved closer and put his hand on her arm. "Not really, but we're not taking any chances. I'm going to send to Chicago for one of the private investigators my law firm uses. We'll do some checking on our own."

"Hey, that's something I can do," Ray said. "I put myself through college and law school by working as a P.I. I'm good at it, and I have a lot of contacts here in St. Louis."

A big grin split Fergus's face. "Great! If you can get started right away maybe you can come up with something I can use at the arraignment tomorrow. Why don't you go over to the Starlight and check into a room for the night. That place is probably buzzing with rumors and gossip. You shouldn't have any trouble tuning in to it. Some of it might even be true."

Ray nodded. "Consider it done," he said. "I'll be in touch with you no later than eight o'clock in the morning."

He left, and as the door shut behind him the phone rang. Fergus answered it, and Sharon went into the bedroom to gather up her things. It was time for her to go home, but first she had to walk over to the Starlight and get her car, which was still parked in their garage.

She was fastening the overnight case, when Fergus appeared in the doorway. "That was Lieutenant Zurcher at homicide," he said. "He wants to question you again in the morning, before the arraignment in the afternoon. I told him we'd be there at nine—" He broke off when he saw that she was fiddling with the suitcase. "What are you doing?"

She turned around. "I'm getting ready to go home," she told him, "but first I have to pick up my car at the hotel."

He looked disappointed. "Oh. But I was going to take you to dinner. Why don't you just spend the night here again since we have to be at the police station so early in the morning?"

That sounded good. So good that she didn't dare accept. It would be pure idiocy to get used to living with him again. It was only a convenience for him, but for her it could spell disaster.

"Oh thanks," she said, trying to keep her tone light and the disappointment out of it, "but I must get home. That is, unless you really don't trust me out of your sight."

He scowled, and waved a hand in denial. "Of course I trust you, and I never thought or said otherwise. I was only trying to make things easier for you."

She picked up her suitcase and walked over to him. "I know," she said gently, "and I thank you for that. Look, why don't you drive me over to the Starlight to pick up my car, then follow me home and have dinner with us? I'd like you to see where I live and get to know the women I share a house with."

His gaze searched her face before he nodded. "Fine. I met Anna briefly this morning when she brought your clothes. She's one gorgeous-looking lady and seemed awfully nice, but I'd like to meet the other woman, too, and see where you live."

Sharon felt a stab of jealousy. It was true, Anna was a stunner. A fact Fergus hadn't lost any time noticing. Did that mean he was attracted to her?

Sharon felt sick, but forced a smile and a light tone. "Tracey's not as beautiful as Anna, but she's awfully cute. Red hair, pug nose and freckles. Neither of them is seriously involved with a man right now, so you can have your pick.''

Fergus caught his breath as Sharon's words landed like a blow to his midsection. She was trying to fix him up with one of her roommates! Damn! So much for any hopes he may have had that someday she'd learn to love and trust him again.

"Knock off the matchmaking, Sharon," he said angrily. "I'm not in the market for a woman."

He reached out and took the case from her. "Come on, maybe if we hurry we can miss the worst of the rush-hour traffic."

After picking up her car, then a quick stop at her favorite supermarket for groceries, Sharon eventually pulled up to the curb in front of her house, with Fergus right behind her. Neither Anna's automobile nor Tracey's was in the driveway, which meant that they weren't home from work yet.

Sharon and Fergus got out of their cars and met on the sidewalk, Fergus carrying the groceries, which he'd insisted on paying for. His gaze roamed over the red brick Tudor house with the gabled roof and the arched doorway. "Nice place you've got here," he said. "Classy old neighborhood, too. No wonder it takes three of you to pay the rent. How many rooms do you have?"

She fingered her keys for the one to the house while she answered. "Four bedrooms, although we use one of them as a family room, a living room, formal dining room, modernized kitchen and three baths. Oh, there's also a full basement, where we do the laundry."

They strolled up the cement walk that bisected the thick green lawn and led to three steps and a landing in front of the solid oak door.

"Surely you have a gardener," Fergus said as he surveyed the large, well-kept lot that bloomed with colorful flower gardens and huge old shade trees.

"Bet on it," she answered with a laugh. "None of us has the time or the inclination to keep up a yard this size. The back is even bigger."

She unlocked the door and walked into the foyer with Fergus right behind her. He pushed the door shut and turned to the right into the living room, while she went left through the dining room and into the kitchen. Fergus joined her shortly, still carrying the groceries. "I'm very impressed with your house," he told her as he set the sacks on the yellow tile counter.

"Thanks," she said, "but it's not mine. I could never afford to buy it. We just keep hoping that nobody else can afford to buy it, either. We love living here."

The sound of a car pulling into the driveway distracted them, and a few minutes later Anna let herself in. "Sharon, are you here?" she called as she headed toward the kitchen. "I saw your car out front— Oh, there you are," she said as she appeared in the doorway and spotted them. "Fergus, hi. You're staying for dinner, I hope."

"He is, and I'm cooking," Sharon answered as she unpacked the groceries.

"Great," Anna said. "I'll go change my clothes and be right back to help."

She turned and walked away just as the door opened again and Tracey's voice echoed through the rooms. "Sharon, where are you?"

They all four met in the dining room, and Tracey grabbed Sharon and hugged her. "Oh, Sharon, I'm so glad they let you out of that awful place. It must have been gross—"

"It was," Sharon interrupted, not wanting to go into a long discussion about her stay in jail. "but I'm home now, and that's all that matters."

She felt Tracey stiffen just before they pulled apart. "Do you mean you'll be spending the nights *here* again?"

Sharon blinked. "Of course. Where else would I stay?"

A high blush of emotion stained Tracey's face. "Oh, I...that is, I thought you'd be staying at the hotel with Fergus. You know, like you did last night."

Sharon's confusion increased. What had gotten into Tracey? She was always a little flaky, but she wasn't usually irrational. "Whatever gave you that idea?" she asked crossly. "Clients aren't chained to their lawyers, you know."

"No, of course not!" Tracey exclaimed quickly. "I didn't mean... That is, I don't know what I was thinking of." She seemed to become more flustered the longer she talked.

"Excuse me, I..." She paused for a moment, then turned away. "I have to go change my clothes," she stammered, and hurried out of the room.

Sharon saw Fergus and Anna exchange a puzzled glance, but no one commented as the three of them headed back into the kitchen.

Fergus volunteered to barbecue the steaks on the grill in the backyard. He also buried foil-wrapped potatoes and corn in the hot coals to bake, but by the time everything was ready a breeze had come up and it was too chilly to eat outside, so they moved into the dining room.

Sharon tossed a green salad with ranch dressing, Fergus's favorite, and later dished up scoops of vanilla ice cream covered with chocolate syrup, again Fergus's favorite, for dessert. Fergus, Anna and Tracey kept up a running conversation of questions and answers in the manner of companionable strangers getting to know one another, while Sharon sat back and listened.

It was a warm, relaxed and intimate setting. Too intimate for Sharon's peace of mind. It reminded her all too sharply of the small friendly gatherings she and Fergus used to host when they were married, and the memories were bittersweet.

Although they'd enjoyed attending large parties, they'd preferred to entertain in small groups, and she'd always planned her menus around his favorite foods. It disconcerted her to realize she'd done the same thing tonight.

Why was she catering to the man who had left her for another woman? She'd have to watch that. It would never do for her to fall back into the habit of doing things for him.

Still, isn't that what he was doing for her? Taking care of her? He'd dropped everything to come when he heard she was in trouble, even though she hadn't asked him to. He'd gotten her released from jail on bail after Ray had been unable to. He'd put his reputation on the line by guaranteeing her appearance in court. The least she could do was make him comfortable.

She really owed him that much. Didn't she?

Her uneasy musing was interrupted when Fergus pushed back his chair.

"I hate to break this up," he said as he put his napkin on the table, "but I have some phone calls to make when I get back to the hotel, and it's getting late."

He stood, and the three women also rose. "It's been a great evening," he said, "and I'm sure we'll get to know one another a lot better as time goes on. Thanks for dinner. It was delicious."

He turned and looked at Sharon. "Come out to the car with me," he said softly, and she nodded, unable to resist.

After a round of goodbyes he took her arm and strolled with her out of the house and down the walk. "Thank you for inviting me over," he said again. "I appreciate meeting your friends and being welcomed at your house."

Sharon was caught off guard and wasn't sure how to answer. "It . . . it seemed like the least I could do after the way you've come to my rescue."

She knew that was the wrong response when his hand tightened involuntarily on her arm, as though he'd been hit by a sudden sharp pain.

"I don't want you putting yourself out for me just because you think you owe it to me," he said briskly. "You

don't owe me a damn thing, and I don't want your gratitude."

He released her arm and started around the car to get in
on the driver's side.

"Wait, Fergus," she cried, and ran to catch up. "I didn't
mean it like that. Really. It's just that I... I don't know how
to talk to you anymore. Everything I say comes out wrong."

He'd stopped in front of the car, and they stood there in
the street just a few feet away from the lamp that provided
enough dim illumination for them to see each other's faces.

He turned and cupped her shoulders with his hands. "I
know what you mean," he admitted. "I have the same
problem. I'm so afraid of saying or doing something you'll
misunderstand that my tongue gets tied and my foot winds
up in my mouth."

She couldn't stifle a giggle. "Good. Then you won't mind
if I try again on that last foot-in-mouth remark I made?"

He chuckled and squeezed her shoulders. "Please do."

She searched his face as she spoke. "Anything you may
have done to hurt me in the past has been canceled out by
the way you've come to my rescue in these past few hours,"
she said slowly as she mentally scrambled for words to express her feelings. "I'd never have survived the night in that
jail cell, and as you've pointed out, I'm totally out of my
depth in handling this horrendous experience."

Unable to resist touching him, she reached out and caressed his cheek with her fingertips. "I always knew you
were an honorable man, and you've more than proven me
right. You didn't have to disrupt your busy life and come
here to defend me. I'm not your responsibility anymore, but
still you did just that and I'll be forever grateful."

He glowered and opened his mouth, but she put her fingers across his lips and smiled. "I know you don't want my
gratitude, but you have it all the same. There's nothing
wrong with that, but I hope we can also be friends. I mean,

good friends. The kind who don't have to pussyfoot around each other for fear of being misunderstood.''

He kissed the pads of her fingers, sending chills up her spine, then put his arms around her waist and pulled her gently against him. ''At the very least I'll always be your good friend,'' he murmured huskily. ''You're special, and from now on I'll always be there when you need me. I pray that someday you'll trust me enough again to believe that.''

He lowered his head and brushed her lips with his, so lightly that she would have thought it was just a soft breeze if her senses hadn't been so fully aware of the touch of his warm, familiar mouth against hers.

It was over before she could react, and he pulled away from her and continued on around the car.

''I'll pick you up at eight-thirty in the morning,'' he said as he opened the door.

''Oh no, don't do that!'' she exclaimed shakily. ''It's so far out of your way. I'll meet you at the hotel and we can go to the police station together from there. Okay?''

He gave a curt nod. ''If that's the way you want it, but don't go near the station without me. I don't want you to even say hello to a policeman again unless I'm with you.''

He climbed behind the wheel and started the engine, and Sharon stepped back up on the curb as he drove off. She stood there watching long after the car was out of sight, shivering in the cool night breeze, but unwilling to go inside until she was sure the enchantment that radiated within her didn't glow from her face and eyes.

Snap out of it, you idiot, she told herself. *You're nothing to him but a big load of guilt, and don't ever lose sight of that fact. His emotions are not to be trusted. Nobody knows that better than you!*

Anna and Tracey cleaned up the kitchen and put the dishes in the dishwasher, since Sharon and Fergus had fixed dinner, but Sharon noticed that Tracey was quieter than usual and again seemed uneasy and preoccupied the way she had been when she'd arrived home earlier.

She excused herself and went to her room as soon as they were finished, and that puzzled Sharon, too. Usually Tracey was the last one to turn in at night. But Sharon was still too bemused by the fleeting kiss Fergus had given her to keep her mind on anything else.

The following morning Sharon was awake early as usual, but stayed in bed until the other two were through in the bathrooms, since she didn't have to leave the house as early as they did. When she did get up she dressed carefully in her softly tailored mauve business suit. This time when she was interrogated by the police she was damn well going to be treated with dignity, and the best way to assure that was to dress the part of the successful businesswoman. Last time she'd been questioned she'd been almost incoherent, and the front of her dress had been stained with blood!

As she walked up the hall she heard Anna and Tracey talking in the kitchen and was on her way to join them, when she heard her name mentioned. Instinctively she stopped a few feet short of the door and listened.

Anna was speaking and she sounded cross. "Tracey, I don't understand you. How could you possibly be afraid of Sharon? Surely you don't think she murdered Floyd Vancleave!"

Sharon gasped and put her hand across her mouth to keep from crying out.

"No...not really." It was Tracey, petulant and uncertain. "That is... Oh, I don't know. She sure had good reason to. I don't think any jury with working women on it would convict her, but how do we know that if she got mad enough to do it once she wouldn't do it again the next time someone upset her?"

Sharon's head began to spin, and she leaned against the wall to steady herself. *Tracey actually thought she'd killed Floyd!*

"That's the most ridiculous thing I've ever heard!" Anna said angrily. "Sharon wouldn't even let us set a trap for that mouse we had a while back. For heaven's sake, Tracey, get a grip on yourself. She's no more capable of killing someone than you are or I am."

Sharon felt a little better knowing that Anna didn't share Tracey's uncertainty.

"But we can't be sure of that," Tracey wailed. "How can you feel safe in the house with her here? I didn't sleep hardly at all last night, even though I propped a chair under the doorknob. I'm sorry, but I can't help it. The possibility that I'm sharing a house with a murderer scares me to death!"

Sharon had heard enough. She wasn't going to force her presence on Tracey if Tracey was afraid of her.

But, dear God, if her housemate, who knew her so well, could believe she was capable of cold-blooded murder, how many other people would believe it, too?

Sharon pushed away from the wall, then realized that her knees were shaking so badly she could hardly stand. She steadied herself with her hand for a minute, then walked into the kitchen.

The two women were sitting at the table, eating breakfast, and when they looked up and saw her standing in the doorway they stopped their argument in midsentence.

Sharon's anguish must have been evident in her expression, because Anna's eyes widened with concern. "Sharon! Oh my God..." She pushed back her chair and hurried across the room. "Here, let me help you," she said, and put her arm around Sharon, but Sharon shrugged it off.

"How long have you been standing there?" Anna asked anxiously.

"Long enough," Sharon answered, and watched as Tracey's stricken face turned several shades of red.

"I...I didn't mean..." Tracey's words trailed away into an uncomfortable silence.

Sharon took a deep breath and tried to pull herself together. "Don't lie to spare my feelings," she said coldly. "You obviously meant every word of what you said. You actually believe I'm guilty as charged."

"She's just confused," Anna interjected as she shot Tracey a quelling look. "When she's had time to think about it she'll know you couldn't have done it."

"It's . . . It's not as if I blamed you," Tracey stammered.

"Dammit, Tracey, shut up," Anna ordered. "You're only making things worse."

Tracey's face crumpled and tears gushed forth. "I'm sorry. . . ."

"I'm sure you are," Sharon said, feeling too betrayed to accept the apology, "but don't worry, I've no intention of staying where I'm not wanted. I'll pack up and leave before you get home from work."

"No!" Anna cried. "This is your home and you have a right to be here. I won't allow you to be forced out because of Tracey's wild imaginings."

Tracey wailed loudly into her napkin, but it was Sharon who spoke. "I appreciate your loyalty, Anna. More than I can say. But I couldn't stay here knowing Tracey's afraid to come home for fear I'll kill her while she sleeps."

Tracey continued to cry, while Anna muttered a few well-chosen oaths. "Promise me that you won't do anything until we've talked to Fergus," she insisted. "He should have a say in this. After all, you were released in his custody."

"That doesn't mean I have to get permission from him—"

"Yes, I'm afraid it does," Anna interrupted. "Almost anything you do now has possible legal ramifications. It's not fair to either of you not to check out any sudden decision with him first."

Sharon shrugged. "I suppose you're right," she admitted. "I'll bring him home with me after the hearing this afternoon. Who knows, maybe the judge will find that there's not enough evidence against me to charge me with anything."

She didn't really believe that, and even if, by some miracle, it did happen she couldn't share a house, or a friendship, with Tracey again, now that she knew how shallow the young woman's loyalty was.

Sharon arrived at Fergus's hotel suite at eight-thirty and knocked on the door. He opened it, then just stood there staring at her. "You look..." He cleared his throat and started over. "I've never seen you looking more beautiful, but it wasn't necessary for you to dress up to be questioned by the police."

Just seeing him made her feel better, and she smiled and walked past him as he stood back to let her enter. "It was necessary for my own morale," she told him as she sat down on the couch. "Wednesday when they interrogated me I was an emotional and visual wreck. My clothes were spattered with blood, and I was so shocked that I could barely function. I looked like a killer and they treated me like trash."

Fergus had been about to sit down in the chair, but now he straightened up again and eyed her. "If you were mistreated by any of the police officers I want to know it," he said grimly. "I'll file complaints all the way from the local chief to the attorney general."

She shook her head. "That's not what I meant," she assured him. "No one laid a hand on me. It was their attitude I'm talking about, and I'm going to insist on being treated with a reasonable amount of respect today."

Fergus appeared relieved and sank back down into the chair. "They won't harass you today," he promised. "I'll be there, and I won't let them."

Again she smiled. "I know. You were always there to fight my battles for me, but I'm not a teenager anymore. I want them to know I'm a woman to be treated with consideration even when my lawyer's not around."

* * *

The interrogation didn't exactly go smoothly, but neither was it as horrendous as before. Fergus was a force to be reckoned with, and he severely limited its scope. He never left her side, and he wouldn't allow her to answer questions that might remotely intimidate her, although they were mainly a rehash of actions and events she'd already admitted to before she'd had the protection of an attorney.

They were finished in time for a leisurely lunch at her favorite Greek restaurant in the University City loop area, far enough away from downtown that they eluded the persistent reporters and photographers who were becoming a nuisance.

Sharon had known all morning that she should apprise Fergus of the scene with Tracey at breakfast, but she kept putting it off, telling herself she'd do it later, after the police questioned her, after lunch, and now, after the arraignment. There were just too many things happening to her all at once. She needed a respite, however short, before she could face this last heartbreak.

The arraignment was short and to the point. The judge informed her that she was being charged with murder in the first degree and asked if she would plead guilty or not guilty. Fergus answered for her. "My client pleads not guilty, Your Honor."

Since she was represented by an attorney, the judge merely noted the plea and dismissed them without advising her of her rights under the law. A preliminary hearing was scheduled for Wednesday of the following week.

Although Fergus had acquainted Sharon with the various steps in a criminal-court procedure, she was still confused, and when they got back to his hotel she asked him to explain once more what happened during a preliminary hearing.

They were having drinks in the lounge, and he put his hand over hers where it lay on the table. "It's the procedure to determine whether there is sufficient evidence to bind you over for trial."

He kept his voice low, but she heard a slight tremor. "The district attorney will present his case against you, and I will cross-examine his witnesses and challenge his evidence. It won't take long, but again I have to warn you, from what I've heard so far he has a strong case."

Fergus squeezed her hand. "Unless we find a witness who saw you during the time you were away from the hotel on that day, you'll almost certainly be indicted."

Sharon had already known this, but hearing Fergus say it again still sent a wave of terror through her and made her moan.

He held up his other hand for silence. *"But,"* he continued, "if necessary, I'll fight for you to be allowed to remain free on bail, and we'll have at least three months before the trial starts to find a way to prove your innocence. You're entitled to a speedy trial, but if that's not enough time we can ask for a continuance."

He brought her hand to his mouth and kissed her palm, almost making her forget how bleak her future looked.

"Believe me, love, I'm not going to let you be convicted of murder."

Sharon didn't doubt but that he'd do everything in his power to prove her innocent, but she also knew he was taking on an almost impossible task.

They finished their drinks, and she realized she could no longer delay wrestling with the latest impediment to her freedom and peace of mind. Was there no end to the problems that confronted her? They just kept popping up, one after the other, with frightening regularity.

When the waiter came to replenish their piña coladas Sharon declined, saying she wanted to get home before the late-afternoon traffic crunch got any worse. They left the lounge, but in the lobby she took a deep breath, then stopped and turned to Fergus. "I . . . I promised Anna I'd invite you to dinner again tonight. Some—something has come up that she says you need to be consulted about."

A flash of apprehension darkened his face. "What's happened?" he asked anxiously. "Dammit, Sharon, are you keeping something from me? How in hell can I defend you if—"

"It's nothing like that," she quickly assured him. "It's something I'm perfectly capable of handling myself, but Anna insists—"

"I'll be the judge of what you can handle," he grated, and took her arm. "Let's go up to my suite, where we can talk in private."

He tried to turn her toward the elevators, but she dug in her heels and resisted. "No. This involves Anna and Tracey, too, and they need to be there when we discuss it. If you'd like to come about six, we'll have dinner and then—"

"I'll follow you home now," he interrupted impatiently, "and forget about dinner. Nobody eats until I find out what happened between the time I left you last night and when you showed up here at the hotel this morning. Honestly, Sharon, I'd hoped you'd outgrown that stubborn independent streak. There are times when you could try the patience of a stone."

His hand still on her arm, he led her to the parking garage and asked the attendant to bring their cars around.

While they waited in silence Sharon cast a furtive glance at Fergus. He was really ticked off with her this time. She could feel the anger radiating from him, and see it in the harsh set of his mouth and the storm gathering in his green eyes.

She hadn't meant to upset him. Once more she'd been overly dramatic. Maybe she should go ahead and tell him now what had happened so he could see for himself that it had no bearing on her case and not worry about it all the way home.

She was thinking about how to phrase the matter, when the attendants drove up with their cars and the opportunity was lost as Fergus hustled her into hers, then got into his own and waved her ahead.

It was rush hour on a Friday, and traffic out of the downtown area was frustratingly slow. By the time they got to the house both Anna's car and Tracey's were parked in the driveway. Sharon breathed a sigh of relief. They were all there and could get this over with.

As she unlocked the door and walked inside with Fergus she sniffed the redolent aroma of Tracey's tuna-and-noodle casserole bubbling gently in the oven, and knew she wouldn't be able to eat. All she wanted to do was get this confrontation over with and leave. The home she'd lived in and loved for the past four years now seemed stark and forbidding.

A feeling of dread stole over her. Was this a portent of what her life was going to be like from now on?

Chapter Six

The house was quiet, with no immediate sign of either Anna or Tracey, but Sharon spotted several envelopes scattered on the small, marble-topped maple chest in the foyer and picked them up as she led Fergus into the living room. She knew they'd all be for her, since she was the last one home.

As she sorted through them she noted that most were junk mail, but the last one was an official envelope from the Starlight Hotel where she worked. A notation on the envelope indicated that it had been delivered by special messenger, so apparently it had arrived while either Anna or Tracey was home to sign for it. She ripped it open, extracted a familiar piece of hotel stationery and unfolded it.

She glanced at the typewritten note, then blinked and reread it as the letters blurred on the page. "Oh no," she moaned, and bent forward slightly. She folded her arms across her waist in a reflex motion to stem the nausea that clutched at her stomach from the force of the emotional blow she'd received.

Fergus was standing beside her. "What's the matter?" he asked anxiously. "Sharon, what's wrong?"

She handed him the letter. "I've... I've been put on administrative leave without pay until the legal charges against me have been resolved." She fought back a sob. "Dammit, Fergus, can they do that? Isn't there something in the Constitution about being presumed innocent until proven guilty?"

He read the letter, then folded it and put it in his suit-jacket pocket. "You bet there is," he assured her as he turned and took her in his arms. "Don't worry, sweetheart." He cuddled her and rubbed his cheek in her hair. "I'll take care of it. They can put you on involuntary leave, but I'll make the bastards pay you for it."

Sharon couldn't hold back the sobs any longer, or the tears that streamed down her face and onto his expensive coat. *This had been a rotten day!* It had started when she'd gotten up and learned that Tracey thought she'd murdered Floyd and was afraid to live in the same house with her. Then there had been the repeated grillings by the police and her arraignment on charges of first-degree murder, and now she'd been fired from her job. Or as close as they could legally come to firing her.

Was there no end to it? The only good thing in this whole sorry mess was that Fergus had reentered her life, and he was only there to defend her. He was a lawyer and that was his job, but once the trial was over he'd be gone again and she'd be alone and...

And what? Free? Or doomed to spend the rest of her life in prison?

A shudder ran through her, and Fergus tightened his arms around her just before they were both distracted by Anna's voice.

"Sharon. Are you here? I thought I heard— Oops! Sorry...."

Fergus and Sharon both looked toward the doorway, where Anna was just turning away. "Anna, wait. Don't leave," Sharon said as she reluctantly slipped out of Fergus's embrace. "It's not what you think...."

Anna turned back, and her expression quickly changed from embarrassment to concern when she saw Sharon's tear-stained face.

"No, unfortunately it's not," Fergus added. "Sharon's just received notice that the hotel doesn't want her to come back to work."

Anna gasped. "But that's—"

"Legal," he interrupted, "but it's going to cost them. I'll see to it that they pay her for her enforced 'vacation,' but right now it appears there's a different problem that needs clearing up. Sharon wouldn't tell me what it is until you and Tracey could be present. Is Tracey here?"

Anna nodded. "Yes, but she's awfully upset. She fixed her casserole, then shut herself in her room. She doesn't want to face the two of you."

Fergus's eyes widened. "Why ever not? What in hell is going on here?"

"I suggest that Sharon and I tell you about it, and then you can talk to Tracey," Anna said. "Forcing her to be here will only make things worse."

"That's fine with me," Fergus replied. "It was Sharon who wanted you both present." He looked at Sharon. "Is that all right with you?"

She was too drained to offer any resistance. "Yes," she said between sniffles, "but let's sit down first." Her knees felt rubbery and she wasn't sure how much longer they were going to hold her up.

Sharon and Fergus settled themselves on the sofa, and Anna chose the wing chair.

There was a rather strained silence as each waited for one of the others to start. Finally Fergus impatiently broke the tension. "Anna, suppose you tell me what everyone is so unwilling to talk about."

Anna leaned back and crossed her long, slender legs. She hadn't yet changed from the blue suit she'd worn to work. "Tracey confessed to me this morning that she's nervous about living in the same house with Sharon now that Sharon's been charged with killing her boss."

Fergus stiffened and bit back an oath as he forced himself to be quiet and not interrupt.

"Unfortunately Sharon overheard the conversation," Anna continued, "and she insists that she'll move out immediately."

Fergus winced with the onslaught of empathetic pain he felt for Sharon. It was almost as if he were connected to her by a physical bond. Dear Lord, she'd been dealing with this alone all day. Why hadn't she told him this morning? Didn't she even want his emotional support? How many more of these continuing setbacks could she bear? How much more of her silent rejection of him could he stand?

He glanced at her, huddled next to him on the sofa, fighting back the tears and sobs she had every right to give vent to. It was sheer agony not to reach out and hold her, comfort her, even though she apparently didn't want his comfort, but if he did he'd lose his objectivity completely, and right now she needed his expertise more than she needed his empty assurances that everything would be all right. They both knew it wouldn't.

"No way are you moving out," he said between clenched teeth.

"But I can't stay here," Sharon protested. "Tracey's scared to death of me. She's afraid I'll murder her in her sleep."

"Then it's up to Tracey to move." His tone made it plain that he was not open to argument. He looked at Anna.

"How do you feel about this? Are you afraid of Sharon, too?"

"Of course not," she said scornfully. "Sharon couldn't harm anybody or anything, and I won't hear of her moving out. The two of us have shared this house for almost four years. I consider her more like a sister than just a friend."

Again Sharon's tears started to flow, and Fergus could no longer resist the urgent need he had to touch her, however lightly. He reached over and took her hand in his.

But before he could say anything Anna continued, "I agree with you that if anyone moves out it will be Tracey. She's the newcomer. She's been with us for over a year and I deeply resent her lack of loyalty. Everyone who knows Sharon at all knows she's not capable of committing any crime, least of all murder."

A sob convulsed Sharon, and she squeezed Fergus's hand in an obvious effort to control her emotions. "Your...your faith in me means more than I can ever tell you, Anna. You're the closest thing I have to family and I love you, but I really think it's me who should leave. After all, I'm the one who's in trouble."

Fergus felt as if Sharon had slapped him. How could she say that Anna was the closest thing she had to family? *He* was her family! He was closer to her than Anna could ever be. Had been ever since her parents had been killed in a boating accident shortly after he and Sharon had become lovers. From then on he'd been father, brother, lover and husband to her.

How could anyone else be closer than that?

But, of course, he'd forfeited that relationship when he'd gotten involved with Elaine. He'd never stopped loving Sharon, but she couldn't believe him then and she wouldn't believe him now. She hadn't even contacted him when she was arrested for a murder she didn't commit, even though he was recognized as one of the top defense attorneys in the country.

His attention snapped back to the subject at hand when Anna spoke.

"You're in trouble, but it's through no fault of your own."

"That's right," Fergus agreed. "And if you move now it's going to look like both of your housemates think you're guilty and have kicked you out. That would be a public-relations disaster, and I can't allow it. I think it's about time we had a talk with this young woman. She's hidden in her room long enough. Do one of you want to go get her or shall I?"

Anna chuckled and stood up. "I think that in the best interest of all of us I'd better do it," she said, and left.

Sharon pulled her hand out of Fergus's and shivered as she folded her arms across her chest. She looked so forlorn and alone that all his good intentions dissolved, and he reached for her and snuggled her in his embrace. She didn't protest, but buried her face in his shoulder and continued to tremble.

He caressed the top of her head with his lips. "Honey, I'm afraid you're going to be sick if you stay this keyed up. Do you have a tranquilizer you could take?"

She shook her head. "I don't take pills. They're nothing but a crutch, and it's too easy to become addicted."

He should have known. While they were married she wouldn't even take an analgesic for menstrual cramps.

"That's true up to a point," he agreed, "but sometimes crutches are necessary in order to give the body, or the nerves, a respite so healing can take place."

She snuggled closer and he tightened his arms until her soft breasts flattened against his chest and her thigh crushed against his. He knew she was too upset to be aware of the intimacy of the contact, but he gloried in it.

He also silently cursed the swift quickening of his body, which was going to torment as well as embarrass him, since there was no way he could act on it, even if they were alone.

She'd be outraged if he made a pass, and he couldn't chance that. Not yet. Not until he found a way to convince her to trust him again.

"I suppose you're right," she said, "but I don't have anyone to rely on but myself, and I need all my wits about me. I can't afford to dull my mind with drugs."

He cringed at her unthinking cruelty. If she'd deliberately set out to hurt him she couldn't have done it more thoroughly.

"What do you mean you don't have anyone to rely on?" he demanded. "You've got me." He heard the pain in his tone, but couldn't disguise it.

He felt her muscles tighten just before she raised her head and looked at him. His expression must have given away his inner torment, because she immediately looked contrite.

"Oh, I'm sorry. I didn't mean... That is, I'm terribly grateful to you for coming down here to defend me, but I was talking about family, or long-time close friends. Ever since...uh...since the divorce I've had to grow up and take care of myself because there's no one to do it for me."

Fergus knew he deserved her rebuff, but he wasn't going to accept it without protest. After all, it was his efforts to take care of her that caused most of the friction in their marriage.

He took her by the shoulders and sat her up and away from him. "Dammit, Sharon, *I'm* your family! And although I can't blame you for not believing it, I'm also your best friend. The divorce didn't nullify that. I'll always be there for you. All you have to do is let me know you need me.

"Who else would you turn to if not me? You're not involved with another man, are you?"

He knew he was coming on too strong, being unreasonable, but he couldn't help it.

For a moment she looked stunned, then she ran the tip of her tongue over her lips. "No, but—"

"Have you been in the past?"

He knew immediately that question was a mistake. Her dewy eyes hardened and her jaw clenched.

"That's none of your business!"

His heart sank. Did her reluctance to answer mean that she had been involved with a man, or men, in the past few years? Or was she just offended by his asking?

He was saved from persisting and making a further fool of himself by the sound of footsteps on the hardwood floor of the hall. Anna appeared in the doorway, followed by Tracey.

It was obvious that Tracey had been crying. Her eyes were red and puffy, and her makeup was streaked with tears. Fergus knew he'd have to handle her carefully. He didn't want her to fall apart on him or, worse, to get mad at him and take it out on Sharon by disclosing her fear to her friends and the media.

Anna walked across the room and sat down, but Tracey stood just inside the door, her head bowed and her gaze lowered. She was wearing jeans and a sweatshirt, and looked like a repentant schoolgirl. Fergus devoutly hoped she'd never be called by the prosecution if this case went to trial. All she'd have to do is get on the stand and the jury would sympathize with her before she even opened her mouth.

"Come on in, Tracey, and sit down," he said as kindly as he could manage.

Without raising her head to look at him, she walked over and sat down on the raised hearth of the fireplace.

Fergus stayed seated beside Sharon as he talked. "I understand you no longer want to live in the same house with Sharon." He kept his tone low and slightly sympathetic.

As if on command, one tear fell from each eye and Tracey sniffled. "I'm ... I'm sorry." She spoke barely above a whisper.

"There's no need to be sorry," he said. "If that's the way you feel, then I agree that you should leave."

That brought her to attention. She raised her head and looked at him. "Me! But I thought..."

"Sharon and Anna are even willing to refund your pro-rated rent for the rest of this month to help with your moving expenses," he assured her, and saw the looks of unpleasant surprise her two housemates threw his way. "Do you have relatives in the area where you can stay until you find another apartment?"

Her eyes widened. "Yes. No. That is... Sharon said she'd move out."

Fergus was having a hard time maintaining his tone of gentle concern when what he really wanted to do was yell at the spoiled brat, who was obviously used to everyone catering to her wishes. "Oh, but that was before she understood her legal rights. She and Anna were here for several years before you joined them, and neither of them has any intention of leaving, so that puts the ball in your court."

Tracey was no longer meek and submissive. "You mean *I* have to leave?" she asked uncertainly.

"Of course not," he answered softly. "You're welcome to stay. Did you say you have relatives living nearby?"

Tracey looked stunned. "Well, yes, fairly close. My parents live just across the river in Mascoutah, Illinois, but—"

"That should be an easy commute," he said thoughtfully. "They wouldn't mind if you moved back home, would they?"

"No, but I don't want to—"

Fergus forced a smile. "Good. Then it's settled. Sharon can stay at my suite at the hotel tonight while you start packing."

He caught Sharon's mutinous expression.

"Fergus, I can't—"

He gave her a warning glance, but kept his tone amiable. "It'll be all right. You'll have your own room, and after all, we were married at one time. Now, I don't know about the rest of you, but I'm hungry, and whatever it is you have cooking in the oven smells delicious. Will it be long before dinner's ready?''

Tracey stood up, looking somewhat stunned at the turn of events. "Ten minutes, fifteen at the most," she said. Then, for the first time since she'd come into the room, she looked directly at Sharon. "Please don't be mad at me, Sharon," she pleaded.

She looked so unhappy that Sharon couldn't be cross with her. "I'm not mad at you, Tracey," she assured her roommate. "But I am sorely disappointed by your lack of trust in me."

With a sob, Tracey hurried out of the room, leaving the other three sitting in silence.

Sharon was the first to break it. "Fergus, you could have at least discussed it with me before you told her I'd stay with you at the hotel tonight. I don't like that idea."

She kept her voice low so it wouldn't carry.

He shrugged and followed her example. "I know you don't. It's uncomfortable for me, too, but it was all I could think of on the spur of the moment. If you'd discussed this with me earlier we could have decided on a plan of action, but since you didn't I had to improvise."

She knew he was right. She'd made a mistake in judgment and had no right to blame him if she didn't agree with his decisions.

It was Anna who brought up the next objection. "Do we really have to give her this month's rent back?" she asked softly. "After all, it was her decision to leave. Nobody asked her to."

Fergus grinned. "That's not altogether true," he said. "I more or less forced the issue, although I doubt she'll ever catch on, but it's important that she continue to think of you both as her friends. She's a self-centered airhead, but she's also expert at playing on people's emotions. If she thinks she's being treated unfairly she could do a lot of damage to Sharon's case. I've had experience with her type."

"Yeah, I suppose you're right," Anna said, "but I hope it doesn't take us too long to find another tenant. It's tough for Sharon and me to split the rent just two ways. Especially if Sharon isn't getting paid during her suspension."

The mention of her suspension brought another wave of despair to Sharon, but Fergus's reply eased it.

"I promise you, Anna, Sharon will be able to keep up her share of the household expenses. I'll talk to the hotel's lawyers in the morning, and I also have a solution to your lack of a third tenant—"

"Dinner's ready," Tracey yelled from the dining room, interrupting the discussion.

"We'll be right there," Anna called, then turned her attention back to Fergus. "You were saying?"

He shook his head. "We'll go into that tomorrow," he said, and stood. "There's not time now, and besides, I think I'd better discuss my idea with Sharon first. She doesn't like for me to make decisions for her."

He reached out his hand to her and pulled her up to stand beside him, leaving her to wonder just what devilish plot he was going to charm her into agreeing to next.

After dinner, while Anna and Fergus did the dishes, Tracey halfheartedly started packing her belongings, and Sharon changed into slacks and a blouse, then gathered up the things she'd need for her overnight stay at the hotel and tossed them into her small suitcase.

It was a little after nine by the time Fergus and Sharon arrived at the hotel, and so far neither of them had alluded to their earlier conversation. She knew him well enough to know that he'd open the discussion when he was good and ready and not before. As for her, she was emotionally exhausted and wasn't sure she could handle an argument if that's what it became.

When he unlocked the door to his suite and stood back for her to precede him she had mixed emotions. She knew she shouldn't have agreed to this. It was not only unwise, but dangerous.

She hadn't realized how dangerous until she'd felt the leap of joy that flooded through her when Fergus told Tracey that Sharon would spend tonight at the hotel with him.

Oh, she'd managed to tamp it down and protest, but it flared up again when he overrode that protest. She hadn't even put up a fight, but meekly, even thankfully, had submitted.

Now they were going to be closely confined all night in these two rooms. How was she going to sleep knowing he was just on the other side of the wall? On Wednesday night when she'd stayed there she'd been so shocked and terrified that sleep had been a welcome escape, but after two days in the company of the man who was her ex-husband, her defender and her protector, she knew that she still loved him as totally as she had while they were married.

As Sharon swept past Fergus and into the living room of his suite he felt a profound sense of relief. All the way over he'd been afraid she'd change her mind and insist on checking in alone at another hotel, or taking a separate room by herself at this one, but she hadn't.

So why was he relieved? Having her share these two rooms with him would guarantee him a hellish night. He'd spend the rest of the evening striving to keep his hands off her, and the remainder of the night fighting the overwhelming temptation to join her in her bed and seduce her into making love with him.

Just the thought of it made him shiver with desire and escalated the tension headache that had been building all evening.

His memory of their uninhibited lovemaking during their courtship and marriage was only too vivid. Her passion had matched his own, and the result was combustible. They'd gone up in flame so often it was a wonder they didn't have scars.

But, of course, they did have scars. At least he did, and he was certain she did, too. Not from the fire that had consumed them during those happy times, but from the holocaust that had ripped them apart when his surprising and totally unwelcome attraction for another woman had blurred his judgment and thrown him a curve. A curve he'd fumbled badly.

His wounds had only partially healed during the intervening years, and now that Sharon was back in his life again, no matter how tenuously, they tended to tear open a little more during each encounter, until they were once more raw and bleeding.

If it was painful for him it must be agony for Sharon. He'd not only wronged and humiliated her at the time of their divorce, but now she was charged with a murder she didn't commit and she was forced to depend on him for her very life.

He knew she didn't trust him, would probably never trust him again, but still she was totally dependent on his skill and knowledge of the law to save her from a terrible miscarriage of justice.

Consequently she was terrified, bewildered and so achingly vulnerable. He'd be a world-class bastard if he took advantage of her temporary susceptibility to appease his own burning need.

The telephone started to ring just as Fergus shut the door, and he answered it while Sharon went into the bedroom to hang up the lightweight coat she'd worn as protection against the chilly spring-night breeze. He was still talking when she came back, and she could tell from his end of the conversation that it was a business call.

Not wanting just to stand there and listen, she began pacing slowly around the room, until she found herself in front of the locked bar cabinet. The key was in the lock, and she opened it and rummaged through the contents until she found a bottle of Perrier and a can of beer.

She caught Fergus's eye and held up the beer in a questioning gesture. He smiled and nodded, and she opened both containers and poured them into two glasses from the cupboard over the cabinet, then opened a package of miniature pretzels and emptied them into a glass bowl.

"I'm sorry," Fergus said as he hung up the phone and joined her. "I left Chicago so suddenly in the middle of the night that I didn't have time to tie up any of the loose ends at the office."

He picked up his glass and the pretzels and strode over to the sofa, followed by Sharon. "I'm afraid I'm going to have to start wearing my beeper so I can be contacted more easily."

They sat down and he put the bowl of pretzels on the coffee table.

Sharon felt a blast of guilt. She'd been so glad to see him and so relieved to have him there, taking over her defense, that it hadn't occurred to her what a huge sacrifice he was making to drop everything the way he had and come to her rescue. How could she have been so thoughtless?

"I'm sorry," she said. "I hate it that I've disrupted your work so badly. If you need to go back to Chicago please don't feel compelled to stay here. I'm sure Ray can carry on, now that you've taken care of all the preliminaries—"

"Stop right there," Fergus said. "Are you trying to tell me you'd prefer to have Ray Quinlan defend you instead of me?"

"No!" She was so startled that she practically shouted the denial at him. "That's not what I mean. I just don't want to be a burden—"

"Burden, hell!" he roared as he slammed his glass down on the coffee table, spilling part of the beer as he jumped to his feet. "Goddammit, Sharon, will you stop being so sickeningly self-sacrificing and face a few hard truths?"

"Self-sacrificing? Me?" Her volume matched his as she also put her glass down and stood. "Aren't you being a tad

overconfident? What makes you think you're the only lawyer on earth who can convince a jury I'm not guilty?''

He glared at her. ''I don't *think* I am, I *know* I am. I'm
the only one who would put up with your stubborn, egotistical insistence that you're invincible and don't need or even
want help from anybody.''

''Stubborn! Egotistical!'' Her voice rose a decibel with
each word. ''Look who's talking. I've never known a more
stubborn, egotistical man than you.''

''Then I'd say you've been damn lucky,'' he said grimly.
''I'll be happy to introduce you to a few, but don't count on
one of them to defend you. They're not burdened with the
same motive I am.''

''Oh.'' Her tone was sarcastic. ''And just what motive are
you saddled with? It sure can't be the size of the fee you'll
get.''

''No, it's not the fee,'' he said, his voice suddenly flat and
back to a normal volume. ''It's a much more compelling
and painful obsession than that. I'm in love with you.''

For once Sharon was speechless. It was as if she'd had the
breath knocked out of her, and for a moment she found
herself struggling just to breathe as she watched Fergus put
his fingers to his temples and turn away from her.

''That... That's a low blow, Fergus,'' she finally stammered. ''I truly didn't expect you to lie to me. Especially not
about... about that.''

''I'm not lying,'' he said dully. ''I told you the same thing
five years ago when you confronted me about Elaine. You
wouldn't believe me then so there's no reason to think you
will now, but it's true.''

She felt a faint flicker of hope, but ruthlessly pushed it
away. ''If you'd loved me then you wouldn't have gotten
involved with another woman.'' Her tone was as lifeless as
his.

He turned around to face her, and she saw anguish in his
tight-lipped expression. ''I didn't get 'involved' with Elaine

in the way you mean until after you and I were divorced, but you wouldn't believe that, either. You just closed your mind and refused to listen to anything I tried to tell you."

"But... but you married her."

He nodded wearily. "Yes, I married her." Again he put his fingers to his temples. "Look, why don't we call it a night? It's been a long day, and I have a pounding headache."

A wave of compassion flooded her as she remembered that during their marriage he'd been prone to headaches when under an inordinate amount of stress. In her eagerness to relieve his suffering she'd borrowed a book on massage therapy from the college library and had worked out a way of manipulating the muscles of his neck, shoulders and back that had effectively relaxed him and alleviated the discomfort.

Now she was the cause of his stress, and she had an irresistible urge to take away his pain. Without thinking past that urge, she got up and walked over to stand in front of him. "Since I'm probably the cause of your headache, will you let me try to relieve it?" she asked softly. "I think I remember how."

With a muffled groan he put his arms around her and pulled her so close that she could feel the tension in him as she slid her arms around his neck. "I'd be eternally grateful to you if you would," he murmured in her ear, "but I have to tell you that stroking me with those soft little hands is definitely not the way to relax me."

She rubbed her cheek against his. "Would you rather I didn't?"

"Oh, please don't back out now." It sounded very much like a plea. "I'll muddle through and enjoy every minute of it."

So would she, but that wasn't necessarily good. She leaned back a little in his arms and started to unknot his tie. "Would you like to take off your shirt?"

A wicked little grin lit his face. "Why don't you do it for me?"

The very thought sent a wave of heat coursing through her. It was easy to see that she'd made a serious mistake by getting herself into this, but she couldn't back out now. Not when he was hurting and she could bring him relief.

"I—I think you'd better do it," she stammered. "It's been years since I undressed a man."

Oh damn! That wasn't what she'd intended to say. Now he'd know there hadn't been any other men in her life since their divorce. He'd either think she couldn't attract another man or he'd know that she'd been pining for him all this time.

She wasn't prepared for the look of contrition—and could it be relief?—that altered his expression as his arms once more tightened around her.

"Oh, Sharon." It was clearly a moan of despair. "You're right. I don't deserve your forgiveness. I didn't have the good sense to hold on to you when I had you, but I loved you then and I never stopped."

She didn't know what to say. How to react. She wanted so much to believe him, but when she'd found him and Elaine Odbert in each other's arms he'd admitted that he cared for the other woman.

She knew with the knowledge of hindsight that if she'd been older and less idealistic she would have fought to keep her marriage intact. But she hadn't, and he'd married Elaine and apparently been happy with her until she'd died so suddenly.

Now he was a lonely widower and it would be easy to convince himself that he was still in love with the ex-wife he'd felt guilty about all those years. It was a good way to assuage his guilt and alleviate his loneliness.

Well, that was nice for him, but she hadn't been willing to be second best with him five years ago, and she still wasn't now.

But how could she hold on to the sensible resolution of her mind, and resist the overwhelming temptation of her psyche to forget the past and give him her heart, her body and everything else he might want from her?

Chapter Seven

Sharon and Fergus just stood there holding each other and savoring the delicious intimacy as the seconds ticked into minutes, until Sharon finally gathered enough self-discipline to again lean back in his embrace.

"Why don't you take off your shirt while I pull down the wall bed?" she asked, changing the subject without comment on his last remarks. "Or better yet, undress and put on the bottoms of your pajamas. Then you won't have to get up again after you're all relaxed."

Fergus gave her one last hug, then released her, but there was a suspicious glint in his eyes. "Now you've hurt my feelings," he said morosely, but his mouth twitched into a tiny smile. "How could you have forgotten that I don't wear pajamas?"

She felt a dizzying rush of blood to her head and knew that her face must be red with embarrassment. How could she, indeed?

Actually, she hadn't. How many hundreds of nights since their divorce had she lain awake in her cold and lonely bed, remembering his powerful, naked body entwined with hers, also nude, as she'd fallen asleep? But as usual with Fergus, she'd let her mouth run off before she'd gotten her brain in gear.

Her teeth worried her lower lip. "That . . . that was a long time ago, and it's not something I needed or wanted to remember."

She hated the waspish tone of her voice, and made a determined effort to banish it when she continued. "Take off everything but your slacks. Then you can pull down the bed while I get into something more comfortable."

She bolted for the bedroom and closed the door before he could reply.

Sharon hurriedly undressed, then pulled on a long, flowing, India-print caftan in bright shades of orange, green and brown. It buttoned at the neck and had wide sleeves with gathers at the high bodice. She'd chosen to bring it instead of a robe because she thought it wouldn't have the same sexual connotation that nightclothes did, but now, as she glanced at herself in the mirror, she wasn't so sure.

If she had a candle holder with a lit candle in one hand and a floppy rag doll clutched in the other arm, she'd look like those pictures of a Victorian maiden on her way to bed.

Oh well, it was too late to worry about that now. She didn't have anything else to put on unless she wanted to get dressed again, and she didn't.

At the door to the living room she hesitated, then rapped. "Fergus. Are you decent?"

He answered with one terse word, "Yes," and she knew he was again displeased about something.

She opened the door and walked into the room, to find him sitting on the side of the bed, glaring at her. He was bare to below the waist, and it was evident the years hadn't aged that magnificent body of his at all. He was still tanned and muscular, with a heavy sprinkling of brown hair on his chest.

He'd also removed his shoes and socks, and she'd never before realized how erotic bare feet could be as she was suddenly seized with a desire to feel them rubbing slowly up and down her calves. She gulped and blinked in an effort to erase such unsettling images, and noticed that his glare had turned into a stare as he watched her.

"You look like Little Bo Peep," he said in a strangled tone, then cleared his throat and changed the subject. "What was that crack about am I decent? Dammit, Sharon, I wish you'd stop acting like Little Red Riding Hood fending off the Big Bad Wolf. My God, you even dress like a nursery rhyme."

He stood up and turned away from her. "We were married for three years, and you never worried about whether I was 'decently' clothed when we were together in our apartment. You've seen me nude more times than you can count, so why are you now acting like a naive virgin who's likely to swoon at the sight of a man in the buff?"

He ran his fingers through his hair in a gesture of frustration. "Are you afraid of me? Have I ever given you cause to be?"

Once more she'd been robbed of speech. Shock and anger warred for dominance in her confused mind, and anger was rapidly winning the battle.

What was the matter with him? He wasn't making sense. He apparently expected her to behave to act like the love-struck young wife she used to be, but that was a long time ago. She was a different woman now and it was about time he understood that.

"I don't know what you expect of me, Fergus," she said, struggling to keep her tone calm and controlled, "but I'll tell you what you're going to get. When you and I were living together we were married. That didn't stop you from being attracted to another woman, but I took the commitment seriously."

He winced and held up his hand to stop her, but she hurried on. "Don't interrupt—just listen. You asked me earlier if I've been involved with other men since our divorce. The answer is no. I date fairly often, but I don't sleep around, and I'm not going to make an exception of you. You lost your husbandly privileges the night I caught you kissing Elaine, and now you're no different than any other man.

"If I act like a virgin it's because, except for you, I am. I'm also not a tease. I'm sorry if my high standards offend you, but I don't parade around in front of men in skimpy, seductive clothes, and I don't allow men to undress in my presence."

Sharon knew that now wasn't the time for this discussion, but as her agitation rose so did her need to speak her mind.

She began pacing around the room. "You asked if I'm afraid of you. You're damn right I am, and yes, you have given me good reason to be."

Again he tried to speak and was cut off. "Five years ago you walked out on me and shattered my whole world—"

"Sharon, I did not walk out on you!" This time he didn't give her a chance to shush him. "I never intended to leave you. I didn't want a divorce—you were the one who insisted on it." His voice was ragged with frustration, and he bowed his head in his hands and rubbed his temples with his thumbs.

The headache. In her anger she'd forgotten about his headache and her promise to try to relieve it with massage. Instead, she was making it worse.

The rage drained out of her, and she hurried across the room to where he sat on the side of the bed. Hunkering down in front of him, she put her hands on his shoulders and felt the tightly drawn muscles. "We've been over all this before. There's no point in rehashing it," she said softly as she removed the pillow. "Lie down on your stomach. Do you have medication?"

He raised his head and looked at her. His face was white and his eyes reflected his torment. "Yes, in my shaving kit, but let's try the massage first."

He cupped her cheeks with his palms and lifted her face to look at her. "Sharon, I'm sorry," he said brokenly.

She reached out and stroked his forehead. "I'm sorry, too. I didn't mean to let you suffer while I railed at you for things neither of us can do anything about now."

Their gazes met, and the magnetism between them was so strong that she knew she'd wind up in his arms again if she didn't move—fast!

She practically jumped to her feet and turned away from him. "Lie down," she instructed again. "I'll be right back."

When she returned from the bathroom, where she'd picked up the sample bottle of lotion the hotel had provided, Fergus had pulled back the covers and was stretched out on the bed on his stomach, with his arms to his sides and his face turned toward her. His back was as muscular as his chest, and all that bare flesh was tempting almost beyond resisting.

She remembered how she used to kiss and lick her way up from the indentation at the base of his spine to his shoulders, and the funny little purring noises that had escaped from deep in his throat. She'd loved the feel of his firm flesh under her hands, and the way his muscles had twitched when her stroking became more intimate.

Enough of that! she admonished herself silently, and pulled the sheet and blanket up to his waist, then sat down beside him.

"Are you warm enough?" she asked as she squeezed some of the lotion that she'd warmed under the hot water onto his shoulders. "If you're chilly I can turn up the heat."

She put her hands in the pools of lotion and began the massage.

He sighed contentedly. "Honey, there's no way I could get a chill with you sitting close and doing such erotic things to me."

His seductive words and tone sent a liquid warmth to her nether region, and her fingers involuntarily dug into him. "I . . . I am not doing erotic things to you," she protested.

"Oh, no?" She heard the exaggerated leer in his voice. "Would you like me to turn over and show you?"

That was exactly the type of thing he used to say to her, and in spite of her good intentions, she choked with laughter. "Darn it, Fergus," she said, intending to sound stern but giggling, instead. "How can I stay mad at you when you say outrageous things like that?"

"I don't want you to be mad at me." This time his tone was serious. "And it's not outrageous. I'm willing to prove it."

She'd take his word, but even so it didn't mean anything special. Any reasonably pretty woman could arouse a half-naked man just by stroking him, and Fergus was no exception.

She decided it was time to change the subject. "I won't be able to help you get rid of that headache if you won't be quiet and relax. Your muscles are tied in knots."

"I feel better already," he murmured, and with a few deep breaths managed to release some of the tension in his body.

For some time after that they didn't speak. Sharon worked to unknot his muscles as the most effective moves came back to her, and he gradually loosened up as she stroked and kneaded his tortured sinews and nerves.

After half an hour Sharon's shoulders and hands were screaming for relief from the unaccustomed pressure she was putting on them. Besides, she was almost sure Fergus was asleep. He was totally relaxed and his breathing was deep and regular.

She squared her shoulders and moved them back and forth in an effort to loosen her own aching muscles, then stood and pulled the covers over Fergus's exposed back. He looked so peaceful lying there. The lines of pain were gone from what she could see of his face, and he appeared younger and less harried.

She suspected that he drove himself mercilessly in his profession, and she made a silent vow to try to ease the extra burden he'd assumed by taking on her defense. She'd stop wallowing in past hurts and start being more helpful.

She tucked the sheet and blanket around him, as she'd have tucked in their child if they'd had one, then gave in to the insistent temptation to lean down and kiss him on his slightly bristly cheek. She caught the faint lingering fragrance of shaving lotion and felt a muscle quiver under her lips.

Before she could pull away his hand came up and wrapped around her wrist. "Don't leave," he whispered.

She brushed a lock of dark-brown hair back from his forehead with her other hand. "I'm not going anywhere," she said softly against his ear.

He caressed her palm with his thumb. "I mean stay with me. Sleep next to me on the bed. I won't bother you."

Her heart raced at the very thought of sleeping in the same bed with him again, but that was out of the question.

She opened her mouth to tell him so, but heard herself saying, instead, "All right, if that's what you really want."

He hadn't moved anything but his lips, and now they turned up in a small smile. "It is. More than anything."

Oh, what the hell, she thought. *It was bound to happen sooner or later. At least tonight he feels too rotten to seduce me.*

She got up and turned off the lights, then climbed in on the other side of the bed and settled down, close to him, but not touching. It was then that she remembered the time shortly after they were married when he'd had the flu with a temperature of 101 degrees.

The temperature had hovered up there for three days, but they hadn't missed a night of making love!

Sharon was exhausted and fell asleep almost instantly, but sometime during the night she surfaced enough to be dimly aware that she was cradled in the circle of Fergus's arms. Her back was against his chest, her derriere nestled in his groin and one of his legs captured between both of hers. It was as if the past five years of separation had never happened, and they were back in their apartment in Chicago sleeping as they always did, with their bodies entwined.

Instinctively she snuggled closer, and his hand moved just enough to cup her breast. With a contented little sigh she sank back into the misty buoyancy of sleep.

Sharon awoke the next morning to the ringing of the telephone, but it wasn't until the second ring that she was conscious enough to open her eyes. When she did she saw Fergus, fully dressed in gray slacks and a blue print shirt open at the throat, rushing to the desk to pick it up.

"Lachlan," he said in a low voice, apparently trying not to waken her. "Hi, what's up? Did you get those affidavits...?"

It was obviously someone from his law firm in Chicago, but did they have to bother him on Saturday?

She knew the answer to that. It was a question she'd asked many times during their marriage. Trial lawyers seldom worked a neat forty-hour week. It was more like fifty or sixty.

She missed part of his side of the conversation, but picked it up again when he raised his voice in indignation.

"You mean now? Today? But I can't leave here yet. The preliminary hearing's coming up next week, and— Oh hell! I was afraid something like that would happen. Isn't there anyone there who can handle it? Yeah, I know, it's my responsibility. I'll check the airline schedules and catch a flight later this afternoon.''

Sharon's stomach clenched into a ball of nausea. Fergus was leaving! He was going back to Chicago. But what about her? She needed him here!

She sat up in bed and combed her disheveled hair back with her fingers as he finished his conversation.

"She said what? Well, that's tough. Tell her if she wants someone to hold her hand to get in touch with one of her rich johns. I'm not available.''

Sharon's eyes widened as he slammed down the phone. "Fergus, are you defending a hooker?'' she asked.

He whirled around, and his expression softened when he looked at her. "Sharon, I'm sorry. I didn't mean to wake you....''

He smiled. "Hookers are entitled to a defense the same as anyone else.'' He walked over and sat down on the side of the bed.

"Of course,'' she agreed, "but I didn't think they could afford you. Besides, aren't they usually just brought in and fined, then released?''

He chuckled. "Most of them can't afford me, and are released, but this one services a very wealthy clientele and prefers to be known as a call girl. She probably has an income higher than mine, and she had the misfortune to, um, be there when her client dropped dead.''

Sharon got the picture. "Oh, my God, really?''

He raised his eyebrows. "Yes, really. It happens now and then, but this time the man died of poisoning, and the district attorney thinks she administered it.''

"Did she?'' Sharon knew better than to ask that question, but it just slipped out.

Fergus patted her leg through the covers. "I have no idea, but she's entitled to a fair and impartial trial, and it's my job to see that she gets one. Now, as you no doubt heard, I have to go back to Chicago this afternoon, so why don't you get dressed while I make some more phone calls. Do you want to go down to the coffee shop for breakfast, or shall I order something sent up?''

She didn't always use the best judgment, but even she knew better than to stay in this room with Fergus when half of it was taken up with this queen-size bed that was warm and rumpled and inviting.

"Let's go to the coffee shop," she said, and moved to slide across the mattress and get up. But Fergus stopped her by putting his hands on her shoulders.

"Just a minute, love," he said tenderly. "I want to tell you how much I appreciate what you did for me last night."

A vision of them curled up together so intimately on the bed flashed through her mind, and she panicked. My God, she'd forgotten about that! She'd been so sound asleep both before and after that it hadn't really registered.

But what else hadn't registered? Had they...? Had she...?

She knew her expression must mirror her shock as she gaped at him. "What did I do?" Her tone was a mixture of gasp and howl. "Fergus, did we...?" She swallowed and couldn't go on.

For a moment he looked puzzled, and then he laughed. Not a polite chuckle, but a full belly laugh. "Sharon Sawyer Lachlan, are you implying that I made love to you and you don't even remember it? Now I really am insulted!"

He sounded more gleeful than insulted.

"Well, did we?" she repeated impatiently.

He made an effort to appear more serious, but couldn't manage to bring it off. "No, my darling, we didn't, but when I woke up this morning and found you snuggled so tantalizingly in my arms I can assure you I had one hell of a time convincing myself that I should put you aside and get out of there."

Relief flooded through her and left her limp. "Ohhh," she said with a sigh as she released the breath she'd been holding. "I...I'm sorry. I didn't mean to imply... That is, I was vaguely aware at one time during the night that we were..." She felt herself blush. "That we were cuddled up together, but you were asleep and I drifted off again right away—"

He put his arms around her and drew her against him. "I understand, but it's a good thing I didn't discover it until I was wide-awake this morning. If I hadn't been fully alert I'd never have been able to resist the temptation to seduce you."

He brushed her hairline with his lips and whispered. "If I had would you have responded?"

She nodded against his shoulder. "Yes, but I would have deeply regretted it afterward."

He rubbed her back gently. "That's what I was afraid of." There was no teasing in his tone now. "That's why I forced myself to get up and take a cold shower this morning. When I make love to you again I want you wide-awake and as desperately in need of me as I am of you."

She had to bite her lip to keep from telling him she was feeling that way right now.

Instead she raised her head and put her hand to his temple. "Is your headache gone?"

He kissed the tip of her nose. "Oh yes. You really do have magic in those pretty hands. You relaxed me and took away the pain last night, and I dozed like a baby. That's what I was thanking you for. That, and for sleeping with me." He smiled. "I promise that's all we did. I don't know how you got in my arms, but it's been a long time since I've rested so peacefully. I suspect it's because I was finally holding you again."

She wanted to admit that she understood because it was the same way with her, but they were playing with fire by sitting there on the bed, talking about their mutual sexual attraction. She knew her self-control wasn't up to it, and it was time to change both the setting and the subject.

Giving him a quick hug, she broke away and scooted across the mattress. "I'd better get dressed or they'll be serving lunch instead of breakfast by the time we get downstairs," she said, and without looking back headed for the bathroom.

Forty minutes later, after Fergus had completed his business calls and Sharon had showered and dressed, they were seated at a table in the open gardenlike restaurant in the hotel lobby. Once the waiter had poured orange juice and coffee and taken their order, Sharon broached the subject Fergus had casually mentioned the day before, then dropped.

"Fergus, yesterday you said you had a suggestion about how Anna and I can find a new tenant to replace Tracey. What did you have in mind?"

He took a sip of his coffee and touched his lips with a napkin. "I'll tell you, but I want you to listen and not interrupt until I'm finished. If you're bound over for trial at the preliminary hearing I'll be here in St. Louis off and on for weeks, maybe months. Obviously I'll need permanent headquarters, somewhere to live and work. In that event I'd like to move into the room Tracey's vacating and assume her share of the expenses."

Sharon felt her eyes widen, but she heeded Fergus's edict and kept quiet.

"There shouldn't be any impropriety. After all, we're all three adults, and you and I were once married. Also, you've been put in my custody by the court, so we can just argue that I'm taking my duties seriously by keeping an eye on you."

That got a reaction from her. "And would you be? Spying on me, I mean. Making sure I didn't knife someone else?"

Fergus frowned. "Don't talk nonsense, Sharon," he said icily. "That remark was uncalled for."

A wave of shame washed over her, and she looked away. "You're right. It was," she apologized. "You deserve a lot better than that from me. I'm sorry."

"So am I," he said grimly, "because it means that you still don't trust me. You have a right to feel that I've failed you personally in the past, but no one has ever accused me of not giving the best possible defense to a client. Please, don't let your dislike of me sabotage my ability to defend you."

Sharon gasped. "I don't dislike you, Fergus."

He shook his head. "It doesn't matter. It's not necessary for one to like one's attorney in order to be well represented in court, but don't impair my efforts to defend you. It's been my experience that juries are usually pretty astute. If you throw barbs at me in the courtroom the way you do in private it could backfire and cause them to question either my competence or your innocence."

His words hit her like blows. Taking a deep breath, she sought his gaze with her own and hoped the tears that burned behind her eyes weren't visible. "Fergus, I'm sorry if I'm coming across as an ungrateful shrew." She heard the tremor in her voice. "Please believe me when I say I don't dislike you. Actually, I like you very much. Maybe that's the problem. It would be easier for me if I didn't, because then I wouldn't have to worry about being hurt again."

Fergus looked shocked. "I'm not going to hurt you, Sharon."

She clasped and unclasped her hands. "I know. You've been so kind, and so helpful. I...I don't know what I would have done if you hadn't come to my rescue when Anna called you. If you hadn't been there to get me out of that dreadful jail..."

Her voice broke and she couldn't go on.

Fortunately the waiter chose that moment to bring their breakfast plates, giving her time to pull herself together while he put the food on the table and poured them more coffee.

When he was finished and had left, Fergus picked up his fork and knife and started cutting his ham into pieces. "I'm not looking for gratitude. What I desperately need now is your faith in my ability and my integrity. I can understand why you have a problem with that, especially the integrity, but I can't defend you without that commitment. If you don't have complete confidence in me, then I have no choice but to help you find another attorney."

Coffee sloshed out of the cup Sharon had just picked up, and she set it back in the saucer with a bang. He couldn't mean that! Such a suggestion was unthinkable. *"No!"* she blurted. "I don't want another attorney. I want you. You're the only person I do have faith in."

Fergus shrugged, apparently untouched by her obvious distress. "If that's true, then you'd better start thinking of me as your defender, instead of as the bastard who broke up our marriage."

Sharon lowered her head and rubbed at her eyes with her fingers. "I'm sorry," she said, for what must have been the hundredth time. "I don't mean to be so... so querulous. I don't seem to be able to help myself. The words just tumble out."

"I'm not blaming you." His tone had softened. "I hurt you badly and I don't deserve your forgiveness, but you'll have to at least appear to respect me when we go to court or..."

He stroked his hands through his hair. "Maybe my sharing a home with you isn't such a good idea after all. I can see that I'm getting on your nerves."

She shook her head. "It's not you, Fergus. It's the shock of what's happening to me that keeps me so off balance. I promise to make more of an effort to control my tongue."

He shook his head. "This isn't going to work if you have to make an effort to be civil to me. You'd be better off with a lawyer you like and trust."

Sharon felt the stirrings of panic. He was serious about getting someone else to represent her. "I'll never agree to having someone else take over my defense!" she said emphatically. "I trust you enough to put my freedom, possibly my very life, in your hands. What more do you want?"

He looked at her, and there was sadness in his expression. "I want you to forget about the past. I want you to love me again, or at least like me, but I'll settle for an unarmed truce. Try to stop thinking of me as the enemy. Focus instead on the fact that I'm trying to keep you out of prison, but I can't do it without your help."

She reached across the small table and covered his hand with hers. "I promise," she said softly, "and I don't think of you as the enemy. Quite the opposite. I find myself thinking of you as my knight in shining armor and it scares me. I guess that's why I get so bitchy sometimes. I don't want to think of you that way."

He turned his hand over and squeezed hers. "Don't be afraid of me, Sharon." His tone was low and husky. "I can stand almost anything but that."

Her love for him almost overwhelmed her. Had he any idea how much she wished she could believe him? She trusted him totally to prove her innocent of murder, but she could never again empower him with her unquestioning faith. She couldn't help loving him, but neither could she let him close enough to break her heart again.

Gently she pulled her hand from his and picked up her fork. "Of course we'll have to talk to Anna first, but I have no objection to your becoming our new housemate," she said, changing the subject and getting back to the original one.

* * *

After Sharon and Fergus finished eating they drove out to the house and confronted Anna. Tracey had left, bag and baggage, just a short time before to move in with her parents until she could find another apartment.

"She cried all morning," Anna said somewhat impatiently, "from the time she got up until she drove off."

Sharon smiled sympathetically. "Tracey wants the whole world to love her, and now she thinks we hate her. There's no half way with that young lady."

"Well, she'd better get over it," Anna said. "Otherwise she'll be an emotional wreck before she's thirty. You'd have thought it was our fault she was leaving."

Fergus shook his head. "Don't let her waterworks bother you. I can almost promise you she was enjoying every minute of it. I see a lot of people like her in my profession. She's not only emotional, but also highly theatrical, and loves to milk every scene for all she can get."

He grinned. "Stop and think about it. She was the one who stirred up the hornet's nest, but now that she's gone she has you both feeling guilty. That type never takes the blame."

Anna shrugged. "I'm sure you're right, but now the question is, where are we going to find another housemate?"

Fergus and Sharon looked at each other, then Fergus took the initiative and told Anna his ideas on the subject.

"You want to move in here with us?" Anna asked. "But is that, um, ethical? You're Sharon's attorney in a murder case."

Chapter Eight

Since Anna had broached the subject of ethics, Fergus had no choice but to answer her honestly. "Sharing a home with my female client could be a gray area," he admitted, "but I won't be here all the time, and when I am you'll be around to chaperon."

Anna's eyes widened. "Me? I'm not going to chaperon anybody. You two are adults. If you want to make love it's none of my business as long as you keep it reasonably private and I don't have to step around you on the floor."

Fergus laughed. Anna was right. She was beautiful, sophisticated and streetwise. Not exactly the type the court would approve as a chaperon if one were needed.

"I agree," he admitted, still chuckling. "The three of us living together are more likely to be looked upon as a ménage à trois, but the last time I checked that wasn't a hanging offense."

He wiped the smile from his face and became serious. "Unless I'm breaking the law, my domestic arrangements are not open to court scrutiny. Sharon and I were married at one time, and we won't be setting up housekeeping alone together. While you're not exactly Mary Poppins, your presence will be noted. I don't anticipate any problem with professional ethics, but is there a man in your life who might object to my moving in?"

Anna shook her head. "No man makes my decisions, and it's okay with me if you want to share our house and expenses. You can bring your things over today if you like."

Fergus breathed a sigh of relief. He was an idiot even to consider this arrangement. Living with Sharon and not being able to touch her would be torture, but living without her was hell. "Thanks, but I'm flying back to Chicago this afternoon, so I'll settle up with you financially now and move in when I return."

A phone call to the airport had secured him a seat on a two-o'clock flight, so now he barely had time to get back to the hotel, repack the few things he'd brought with him, check out and return his rental car before takeoff. Anna had disappeared after he'd signed the limited-lease agreement and had given her a check, so he was alone with Sharon as he prepared to leave.

He toyed with the idea of asking her to ride to the airport with him, anything to keep her by his side as long as possible, but decided against it. He was afraid she'd refuse, and he'd had all the rejection from her he could handle for a while.

He wanted to take her in his arms and kiss her goodbye. God how he wanted that, but he knew it would be a big mistake. He'd lose all his carefully constructed control. It was precarious at best, and he couldn't chance scaring her or making her so mad that she'd fire him on the spot and tell him never to come near her again.

He was living in a hades of his own making, and it was doubtful that she'd ever even let him back into her good graces, let alone into her life, into her bed.

As they walked together toward the front door he was careful not to touch her. "You have both my business and home addresses and phone numbers," he said urgently, "so, please, call me if anything comes up that upsets you or you think I should know about. I'll be back in two or three days. Meanwhile I'll be in close touch with Ray Quinlan. If you need anything call him."

"Fergus, I'm not a child," she said firmly. "I don't need a baby-sitter or a surrogate parent. I know how and where to get help if I need it. Don't worry about me. Concentrate on defending your hooker."

Dammit, she was being spiteful again. "She's not *my* hooker," he growled.

Sharon looked genuinely startled and put her hand on his arm, stopping him. "I didn't mean it that way," she said apologetically. "Truly I didn't. It was just a figure of speech."

Her wide blue eyes were filled with regret, and all his good intentions melted as he gathered her in his arms and held her close. "I believe you," he murmured into her silky hair. "I shouldn't have snapped at you. Oh, Sharon, I don't want to leave. I don't want to let you out of my sight. I'm afraid if I do you'll disappear, like you did before, and I'll never see you again. Come to Chicago with me."

She didn't try to pull away. Instead, he felt her arms slide around his waist and she snuggled into his embrace.

"I don't want you to go, either," she admitted, much to his relief. "But I can't go with you. When they released me on bail they told me I couldn't leave the jurisdiction of the court. Doesn't that mean I have to stay here?"

Fergus groaned and cursed himself for an idiot. "Yes, of course it does. I'm not thinking straight. I'll be back Tuesday at the latest. Meanwhile Ray will continue his search for potential witnesses."

It took all the effort he could muster to release her and step back. "Don't forget, call me if you need me." He turned and walked away while he still could.

Time seemed to stand still for Sharon after Fergus left, and as the hours dragged into days her apprehension increased. What had she gotten herself into? How could she be happily contemplating a promotion at work one day and be arrested for murder the next? Things like that just didn't happen to people like her!

On Sunday morning Ray Quinlan called to say he was going to be visiting his parents next door to her that afternoon, and would it be convenient for him to stop by for a talk? Sharon said yes. Anna would be tied up all day with an open house at one of the homes she had listed for sale, and Sharon was glad to have the company.

Ray arrived at a little before two, and after the usual coffee and chitchat he got down to business. "I've talked to the three women whom you said were also rumored to be victims of Vancleave's sexual advances. They all admitted it, but none of them want the publicity that their testimony in open court would attract. With a big-shot attorney like Fergus Lachlan representing you there's bound to be a lot of media coverage."

Sharon's hopes plummeted. She could understand the reticence of the women, but if they didn't come forward how was she going to prove what a bastard Floyd was?

"Elizabeth Williams admitted that she'd given in to his threats and intimidation and had a short-term affair with him," Ray continued, "but she doesn't want her teenage daughter and her daughter's friends to know."

Sharon sighed. "I don't blame her, but how about the other two? They don't have children."

Ray made a face. "No, but they have significant others. Judy Irwin told her hot-tempered boyfriend about the harassment, and he confronted Vancleave and threatened him with bodily harm if he didn't back off. There were witnesses, and Judy's afraid the guy will be a suspect if that ever comes out."

Sharon blinked. "Are you sure he isn't? I mean, maybe he was still mad enough to—"

"Nah, I checked him out. He has an alibi that isn't exactly airtight, but it's good enough to hold up in court. Besides, that incident happened over a year ago, and Vancleave hasn't bothered Judy since, so there's no reason to think the boyfriend was still upset about it."

Sharon felt a chill of foreboding. "What about Delores?"

Ray shook his head. "Delores Garroway has a rich and snobbish fiancé, who has her convinced that he's doing her a favor by marrying her. She says if he knew she'd been sexually harassed he'd claim it was her fault for leading the man on and break the engagement."

Sharon was dumbfounded. "Why would she want to marry a man like that?"

Ray shrugged. "It takes all kinds. I guess she loves the guy. Is there anyone else who was bothered by this supervisor? What about his wife? Did she know what he was up to? Not many wives will put up with that sort of behavior."

Sharon slumped against the back of the chair. "Oh Lord, that's really grabbing at straws. Floyd sure wouldn't tell her, and Helen Vancleave is such a shy, trusting, almost fragile woman that it's not likely anyone would want to be responsible for informing her that her husband was cheating on her. Besides, she's not the type to stab him in a jealous rage. She'd be more apt to let him convince her it was all her fault."

"Do you know her well?" Ray asked.

"Not really. I've met her a few times. She's the stereotypical subservient wife who watched him adoringly and never disagreed with him or had an opinion of her own. Besides, she wasn't there."

Sharon sighed heavily. "Ray, can't these other people be compelled to testify?"

Again he shook his head. "We could subpoena them, but even if we did they could deny it ever happened."

"But that's perjury!"

Ray spread his hands in resignation. "Honey, it happens. Unless you have proof to the contrary, you can't force a person to tell the truth if he or she doesn't want to."

Sharon gave in to defeat. So much for her faith in the American system of jurisprudence.

On Tuesday Fergus drove his black Lincoln back to St. Louis. It was midafternoon when he approached the bridge that took him across the Mississippi River and into the sprawling downtown area, ahead of the peak traffic hours.

He was anxious to get home!

But since when had St. Louis been home? He resided in Chicago. He'd been born there, owned real estate there, including the apartment he lived in. He was a senior partner in a law firm, and Chicago was his legal voting residence.

So why was he rushing to get back to a redbrick house in St. Louis that he hadn't even moved into yet? The answer was so simple he was surprised he'd ever questioned it.

It was because that's where Sharon lived.

A spurt of excitement set his blood to pounding, and he pressed his foot harder on the gas pedal. Would she be there? She wasn't working, but he'd had a firm talk with the attorneys for the hotel chain, and it had been agreed that she would be paid full salary until the matter of her guilt or innocence was settled. If she was found innocent her job would be there for her to return to.

The traffic slowed, and he slowed down with it. Guilty or innocent? There was no doubt in his mind, but how was he going to prove that she hadn't killed Floyd Vancleave? The evidence was stacked a mile high against her.

Turning off the highway at the next exit, he wound through the peaceful, upper-middle-class streets until he spotted the house and pulled the car to a stop at the curb in front of it.

He got out and was rounding the front of the car, when the door was thrown open and Sharon came running across the yard to meet him. Picking up his pace, he caught her as she threw herself into his arms. She was soft, and pliant, and smelled of wildflowers and clover. His heart was beating so erratically that for a moment he didn't even try to speak but just held her.

He could feel her heart beating, too, as she clung to him, her arms around his neck and her body pressed against his own. He hadn't expected such an enthusiastic reception. Surely it meant that she'd missed him! That she was glad to see him!

"Fergus, I'm so happy you're back," she said breathlessly as she hugged him. "Ray just called a few minutes ago. He said he's found another woman that Floyd hit on, and she'll be happy to testify for us. This one isn't afraid of the publicity."

Fergus almost groaned aloud as disappointment rolled through him in waves. It was his own fault that he'd jumped to the wrong conclusion. She'd told him often enough that she had no intention of getting personally involved with him again. He should be sharing her jubilation instead of wallowing in self-pity.

Well, he'd put on a good show. After all, that's what he'd been trained to do. The art of being a good trial lawyer depended as much on theatrics as skill.

She'd already started to wiggle out of his embrace, when he found his voice and managed to instill the proper amount of enthusiasm in it. "Hey, that's great, but you mustn't get your hopes up too high, honey. We'll have to check out this woman's story first."

He hated to dampen her excitement, but he'd learned not to put too much faith in a witness who was eager to testify at a criminal trial. They often had an ax to grind with either the accused or the defendant, and weren't above embellishing the facts. That type could do more harm than good to whichever side they were championing.

Sharon backed away from him, and the radiance that had shimmered around her had been replaced by a cloud of dejection.

"But why do you think she might not be telling the truth?" she gasped. "She called Ray with her story. He didn't coerce her or anything, and *she's willing to testify.* None of the women I told him about will."

Fergus felt like the lowest form of life for quelling her optimism. Who knows, maybe this witness was just the one they'd been looking for? But then again, maybe she wasn't, and it would be just that much more painful for Sharon if he encouraged her to build her hopes and dreams around a phantom.

"I know, Sharon," he said, hoping he could make her understand. "Ray and I have been in close touch while I've been away. I know our other witnesses have been reluctant to get involved, but we can't pin our hopes on someone who walks in off the street, either."

He put his arm around her waist and led her back toward the car. "Let me take my suitcases in the house so I can freshen up a little, and maybe you'll offer me a drink. Then we can relax and talk. Okay?"

Half an hour later Sharon was in the kitchen, fixing Fergus a tall cool vodka tonic, when he came downstairs and joined her. His hair was still damp from the shower, and he'd changed into crisp, tan Dockers and a green plaid short-sleeve shirt open at the neck.

She wondered if she'd ever get her feelings under control enough that her heart wouldn't pound at the sight of him.

"Sorry I took so long," he said with a smile, "but I've been on the road all day, and that brisk stinging shower was a godsend. Can I help you with that?"

He held out his hand and she put the chilled glass in it. "It's all finished," she said with an equally determined smile. "Why don't you go into the living room and sit down? I'll be along as soon as I pour myself some plain soda."

He didn't leave, but leaned back against the counter and crossed his ankles. "I want to stay here and watch you. I missed you, Sharon."

He sounded wistful, and his admission flustered her. "I've missed you, too," she said softly, and knew that was a deliberate understatement.

She'd missed him in ways he'd never believe. In ways she'd neither expected nor wanted to. She'd missed that curious blend of expensive shaving lotion and male scent that was so uniquely his. The one that was nearly her undoing when he'd clasped her in his arms outside on the lawn after she'd run out to meet him.

She'd missed that aura of protectiveness that wrapped her so securely in its cloak. In the five years that she'd been alone she'd learned not to need a man to lean on, but now she knew that she'd never learned not to need Fergus.

She was alarmingly certain that was one lesson she'd never master.

And most of all she'd missed *him*. His tender smile, his tough yet gentle hands, his green eyes, hooded but watchful, and his arms. Oh yes, his strong, sheltering arms that told her far more efficiently than words that she was a vulnerable woman who longed for his deep and undivided love.

But was he capable of giving that? He hadn't been before, and she wasn't capable of sharing his love with another woman.

"Are you anxious about tomorrow?" he asked. "You needn't be. It's just a hearing to determine if there's enough evidence to go to trial."

Apparently that was supposed to make her feel better, but in reality she was terrified. "So you've said, but could you give me some idea of what's going to happen?"

She picked up her glass and headed for the living room. Fergus followed and they sat down together on the couch facing the fireplace.

"Will I have to testify?" she asked as she sipped her soda.

"No," Fergus said. "The state will produce witnesses and I'll cross-examine. I'm allowed to try to discredit their witnesses, but this is the district attorney's show. We don't present a defense at this time."

"But... but that's not fair!" she sputtered angrily.

Fergus took a large swallow of his drink. "I know it seems that way, but you don't need to defend yourself until you've been charged with something. This is just another step in the justice system. The state doesn't need to show proof of guilt beyond a reasonable doubt. All they have to show is probable cause. A reasonable suspicion that Vancleave was murdered and you did it."

Sharon shrank against the back of the sofa. "And if the judge finds probable cause?"

Fergus set his glass down on the coffee table and looked at her. "Barring a miracle, he will, Sharon. You'd better accept that as fact. The case against you is too strong to find otherwise. You'll be charged and bound over to superior court for trial."

Even though she'd known that was likely to happen, the horror of Fergus's words sent chills down her spine.

"But I didn't do it!" she cried plaintively. "Why won't anyone believe me? I wasn't even there!"

Fergus reached out and gathered her into his embrace, warming her with his heat and his compassion. "I believe you, sweetheart," he murmured as he trailed kisses in her hair. "I'll find a way to make the jury believe you, too, but you will have to stand trial. There's no way I can prevent that."

Another terrifying thought crossed Sharon's mind. "Do you think the charge will stick?"

"Not as long as I have a license to practice law," he said grimly. "They'll probably go for murder two, but I'm going to argue for involuntary manslaughter. That way, we can compromise on voluntary man."

She shivered and forced herself to ask, "What is the sentence for that?"

Fergus tightened his arms around her. "It doesn't matter, because I'm not going to let you be convicted. We'll waive your right to a speedy trial so we'll have time for a thorough investigation."

She pushed back and looked at him. "But I want a speedy trial."

He blinked in surprise. "No, honey, you don't understand. We need all the time we can get to prepare a defense. The district attorney is the one who usually benefits from a speedy trial, while the witnesses are still sure of what they saw and heard. While the evidence is still fresh and the case is being tried in the press."

She wasn't getting through to him. "No, Fergus, you're the one who doesn't understand. My life has been put on hold until this mess is settled. I can't work, I can't leave town, some of my friends think I'm guilty. I won't live like this. I need to be exonerated."

His demeanor changed to that of a man trying to reason with a child. "Of course you do, but a speedy trial isn't the way to do it. I won't let you put yourself in jeopardy just because the waiting is unpleasant and you're impatient."

He hesitated, then continued. "Surely I don't have to remind you what it's like in jail? Well, prison is a hell of a lot worse."

Sharon shivered, and Fergus again cradled her against him. "I'm sorry," he said gently. "I hate having to scare you into anything, but you've got to be realistic. Right now our case is practically nonexistent. We need to find someone who saw you leave Vancleave's office. There were people in the pool area, but it may take a long time to find them. Guests at a hotel usually don't stay long. Ray has gotten access to a list of guests who were registered at the time of the murder, but so far he hasn't found anyone who was out at the pool on the morning in question."

She was torn between fear of conviction and frustration at the limitations placed on her until this was settled. "I don't know," she said mournfully against his hard-muscled chest. "I'll have to think about it."

He caressed her back with his hand. "Do that," he agreed reluctantly, "but you'll have to let me know before we go into court in the morning. If you're bound over they'll set a date for the trial at that time."

Sharon slept fitfully that night. Her mind kept twisting and turning, wrestling with the dilemma of her own making. She trusted Fergus completely on this issue, but even if she hadn't his argument would have made sense. He needed all the time he could get to prepare a defense. The evidence was all stacked against her, and just the thought of going to prison made her break out in a cold sweat.

So why couldn't she give him free rein to postpone the trial as long as possible? Her stubbornness was making his job much more difficult, and it was so unnecessary. Why couldn't she just let him handle things the way he'd been trained to do?

It sounded so simple, but how could she survive for a year or more in this purgatory of suspense and degradation? She was a virtual prisoner, even though the bars were invisible, and how long would the hotel keep paying her a salary not to work? She doubted that even Fergus could compel them past a certain length of time.

Then what would she do? No one would hire her with a charge of murder hanging over her head. The newspapers were eagerly printing every bit of fact or fiction pertinent to the case, complete with pictures, and their readers were gleefully taking sides. One faction thought she should rot in prison for killing her boss in an angry rage. The other faction proclaimed that she'd struck a blow for women's liberation and deserved sainthood.

But both sides never doubted that she was guilty!

When it became obvious that she wasn't going to fall asleep until she stopped worrying about that she tried to focus on a different subject. Unfortunately her mind flip-flopped over into even more dangerous territory. The fact that Fergus was sleeping just across the hall from her!

A picture of his slender, but muscular, body lying naked and relaxed in sleep between the crisp brown sheets sent prickles of passion to her core. It would be so easy for her to go to him, climb into his bed and take refuge in his arms, in the delicious oblivion of his lovemaking. She knew he'd welcome her. He'd made no secret of his desire for her, and God knows, she was burning with fever for him.

Their lovemaking had always been glorious. They'd had only to climb into bed at night and curl up together to ignite the flame that consumed them. It never failed to happen, and that's why it had been such a gut-wrenching shock to her when she was confronted with the fact that Fergus was involved with another woman.

Her heat cooled and she pounded her pillow in frustration. Damn him! How dared he toy with her that way! He'd taught her the enchantment of ecstasy, then left her bereft and alone.

When she finally fell asleep she had strange and frightening dreams that left her dispirited and sad when she awakened the following morning, even though she couldn't remember the content of them.

The preliminary hearing was set for ten o'clock that Wednesday morning, but Sharon was awake and out of bed by five-thirty. She pulled a lavender-and-white checked cotton robe on over her nightgown, then brushed her teeth and made halfhearted passes at her hair with a comb. A glance in the mirror at her drawn face and bloodshot eyes made her wince, but what the hell? No one would expect her to look like a cover girl when she appeared in court as a murder suspect.

At least it was plain to her now what she was going to do about setting a time for the trial. Although she wasn't conscious of having come to a decision during the night, this morning she knew that her only choice was to get it over with as quickly as possible so she could send Fergus Lachlan back to Chicago and get him out of her life.

His brand of loving had nearly destroyed her once. She wasn't going to give him a second try at it, but the longer they were together the more difficult it was to remember that.

She'd thought she was the only one stirring so far, but halfway down the stairs she was met by the aroma of coffee and bacon. Anna hadn't mentioned having to go to work early, but business hours in real estate were pretty erratic.

When Sharon got to the kitchen she found Fergus breaking eggs into a skillet. For some reason she hadn't considered that it might be him, and his presence startled her. She wondered if he'd been unable to sleep, too.

He heard her and turned around. "Sharon, what are you doing up so early?"

He looked more closely at her. "Did you get any sleep at all?" he asked.

She shook her head. His compassionate tone melted her bones, but she kept her distance. "Not much, and when I did I had bad dreams. I didn't hear you leave your room. I thought you were still in bed.''

"I didn't sleep very well, either, but I usually get up about this time.''

"You didn't use to,'' she blurted, then wished she'd bitten her tongue, instead.

"That's because I had you in bed with me,'' he said simply.

The longing that coursed through her made her gasp. "Dammit, Fergus—''

He held up his hands in surrender. "Okay, I'm sorry,'' he said, and turned his attention back to his eggs. "Are you afraid of what's going to happen today? Is that why you couldn't sleep?''

Yeah, Sharon, go ahead and tell him why you couldn't sleep. Tell him it was because you were lusting for him, and see how long it takes him to get you back upstairs and into his bed.

"I...I guess so,'' she said instead, "but I did come to a decision about the trial date. I'm sorry, Fergus, I know it's going to put a lot of pressure on you, but please tell the judge I want a speedy trial.''

He whirled around, shocked. "Sharon, are you sure? Why are you in such an all-fired hurry? You're too bright not to understand the risk as I've explained it.'' His tone was brusque.

"You're right, I do understand,'' she told him, "and I apologize for being so difficult, but I need to get on with my life. I can't live in a perpetual cloud of suspicion and frustration. All I did was yell at Floyd Vancleave, tell him what a bastard he was and then leave.''

"And that's the crux of the problem,'' Fergus snapped as he turned back to the stove and shut off the heat under the skillet. "Everyone in the reception area saw you storm into his office unannounced and heard you shouting at him, but then you went out the back door, so none of them saw you leave. Minutes later when the receptionist went in she saw you bending over his corpse with a knife in your hand, dripping blood.''

He turned around and ran his hand through his hair in a gesture of irritation. "No responsible juror is going to acquit you unless we either find the real murderer or a witness who saw you outside the building when Vancleave was killed, and that's going to take time."

He turned his back on her once more to move the skillet from the hot burner to a cool one, then walked across the room to where she stood by the table. "Don't do this to me, Sharon," he pleaded. "Don't deliberately tie my hands. I'd never forgive myself if a jury found you guilty. Please, work with me, not against me."

Chapter Nine

The news media were waiting for Fergus and Sharon as they approached the courthouse. Cameras clicked and microphones were shoved at them as reporters yelled questions and jostled to get closer, impeding their progress.

Fergus had warned Sharon this would happen and had instructed her on how it should be handled, but even though she thought she was prepared, it was a frightening experience. She'd never been the center of so much howling attention before, and it all merged into an undecipherable roar. Fergus tucked her arm through his and pushed their way through the wall of bodies with a terse "No comment" to shouted questions.

Sharon, following his orders, kept her head down and her mouth shut. He had selected the celery-colored business suit she was wearing, a well-tailored outfit that was stylish but not eye-catching or sexy.

"You'll make a better general impression if you're neither too beautiful nor too confident," he'd explained. "A jury is mostly made up of middle-class working people who will find it difficult to empathize with you if you look like a beauty queen or a chairman of the board. The same goes for the reporters and the TV audience.''

In spite of her nervousness, Sharon hadn't been able to quell a chuckle. ''In other words, you don't care for this suit?''

Fergus had smiled and winked. ''Right,'' he'd said, then sobered. ''If this case goes to trial the jurors will be people who have watched you on television, so you'll have to be careful of your image from now on.''

That pronouncement had depressed her then, and it continued to do so as she stifled her natural inclination to look her best and speak her mind. At least now she knew she was right to insist on a speedy trial. She was innocent and she'd go out of her mind if she had to play games with the public for a year or two!

When they finally got to the courtroom the entourage followed them inside, all but the cameras. The din was deafening as Sharon and Fergus took seats at the defense table in front. A few minutes later Ray Quinlan, in his role as co-counsel, joined them. In a matter of seconds the bailiff called for order and declared the court in session. A black-robed judge walked out of chambers and took her seat at the bench.

It all happened quickly, leaving Sharon off balance and confused. The courtroom was packed, but the only people she knew were Fergus and Ray. Were all these curious strangers going to influence whether or not she was charged with murdering Floyd?

It was like a nightmarish circus. Did anyone there care what really happened? Or did they just want to be entertained? To hold off the numbing boredom of their dull lives by watching the wheels of justice grind a likely suspect into oblivion?

Sharon's case was called, and after some "preliminaries," as the judge called them, motions that needed to be decided on before the hearing started, an assistant district attorney, a man named John Hollingsworth, stood to make an opening statement.

"Your Honor, on Wednesday of last week, June 15, the police were called to the Starlight St. Louis Hotel, where the defendant, Sharon Sawyer Lachlan, an employee, had been discovered crouching over the body of her immediate supervisor, Floyd Vancleave, clutching a bloody letter opener in her hand. The victim had died of a stab wound in the heart."

Sharon gasped and grabbed Fergus's arm. "I haven't used the name Lachlan since I filed for divorce," she whispered.

Fergus frowned. "Did you petition the court to have your maiden name restored?"

She tried to think. "I'm not sure. I was too upset to—"

No, she wasn't going to whine about how totally wiped out she'd been at the time of their divorce. He already knew that, he didn't need to hear it again.

She stopped and started over. "My attorney handled everything and I asked him to do that. I assumed that he did. I've been signing my name Sawyer for the past five years."

Fergus nodded and stood up. "Your Honor," he said in his musical baritone voice that was pleasingly pitched but still carried to all corners of the room. "So that there will be no confusion, I'd like it noted for the record that Ms. Sawyer is my ex-wife. We were divorced five years ago, and since that time she has not used my name, but has reverted to her maiden name, Sharon Elisse Sawyer, for all personal and legal purposes. We request that the name Lachlan not be used when referring to her."

The judge indicated that the record would so show, and the request was granted.

The assistant district attorney frowned at Fergus and continued. "We will show that Ms. Sawyer had ample motive and opportunity, and that she did in fact kill Floyd Vancleave, deliberately and with malice."

John Hollingsworth sat down, and the judge turned to Fergus. "Did you wish to make an opening statement, Mr. Lachlan?"

Fergus stood. "A brief one, Your Honor. My client is innocent of any and all charges against her. She has been a respected and productive member of this community for the past five years. Before that she was an honor student at Northwestern University in the Chicago area, where she graduated in the top ten percent of her class."

He put his hand on Sharon's shoulder and smiled when she looked up. She saw affection and trust in his gaze, and she was grateful for his effort at reassurance.

"Sharon is known to all her friends and acquaintances as a warm and compassionate woman," he continued, "and it is inconceivable that she would commit an act of violence. She has no criminal record, not even a parking ticket, and it is a travesty of justice that she was ever arrested for this crime."

He sat down, and the judge turned toward the A.D.A. "Do you wish to present witnesses, Mr. Hollingsworth?"

"Yes, Your Honor," he answered. "I call Ms. Beverly Maitland to the stand."

Sharon's heart sank. *Floyd Vancleave's secretary.* Her testimony would be the most damaging.

The door at the back of the room opened and Beverly walked down the aisle. She was dressed in a navy blue suit, with matching pumps and a crisp white blouse. Her curly brown hair framed her face and tumbled to her shoulders.

When she got to the witness chair she was sworn in, and as she sat down her gaze met Sharon's, but Beverly looked away quickly and Sharon couldn't tell whether she was sympathetic or antagonistic.

Hollingsworth stood and led her through a series of questions that established who she was and her connection with the victim and the defendant. When that was accomplished he changed tactics.

"Now, Ms. Maitland," he said, "tell us what happened at approximately 10:30 a.m. of last Wednesday, June 15."

Beverly looked nervously around the room, studiously avoiding Sharon, then cleared her throat. "Well, I ... That is, I was sitting at my desk in the reception room of Mr. Vancleave's office, when the door was flung open and Sharon—uh, Ms. Sawyer, came storming in, carrying a crumpled piece of paper in her hand and headed for Mr. Vancleave's door. There were several people waiting to see him, and when I realized that she intended to go into his office I called to her to tell her she'd have to wait her turn, but she opened the door, shouted 'You bastard,' and walked on in, slamming it shut behind her."

The secretary looked down and fidgeted with the clasp on her purse.

"Are you saying she was angry?" the A.D.A. prompted.

"Objection," Fergus said from his seat. "Calls for a conclusion."

"I'll allow it," the judge ruled. "You may answer," she said to Beverly.

"Oh yes, I've never seen her so mad," Beverly said. "Her face was red, and her eyes were positively spitting fire—"

"Objection," Fergus said.

"Just confine your answers to the questions asked," the judge instructed Beverly.

Beverly hung her head and worried her lower lip with her teeth. Sharon couldn't help feeling sorry for her. She'd probably never been in a courtroom before, and this one was full of spectators. Besides, she was only telling the truth. Sharon knew she'd been breathing fire and smoke.

Hollingsworth spoke again. "What happened after Ms. Sawyer went into the office and shut the door?"

Beverly raised her head. "Well . . . they started yelling at each other. Everyone in the room heard them—"

"Objection," Fergus said again. "She can't know what 'everyone' heard."

Hollingsworth glared at Fergus. "I'll rephrase the question. Did you hear them yelling?"

Beverly nodded. "Oh yes."

"And did others in the room indicate that they had also heard?"

"Yes, they did. They were all looking toward the door and shaking their heads. One man even suggested that I should call security, but then the shouting stopped."

"It stopped?" Hollingsworth asked.

Beverly nodded. "Yes. We . . . I could no longer hear them. I kept expecting Sharon to come back out, but she didn't. Quite a bit of time went by, and the people waiting to see Mr. Vancleave were getting impatient—"

"Just a minute," the A.D.A. interrupted. "Can you be more specific about the time lapse? Was it two minutes? Ten minutes? Twenty?"

She appeared thoughtful. "I didn't look at my watch, but I'd say not more than ten minutes."

"Then what happened?"

"Uh . . . well, like I said, the people waiting in the outer office were getting impatient, and finally one of them came up to my desk to say that she had another appointment and couldn't wait much longer. I was getting concerned, too, so I got up and walked over to the door and knocked. There was no response, so I turned the knob and opened it. That's when I saw—"

Beverly's voice broke, and she closed her eyes and put the back of her hand to her mouth.

"I know this is difficult," Hollingsworth said sympathetically. "Just take your time. There's no hurry."

Sharon could see that Beverly's hand was trembling, but she opened her eyes and took a deep breath, then continued. "I saw both Sharon and Mr. Vancleave on the floor in front of the desk. He was lying on his back, with his legs sort of crumpled up, and she was crouching over him, with a bloody knife in her hand—"

Beverly's voice broke again, this time on a sob.

Sharon moaned and covered her face with her hands as the horror of that moment replayed in her mind, like a videotape through a red haze of blood.

Fergus stood. "Your Honor, I suggest a short recess to allow the witness and the defendant to compose themselves."

The judge nodded. "We'll take five minutes." She stood and walked into her chambers.

Fergus sat down and put his arm across Sharon's hunched shoulders, then spoke softly close to her ear. "Are you all right, love? Do you want to go to the ladies' room or anything?"

She shook her head. "No, I'll be okay. Besides, the reporters would corner me if I went out in the hall, and just make everything worse."

He muttered an oath. "It's a wonder you haven't fallen apart. You didn't get much sleep last night, and you ate hardly anything for breakfast."

He squeezed her shoulder. "Just hang in there. This won't go on much longer. I expect Hollingsworth will wrap it up before lunch, then I'll get you out of here."

Sharon lifted her head out of her hands and straightened up, dislodging his arm. The courtroom was no place for signs of devotion, no matter how innocent. She'd never forgive herself if the bar association frowned on Fergus for being too affectionate with a client, even if that client was his ex-wife.

"I'll be all right now," she assured him. "I... I lost it there for a minute because I had an especially vivid flashback of that scene she was describing."

In spite of her determination not to react again she shivered. "I'll probably have nightmares about that for the rest of my life."

"Not if you spent the rest of your life with me," he said tenderly. "I'd hold you in my arms at night and keep the bad dreams away."

She could see that he was serious, and the thought of being wrapped in his embrace as they slept in the same bed every night filled her with longing. She felt warmed by his loving assurance. He obviously believed what he said, and she wasn't going to hurt him by telling him that for the past five years *he* had been the source of her nightmares.

The judge returned and the hearing resumed with Beverly again on the witness stand.

"Do you feel up to testifying again now?" the assistant district attorney asked softly.

Beverly looked slightly more relaxed. "Yes, thank you."

He walked back to his table, picked up something in a plastic bag and returned to the witness stand. "Is this the object the defendant was holding?"

She looked at it, but made no move to touch it. "I . . . I don't know. I was too shocked and too far away to notice details. My impression was that she was clutching a knife, but this looks like the letter opener he kept on his desk."

"It is the letter opener, and it's also the murder weapon—"

"Objection," Fergus said grimly. "No foundation. There's no evidence before this court to substantiate that claim, and the witness has just stated that she doesn't recognize it."

"I'd like to submit this letter opener as state's exhibit A," Hollingsworth said before the judge could rule on the objection, "and I'll substantiate it with my next witness."

"All right, but see that you do," the judge said sourly.

The A.D.A. nodded and turned back to Beverly. "Tell us what happened after you opened the door and saw Mr.

Vancleave's body lying on the floor and Ms. Sawyer bending over him with a daggerlike weapon in her hands.''

Fergus cursed under his breath and Sharon winced. Had it really been necessary to describe that scene so vividly again? Obviously the man was determined to wring all the drama he could out of the grisly facts he was presenting.

Fergus didn't object, although he was obviously furious, but maybe he knew the damage had already been done and objecting would only call that much more attention to the gory mental picture of her brandishing the weapon dripping with blood.

Beverly hesitated a moment, as though she, too, was shaken by the image. When she spoke her voice shook slightly. "I . . . I was too shocked to do anything for a few seconds, then I screamed. After that I'm confused as to just what happened. People crowded around, and there was a lot of talking and hullabaloo, and then the police were there."

Sharon shuddered. That had been her impression, too. Shock, loud voices, people running back and forth, police asking questions she didn't understand . . .

"Just a minute, Ms. Maitland," Hollingsworth interrupted, "let's go back a bit. What did Ms. Sawyer do when you opened the door?"

"Objection!" Fergus said angrily. "The witness has already said she's confused as to what happened then."

"I just want to lead her through the events step by step and help her sort them out," the A.D.A. said.

The judge looked from one man to the other. "I'll overrule the objection, but you're in a minefield here, Mr. Prosecutor. Be careful that it doesn't blow up in your face."

She turned to Beverly. "You may answer the question."

"She looked up at me," Beverly said. "I remember that because her eyes had such a wild expression—"

"Your Honor, I object!" Fergus thundered. "This witness is not qualified to diagnose the expression in my client's eyes. I request that be stricken from the record."

"So ordered," the judge said. "That last sentence shall be stricken."

Hollingsworth continued. "Did Ms. Sawyer say anything?"

"No, but she dropped the knife—uh, the weapon. It fell on the floor between her and the desk. That's when I screamed, and after that... I turned and tried to leave. People were crowding behind me and I couldn't get away. I think I kept on screaming. At least somebody did."

The prosecutor nodded. "Do you recall what she was wearing that day?"

"She wore a light-blue linen-weave dress. The color was very becoming, and I'd commented on it when I saw her earlier. She said it was new, and she was wearing it for the first time."

"Was there blood on her clothing after Mr. Vancleave was killed?" Hollingsworth asked.

Beverly paused. "Yes. My thoughts were too scrambled to notice it at first when she was on the floor, but when the police came and took her away there was blood all over the front of her dress."

The prosecutor went over to his table and picked up a large plastic bag. Back at the witness stand he removed a blue garment and showed it to Beverly. "Is this the dress Ms. Sawyer was wearing that day?"

Beverly shuddered at the sight of the rumpled blue dress with large brown stains on the front. "Yes," she said, and looked away.

Hollingsworth addressed the judge. "We'd like to enter this garment in evidence as state's exhibit B."

"So ordered," the judge said.

The A.D.A. returned his attention to Beverly. "Thank you, Ms. Maitland. Those are all the questions I have for you, but the defense may wish to cross-examine." He returned to his seat at the table.

What little hope Sharon had clung to was crushed by Beverly's testimony. How could anybody believe she was not guilty in light of the evidence against her?

Fergus stood. "Yes, I do have some questions," he said amiably, and walked over to the witness stand. "My name is Fergus Lachlan, Ms. Maitland."

He had his back to the spectators, so Sharon couldn't see his face, but she was sure he was smiling, because Beverly smiled, and hers looked like the answering kind. "How do you do," she murmured.

He tipped his head in acknowledgment. "Now, I know this is a frightening ordeal, but I'll make it as easy for you as I can. Just relax and think about the questions I'll ask you. Don't feel rushed or intimidated. I'm not going to try to trick you, or get you to say something you don't want to. All I want is the truth. Do you understand?"

She smiled again and nodded, and Sharon could see that Beverly was melting under Fergus's very real charm.

"All right, then, we'll start with an easy one," he said softly. "How long have you known Sharon Sawyer?"

"I met her two years ago when I first started working at the Starlight St. Louis. She'd just been promoted to assistant front-office manager."

"Was Floyd Vancleave front-office manager at that time?"

"Yes."

"How did Floyd and Sharon get along? Did they quarrel often?"

Beverly shook her head emphatically. "Oh no! Sharon never quarreled with anybody. In fact, she was about the only one who could get along with Mr. Vancleave—"

"Objection," Hollingsworth said. "Relevance."

"Goes to state of mind and motive, Your Honor," Fergus answered.

"Overruled. You may continue, Mr. Lachlan," said the judge.

"Was Mr. Vancleave a difficult man to work for?" Fergus continued.

"He could be, yes."

"How so?"

Again Beverly bit nervously at her lower lip. "He was very autocratic, wouldn't listen to anyone's opinion but his own. He was good with plans and figures and the business end of management, but he antagonized people. When any of the employees under him had a problem they took it to Sharon. She could usually placate anybody—"

"Objection," Hollingsworth shouted.

The judge agreed. "The clerk will strike that last sentence."

Sharon caught the quick smile Fergus flashed at her, and knew what he was thinking. The comment may have been stricken from the record, but it would stay in the mind of the judge and possibly soften her judgment.

He turned back to Beverly. "Would you say that Sharon had a hot temper?"

Beverly's eyes widened. "No. I never saw her display any temper at all. That's why people discussed their problems with her. She has a knack for being cool and rational and sympathetic, even when she has to tell them they are in the wrong. Mr. Vancleave was brusque and rude and always assumed the employee was at fault."

"Your Honor," the A.D.A. said as he got to his feet. "Mr. Vancleave is not the subject of this hearing. He's the victim."

"Yes, Mr. Prosecutor, point taken, although I must remind you that this is your witness. However, the last sentence will be stricken."

Hollingsworth sat back down, looking frustrated.

Fergus again turned his attention to Beverly. "Do you know what Floyd and Sharon were quarreling about? I mean, of your own knowledge, not hearsay. Could you distinguish what they were saying to each other?"

"No, sir, I had no idea what they were quarreling about. I'd never seen Sharon really mad before, and once she closed the door after entering his office I could hear them shouting, but I couldn't make out what they were saying. The words were muffled."

"Now, Beverly, I'd like you to tell me about that office," Fergus said. "Is the door to the outer office the only way in and out of that room?"

"No. The office is on the first floor, and there's a wide sliding-glass door that opens onto the pool and garden area."

"Is this area fenced?"

Beverly nodded. "Yes, but there's a gate that opens onto the street."

"So it's possible for a person to leave or enter Floyd Vancleave's office without ever going through the reception area?"

"Yes."

Mark one for our side, Sharon thought, as Fergus concluded his cross-examination.

But then Hollingsworth stood. "I have one more question, Your Honor," he said, and the judge nodded her permission.

"Is that sliding-glass door left unlocked so that anyone can wander in or out?"

Beverly shook her head. "No, it's always locked. It can be easily unlocked from the inside by just pushing the latch up, but it can't be unlocked from the outside without a key."

"Does the door lock automatically when it is shut?"

Beverly lowered her gaze. "Yes, it does."

"And who has keys to that door?"

"Only Mr. Vancleave and the security department. Mr. Vancleave always keeps his on his key ring."

"So if anyone left the room through that door, then returned a few minutes later, someone on the inside would have to let them in?" the A.D.A. asked.

Beverly nodded. "Yes."

Sharon groaned. The implication was only too clear. If Sharon had left and then returned, as she'd told the police, Floyd would have had to be alive to let her in.

Except that wasn't how it happened. She'd unlocked the door to get out, but she hadn't slid it shut again. It had still been open and unlocked when she'd returned for her purse, and Floyd was lying on the floor with a sharp letter opener in his chest!

The state called its next witness, Officer Edward Jackson, one of the first policemen to arrive on the crime scene. He looked like a seasoned veteran of the force, and she remembered him questioning her that day, but none of the details.

Once he'd been sworn in and identified, Hollingsworth began his interrogation. "When you arrived at the scene what did you find?"

"There was a man's body lying on the floor, and a woman in a bloodstained dress, sitting in the chair behind the desk. There were also two uniformed security officers employed by the hotel."

"Is that woman in the room now?"

"Yeah," Officer Jackson said, and pointed. "That's her sitting over there at the defense table."

"Let the record show that he identified the defendant," the A.D.A. said, and the judge nodded.

"Were you able to identify that man and woman at that time?"

Officer Jackson said yes, and gave Floyd's and Sharon's names and their employment records at the hotel.

"Were there any wounds on the body?"

"Yes, there was a puncture wound in the chest, and we found a bloody letter opener on the floor beside the victim. It was later identified as the murder weapon."

Hollingsworth walked over to the exhibit table, picked up the small plastic bag and gave it to the witness. "Is this the letter opener you found?"

Jackson nodded. "It is. It has my mark on it."

"Were there signs of a struggle in the room?"

Jackson thought for a moment. "Only on the desk. The objects on top of it were scattered, and the desk lamp was overturned on the floor. There was a lot of blood on the victim and some on the carpet where he was lying. It looked to me like he was taken by surprise. Like he was stabbed by someone he knew and trusted."

Fergus tensed, but then settled back again. Sharon wondered for a moment why he didn't object. After all, that was only the man's opinion, but then she realized that the officer would be qualified as an expert on such matters.

"Were there fingerprints found on the weapon?" Hollingsworth asked.

"Yes, Mr. Vancleave's and one other set."

"And were you able to identify whom they belonged to?"

The officer looked directly at Sharon. "We were. They belonged to Sharon Sawyer, the defendant."

There was a ripple of voices in the room, and the judge banged her gavel for order.

Sharon felt battered, even though she'd known roughly what his testimony would be. Still, it was frightening to listen to the evidence, so overwhelmingly against her.

Now it was Fergus's turn to cross-examine, and she tried to pull herself together and pay attention. He walked over to the witness stand and when he spoke his tone was friendly. "Officer Jackson, I understand you've been on the police force here in St. Louis for quite some time."

The officer tilted up his head. "Twenty-one years," he said proudly.

"I'm also told that you have a number of commendations." Fergus's tone was laced with admiration.

Jackson beamed and named off several awards, but Sharon didn't catch the names.

"Congratulations. That's an impressive list. You're very thorough and professional, so I won't waste the court's time by asking obvious questions. There are a few things, though, that I need to know. You said that when you arrived on the scene Ms. Sawyer was sitting in a chair, but when Ms. Maitland went into the office earlier she said Ms. Sawyer was kneeling on the floor beside the body. Do you know how she got to the chair?"

"Yes, I do. When Ms. Maitland told me that Ms. Sawyer had been on the floor I asked the security guards about it. One of them said he'd helped her to stand and led her over to the chair so she wouldn't disturb any evidence."

"*Helped* her and *led* her?" Fergus sounded puzzled. "Was she injured, too?"

"No," the officer said. "She was just a little shocked. Disoriented."

"But why would she be shocked and disoriented if she went to Vancleave's office with every intention of killing him, as the charge of first-degree murder would indicate?"

"Objection!" the A.D.A. shouted. "Calls for a conclusion."

Fergus turned and looked at the prosecutor. "But I understood that Officer Jackson was testifying as an expert witness," Fergus said, sounding perplexed. "In which case his conclusions should be allowed. However, I'll withdraw the question."

He sounded accommodating, but Sharon knew him well enough to recognize that he was pleased. Apparently he'd managed to have the testimony he was after inserted into the record.

He turned back to the witness. "In your twenty-one years on the force have you seen many violent crimes?"

"Dozens of them," Jackson said. "No, make that hundreds."

"And in all that time have you ever known the persons who either witnessed the crime or were first on the scene to be shocked and or disoriented? Even though they were innocent bystanders?"

The officer nodded. "Many times. In fact, most of the time."

"So you would recognize someone in that condition?"

"Sure."

"Did Ms. Sawyer show signs of shock?"

"Yes, very much so."

"Can you tell us what some of the symptoms were?"

The officer hesitated, as though searching for the right words. "She seemed dazed. Her eyes didn't focus properly, and at first she didn't respond to me at all—she just sat there staring down at her hands folded in her lap. Later she started to comprehend a little, but she was confused and had trouble understanding the simplest questions."

"When you arrested her did you read her her rights?"

"Yes, that's standard procedure."

"Did she understand what you were telling her?"

The officer shrugged. "She said in front of witnesses that she did, so we went ahead and booked her."

Fergus walked over to the defense table and stood in front of it as he continued. "Was the sliding-glass door in the office open or closed when you got there?"

"It was open."

"Was it dusted for fingerprints?"

"Yes, it was."

"Were Ms. Sawyer's prints found on it?"

He nodded tersely. "Yes, they were."

"Both inside and outside?"

Jackson's gaze shifted slightly away from Fergus's. "Yes."

"And wouldn't that suggest to you that she had left and returned through that door?"

"Objection," Hollingsworth said.

"Overruled," the judge said. "The witness may answer."

"I suppose she could have," the officer answered.

"Were there other prints besides Ms. Sawyer's?"

"Only Mr. Vancleave's. They were on the inside."

Fergus hesitated a moment, then moved closer to the witness stand. "Now, about your statement that Mr. Vancleave was probably killed by someone he knew and trusted. How did you come to that conclusion?"

The officer shifted in the chair. "Because the victim didn't appear to have put up a fight. He was a good-sized man, and muscular. It's reasonable to assume he would have grappled with a stranger."

"But isn't it also reasonable to assume he would have grappled with anyone who threatened him with a weapon, stranger or not?"

"I suppose," the officer admitted, "but if it were a woman and somebody he knew he'd be more apt to try to placate her."

"A woman? Are you implying that only a woman could have committed this crime?" Fergus's tone was low, but sharp.

Officer Jackson looked startled. "Ah...no, but since the suspect is a woman—"

"Then you didn't bother to look for other suspects, since you had one so conveniently close by?" This time Fergus's tone was deadly.

"Yes... I mean no!" Jackson was obviously rattled. "Ms. Sawyer was found bending over the body with the murder weapon in her hand."

"But you didn't actually see her like that, did you? You testified she was sitting in a chair behind the desk when you arrived."

"She was, but we had statements by witnesses—"

"Did any of those witnesses see Ms. Sawyer stab Mr. Vancleave?"

"Of course not," the officer said, red faced.

"Tell me, Officer Jackson, have you made any effort to find someone else who could have committed this crime?"

"You know damn well I haven't," he answered angrily. "I don't do follow-ups. That's the detectives' job, and once they got there they took over. You'll have to ask them whether or not they're looking for other suspects."

Fergus seemed to relax somewhat. "I did," he said, "and they're not."

The prosecutor was on his feet. "Objection!"

Fergus turned away. "I have no more questions," he said, and sat down next to Sharon.

After that Hollingsworth rested his case and gave a closing argument, which was little more than a replay of his opening.

"Do you have a closing statement, Mr. Lachlan?" the judged asked after the prosecutor had finished.

"A short one, Your Honor," Fergus said as he got to his feet. "I submit that there's not enough evidence to proceed with this charge against my client, and certainly not when the charge is first-degree murder. Although the state's own witness has admitted that Floyd Vancleave was a man who antagonized people and was difficult to get along with, no effort has been made to find out if someone else had good reason to kill him.

"Ms. Sawyer admits that she went into the victim's office through the reception area, then quarreled with the victim. But that door is not the only one leading into or out of that room. There was another one that led to the outside area, and Sharon Sawyer's fingerprints were found on both the outside and the inside of that door.

"There's every reason to believe that she left the room as she claimed in her statement to the police, in which case someone else also had access to the office for several minutes before she returned."

Fergus sat down, and the judge was silent as she sifted through her notes. Finally, she raised her head and looked at both the prosecutor and Fergus.

"I've heard all the testimony presented and examined the evidence. It is the judgment of this court that there is probable cause to find that Floyd Vancleave was criminally assaulted and died as a result of that assault. There is also probable cause to find that Sharon Elisse Sawyer had the opportunity and the motive to commit that crime.

"However, I do not find enough evidence to support a first-degree murder charge, but will bind her over to superior court on a charge of murder in the second degree."

Her gaze sought Fergus. "Mr. Lachlan, are you still willing to be responsible for Ms. Sawyer and guarantee her appearance in court when she is summoned?"

"Yes, I am, Your Honor."

"Then the defendant will remain free on bail under that condition."

Hollingsworth got to his feet. "Objection!"

"Overruled." The judge banged her gavel. "Court's adjourned."

Chapter Ten

Sharon felt numb.

Fergus had warned her that the district attorney's case was strong and she would almost certainly be bound over for trial. She thought she'd accepted it, but in truth she'd had no idea of the emotional havoc this hearing would cause her.

She knew Fergus had done everything he could to keep her from going to trial. She trusted him completely, but, given the weight of the evidence against her, no one could have saved her from this indignity.

She knew all of this, so why did the words *bind her over to superior court on the charge of murder in the second degree* come as such a shock and fill her with hopelessness and dread?

Gradually Fergus's voice intruded into her fog of despondency.

"Sharon. Honey, look at me. What's the matter?"

He sounded disturbed, and slowly she became aware of the sound of shuffling feet hurrying toward exits and excited voices debating the judge's decision. Fergus had his arm around her shoulders and was gently shaking her. "Sharon, talk to me. Are you sick?"

She shook her head, then turned it to look at him. "I didn't kill Floyd," she said barely above a whisper.

His eyes were soft with compassion. "I know you didn't, sweetheart," he said tenderly.

Ray appeared with a glass of water and ice, which he handed to her. "Here, Sharon, drink some of this. You'll feel better in a few minutes." He looked worried.

She reached for the glass, but when she took it her hand shook so, it rattled the ice. Fergus wrapped his hand around hers and steadied the glass as he guided it to her mouth. His hand was warm and strong and comforting, and she took several swallows of water. It felt cool and soothing on her dry throat.

"Better?" he asked anxiously as he put the glass down.

She nodded, then clutched at his hand when he moved it. "Fergus, can we go home now?"

His troubled gaze searched her face. "You bet," he said, then turned his attention to Ray. "We'll leave in your car. I don't think the reporters will recognize it. Bring it around to the back, as close to the door as you can get. We'll be waiting there for you."

Ray left, and Fergus returned his attention to Sharon. "Can you stand up and walk?"

"Yes," she said determinedly, although she wasn't really sure. She felt as if all the stamina had been drained out of her. There was no way she was going to admit that, though.

Apparently Fergus wasn't sure, either, because he practically lifted her out of her chair and held her until she got her balance. Her legs felt rubbery and her head light, but it only took a few seconds for her to steady herself.

The hall in front of the courtroom had been cleared, but even so a bailiff escorted Fergus and Sharon to the express elevator and down to the basement in an effort to avoid the reporters gathered at the elevators on the main floor. Then they walked up one flight of the back stairs, where Ray was waiting in the car outside.

Fergus helped Sharon into the rear seat, then walked around and got in beside her. "Do you want to stop someplace for lunch?" he asked as Ray drove without a ripple of recognition past the crowd waiting at the front of the building.

"No," Sharon answered promptly. "I just want to go home."

As Ray wove in and out of the downtown traffic, Sharon was only vaguely aware of what was going on around her. Fergus took her hand, and she clung to his like a lifeline. He was all that stood between her and a long prison term, but even more than that, he and Anna were the closest thing she had to family. She had an aunt who lived in Alaska, but they'd lost touch years ago.

She'd never felt the need for relatives so acutely before. She'd been nineteen and in college when her parents were killed, but she'd always been independent and self-sufficient, and she'd been able to work through her grief and get on with her life.

The following year she'd met and married Fergus, and even though she'd nearly been destroyed when their marriage had broken up three years later, she hadn't needed a shoulder to cry on. Far from it. She'd shied away from sympathy and offers of help. Instead she'd moved to a new city in a different state and started over again—new job, new friends, new interests.

So why was she so shattered and frightened now? Why did she feel so needy? So dependent? So desperate for someone to lean on?

Again Fergus had to rouse her from her mental fog when they arrived at the house. He helped her out of the car, and Ray drove on as they walked up to the door and let themselves in. She loved this gracious old redbrick house that had been home to her for the past four years, and for the first time she allowed herself to dwell on the fact that her days in it might be numbered.

Would she ever live here again after the trial was over? Or would she spend the next thirty or forty years in prison?

My God, she'd be an old woman by the time she got out!

A chill swept through her and she began to shiver. Not a polite tremor, but a convulsive shaking that rattled her teeth.

Immediately Fergus swept her up in his arms and carried her to the sofa, then sat down with her on his lap. "It's all right, Sharon," he said softly, but she heard the doubt in his voice. "Everything's going to be all right."

He wrapped her in his embrace and rubbed his cheek against hers. "I'm not going to let anything bad happen to you. I love you. I'd never forgive myself if you were convicted of this crime. I'll find out who killed Floyd Vancleave if I have to track him or her down myself."

Sharon buried her face in his shoulder and let his low comforting voice and his reassuring words, murmured over and over again, flow through her like a soothing caress. She basked in the body warmth that radiated from him, and made little mewling sounds when his fingers stroked and his lips nibbled lovingly.

As she slowly relaxed she became aware of a different set of sensations. The strength of his arms that promised protection; the softness of his cheek as it pressed against her own; and the hard muscles of his thighs beneath her bottom.

A wave of heat swept through her and caused a twitching at her core. The swiftness and the strength of it caught her off guard, and she squirmed on his lap.

He moaned and she felt another hardness in him, as familiar as the throb of desire that rocked her and as welcome as the burst of excitement that set her on fire.

With an answering moan she lifted her head and fastened her open mouth over his. He gasped with surprise, but his lips parted to receive her, and his arms tightened as he strained to pull her hip against his groin. Their tongues thrust and withdrew, sometimes in his mouth and sometimes in hers, while their hands expertly explored each other with the haste of long-denied craving.

Neither of them spoke. There was no need, their bodies were out of control in full, rapturous harmony that sent them spiraling higher and higher.

With frantic haste they tore at their clothes, removing only what was necessary before Fergus lowered her to the carpeted floor and joined her body with his own.

There was no time for tenderness or murmured endearments as the burgeoning urgency drove them harder and faster until the whole world exploded and sent them rocketing into ecstasy.

For a long time they lay there on the floor, still joined, but now with Sharon on top, as they waited for their hearts to stop pounding and their breathing to slow to normal.

Fergus was afraid to speak. Afraid of breaking the spell that had gripped them so unexpectedly and sent them on a journey to paradise and back. But what now? Was she finally ready to forgive him and resume their life together? Or was this just a mistake that would make her even more unforgiving when the magic wore off?

Sharon slid off him, but she offered no objection when he reached for her. Instead she curled up in his arms beside him, and he breathed a grateful sigh of relief.

He nuzzled her temple and murmured, "I'm not going to say I'm sorry, because I'm not."

"Neither am I," she said, still a little breathless.

Fergus smiled. "I'm glad, but you deserve a hell of a lot better setting than the hard floor."

"Didn't you like it?" she asked with a small pout.

"Like it!" he exclaimed. "Oh God, I loved it. I've never experienced anything so intensely shattering before, but it doesn't surprise me. For over three years you kept me in an almost constant state of arousal.''

He knew he shouldn't have said that when she frowned. "Not always—" she began.

But he quickly covered her mouth with his to shut off her words and hopefully the thoughts that prompted them. She'd never understand his feelings for Elaine.

She responded immediately to his kiss, and in seconds he was hard and throbbing again. He was reacting like a teenager who hadn't yet learned to control his lusty urges, but that's exactly how he felt, urgent and out of control.

Her mouth was soft and sweet, and the familiar taste of her was driving him out of his mind, but he wasn't going to take her again like a rutting boar. She'd surprised him the first time, and then it was too late to stop, but he was determined not to let that happen again.

It took all his willpower to ease his mouth from hers and lift his head. "Not yet," he said, his tone scratchy with frustration. "Not here. I want to make long, slow, euphoric love to you in a bed where you can be comfortable.''

She nibbled at the sensitive hollow on the side of his neck, scattering his good intentions.

"I sort of like the floor," she said lazily, as she slowly slid her tongue over the area she'd just kissed.

He tightened his arms around her even as he protested, "Now, stop that, dammit." Then immediately he negated his command by shivering with desire and bucking against her as her unruly tongue continued up to his ear.

With one last burst of determination he managed to pull away from her and sit up, then looked back down at her. "Humor me just this once, sweetheart. I don't want Anna to come home and find us making love on the floor. As I remember she threatened us with eviction if that happened.''

Sharon chuckled and sat up beside him. "Picky, picky," she scolded teasingly as they both got to their feet.

Fergus pulled up his briefs and trousers and zipped his fly while Sharon pulled down her skirt and slip, then picked up her panties and panty hose off the floor. He put his arm around her and they walked up the stairs together, then down the hall to her bedroom, the one nearest the bath.

He began removing his clothes. "Shower with me?" he asked as he watched her step out of her celery-colored skirt and start unbuttoning her creamy silk blouse.

She looked at him, her eyes focusing on his bare chest. "I'd be delighted," she answered and removed the blouse, revealing a lace-trimmed ivory satin slip.

He remembered that she'd always worn sexy underwear, even under jeans and an old sweatshirt. That was one of the reasons he'd never been able to keep his hands off her. The soft satiny texture of the material added an extra dimension to the round curves underneath, so that now just the memory of it made his hands itch.

Quickly he stepped out of his pants and briefs. He didn't remember taking off his shoes and socks, but he must have done so downstairs, because he wasn't wearing them. He glanced up to see that Sharon was also naked, and it took his breath away.

She was even more luscious than before. In the five years they'd been apart she'd ripened. That was the only word he could think of to describe her. She may have gained a few pounds, but they enhanced rather than detracted. Her breasts and hips were fuller and even more enticing, although he was sure he could still span her tiny waist with his two hands, and her nipples were rosier and even more tempting.

The painful tightening in his crotch alerted him to the fact that he was staring, and he was jolted back to reality to find that Sharon was also staring at him. He took a deep breath and walked across the room to where she stood beside the bed.

Reaching out his hand, he took hers, and they walked into the bathroom, where Fergus adjusted the water to a pleasingly warm setting before they stepped into the stall. He picked up the bar of soap, then put his arms around her waist and pulled her back so her derriere settled into his groin, eliciting a groan of pleasure he couldn't suppress.

The water sprayed over them in a pulsating rhythm as he lathered the soap into a mass of suds, then rubbed them over her breasts, slowly, with circular motions, paying special attention to her firm, erect nipples, which were ripe for suckling.

She leaned her head back against his shoulder and made little panting sounds as he soaped his hands again and lowered them to her belly. It was flat and firm, and as he kneaded it her hips undulated against his already overheated manhood, making him gasp and fight to restrain his own desperate need.

Unable to wait longer, he slipped his hands downward and cupped her mound of soft brown curls. His finger found the crevice it was seeking, then her core, and he felt her muscles tighten and convulse just before he lost his tenuous control. They both cried out and were racked by shudders of exhilaration.

Sharon came back to earth slowly, reluctantly, as the water continued to pour over them. She'd never had a lover other than Fergus. She'd never wanted anyone else, but even when she was the maddest at him, when she thought of him as a cheat, a liar, an adulterer, she still missed their loving.

Over the years she'd come to understand that he was none of those things, just a confused man who'd found out, too late, that he didn't love her. Even so, she was a highly sensual woman, and her years of self-imposed celibacy had been frustrating and lonely. Several times she'd vowed to herself that she'd break that cycle and sleep with some of the men who took her out. A woman didn't need to be married or engaged to have sex anymore.

But she was never able to do it. Even though she'd longed
for that joyous release, she'd never found another man who
appealed to her enough to succumb. It was no wonder she'd
burst into flame when Fergus had kissed her... or had she
kissed him first? It didn't matter—the results would have
been the same either way—and she wasn't ready yet to deal
with the guilt that she knew would follow.

Later she would, but not until after that long, lazy, incredibly romantic lovemaking on her Victorian-style brass
bed that he'd promised her.

She turned in his arms and lifted her face for his kiss. He
obliged and their mouths clung. The passion was banked,
but in its place was a fresh sweetness that was even more
satisfying. Like a vow of eternal love, and a preview of re-
newed ardor.

"You promised me a bed," she whispered against his ear.

He caressed her bottom. "I know, but it took too long to
get there. I couldn't wait."

She nibbled on his lobe. "Neither could I, but if we hurry
maybe we can make it this time."

He groaned. "Sweetheart, I hate to tell you this, but I'm
not as young as I used to be. I'm going to need a little while
to, uh, shall we say, replenish my energy?"

She indulged in a disbelieving snort. "Really," she said,
"I hadn't noticed any problem."

She reached between them and captured him in her hand.
Almost immediately she felt the familiar stirring of muscles
as he started to harden.

He chuckled and kissed her again as his rod grew upright
and ready. "You little tease. You could arouse a marble
statue."

"You're the only one I want to arouse," she murmured
against the side of his mouth. "I've never wanted any other
man but you."

Fergus was both deeply ashamed and outrageously
pleased. Ashamed that he'd hurt her so badly she couldn't

respond to any other man after their divorce, and pleased that she couldn't; that he was still the only man she'd given herself to.

That was inexcusably selfish of him, but he couldn't help it. What he was determined to do, though, was treat her with the loving respect she deserved and practice a little restraint. She'd been profoundly shocked when she'd finally been forced to face the unthinkable in that courtroom—that she was seriously in danger of going to prison for a crime she hadn't committed.

He knew that up to now it had been like a bad dream for her, or a vicious game that had to be played out to the end. In spite of his efforts to convince her to take the charge seriously he'd sensed that she hadn't really believed it would happen, but today the outcome of the hearing had jolted her out of her delusion. She could no longer hide behind the knowledge of her innocence. Now they had to convince a judge and jury that there had been a horrendous mistake.

It was no wonder she'd been dazed and depressed by the decision to bind her over for trial. He didn't need a psychiatrist to tell him she'd turned to him now to distract her and help her bear the unbearable, even though it meant lowering the barriers she'd raised between them and unleashing the most powerful distraction of all, unrestrained sex.

He was no saint. He sure as hell wasn't going to say no to her, but neither was he going to ravish her when she was emotionally incapable of making a rational decision about whether or not she wanted him to.

Gently he disengaged himself from her. "If we don't get out of here we're going to be waterlogged," he said, and turned off the shower.

He opened the stall door and stepped out, then extended his hand to help her. There were large thick bath towels hanging on the metal rods affixed to the walls, and he took one and wrapped it around her, then took another to dry her hair. When they were both dried off except for damp hair, they hung their towels back up and walked into the bedroom, where they climbed into bed and cuddled up between the sheets.

Passion had been overwhelmed by exhaustion and they slept in each other's arms.

The insistent ring of the telephone woke Sharon up, and without opening her eyes, she rolled to her side and reached for it on the nightstand. It was Anna. She sounded hurried and anxious.

"Sharon, sorry I couldn't check in with you earlier, but I've been showing a client farms out in the boonies all day and just got back to the office. How did it go in court this morning?"

Sharon told her, and they talked about it for a few minutes until Anna was interrupted. When she got back to Sharon she sounded disgruntled. "Damn! A distinguished-looking gentleman wearing a fifteen-hundred-dollar suit and driving a Rolls, no less, just wandered in and asked to be shown the La Rochefoucauld estate. Look, Sharon, are you all right? Is Fergus there with you? I can come home if you need me."

Sharon glanced over her shoulder and saw Fergus lying beside her, watching. She smiled at him and he smiled back and winked. "I'm fine," she said, returning to the conversation. "Fergus is here, and I won't hear of you maybe losing out on the sale of a multimillion-dollar estate just to come home and hold my hand. Take all the time you need."

Anna hesitated. "Are you sure? It's dinnertime now. I may not be back till the wee hours of the morning. It's a long way out there."

Sharon felt a rush of affection for this woman who had consistently been such a true and caring friend. "I can't tell you how much I appreciate your concern, Anna," she said, and hoped her tone would relay the depth of feeling that was impossible to put into words, "but really, I'm okay. Fergus will stay with me. Now, for heaven's sake, go make a big fat commission."

They talked for another minute or two, then Sharon put down the phone and turned to Fergus. He welcomed her with open arms and she snuggled against his warm, firm body. It was so much like old times that she could almost forget the five years they'd been apart. Almost, but not quite.

She could feel the hardening of him that matched the quickening of her own body, and she wasn't going to resist it. Today she needed him, totally and without restraint. She'd worry about the consequences tomorrow.

He rubbed his palms in long, slow strokes down her back and her buttocks, awakening delightful sensations all through her.

"I gather Anna won't be home for a while?"

"No, she has a client who wants a tour of an obscenely expensive estate downriver about fifty miles. What time is it?"

Fergus held up one arm and looked at his watch. "It's almost six-thirty. Are you hungry?"

She grinned. "Yeah, but not for food."

He nuzzled her neck. "I've no intention of letting you starve," he murmured, and stroked her breast.

Eager to give him the same pleasure he was giving her, she turned her head and took his earlobe in her mouth to toy with while she kneaded his back and shoulders. His hand inched with tantalizing slowness down to her groin and stopped while his fingers made forays close to, but not touching, her heat. She writhed under his touch as she worried his lobe with her teeth, then sucked gently, causing his fingers to clench and unclench on her sensitized flesh.

For a long time she was lost in a haze of erotic stimulation as they leisurely touched, and licked, and nibbled, each intent on pleasuring the other, until their rhythm escalated, their breathing came in short gasps and their nerve ends screamed for release.

When it happened the eruption sent them soaring into a vast universe where time stood still and nothing mattered but the fiery fusion of their bodies and their souls.

By the time Sharon drifted slowly back from her journey to euphoria enough to open her eyes and rejoin the real world the sun was setting and she realized she was hungry. No, not just hungry, famished!

She was still wrapped in Fergus's embrace, and could feel his heartbeat against her chest and his breath against her cheek. She kissed his shoulder, then raised her head to look at him. "Tell me again about how you're too old to make love to me three times in a row," she teased.

He grinned and patted her on her bare bottom. "I suspect I could keep it up all night, uh, so to speak," he amended with a chuckle, "so unless that's what you want I advise you to be careful about how and where you touch me."

"Oh, you mean like here . . . or here . . . ?" She caressed a couple of highly responsive areas and felt his muscles clench as his arms tightened around her.

"Sharon," he groaned. "I can't think of a happier way to die, but I'm not ready to go yet. Besides, I need nourishment to replenish my energy. We haven't eaten all day. Aren't you hungry?"

"Starved," she answered.

"Do you want to go out or eat here?"

"I want to stay here," she said quickly. "I feel safe here. I don't ever want to leave home again."

Fergus sobered. "You are safe here, love, but don't ever talk about giving up. We're going to fight this thing, and we're going to win. Always believe that."

Sharon knew he was right. Giving in to despair could only defeat her, and she wasn't a quitter.

She lifted her chin and brushed his lips with her own. "I will," she vowed. "I do. How could I lose when I have you to defend me? But I still want to eat in. There're lots of frozen dinners in the freezer. All we have to do is stick a couple of them in the microwave for a few minutes."

They dressed in comfortable jeans and pullover shirts, but left their feet bare. There was something earthy and sensual about the feel of thick carpet under bare soles.

In the kitchen they each chose a favorite frozen dinner to heat up and made a pot of coffee. They ate hungrily and finished off with bowls of ice cream topped with chocolate syrup. Fergus finished the last spoonful and leaned back in his chair with a sigh.

"You heat up a great dinner, Mrs. Lachlan—uh, I mean Ms. Sawyer," he said, correcting himself sheepishly. "Obviously that was a Freudian slip. Wishful thinking."

Sharon had noticed it at the same time he did, and it shook her all the way to her toes. For three years she'd loved being Mrs. Fergus Lachlan, but once she'd filed for divorce she'd never used that name again.

"I'll accept your apology, but—"

"It wasn't an apology," he said firmly, breaking into her sentence.

She gritted her teeth and started again. "I'll accept your apology," she repeated, "but please don't call me that. I don't ever again want to be known as some man's property. If I should remarry I'll keep my own name."

She couldn't miss the cringe of pain her words caused him, and she was immediately ashamed of herself. Dear God, she was turning into a sharp-tongued harpy.

Reaching out, she put her hand over his on the table. "I'm sorry, Fergus, and that is an apology." Her voice quivered with regret. "I'm afraid that subconsciously I'm harboring more bitterness than I realized. It just pops out sometimes. I don't deliberately set out to hurt you, and when I do anyway I hurt myself, as well. I promise to keep a tighter rein on it.''

He turned his hand over and clasped hers. ''No, don't do that, Sharon. Bitterness and anger have to have an outlet. Otherwise they fester and grow ugly. If you want to rail at me, then go ahead. Get it all out in the open so we can deal with it.''

She bit back a sob. How could she want to hate him, when he was so sweet? How could she keep from loving him, when he was so loving, so self-sacrificing toward her? He'd left a mountain of high-fee cases in Chicago to come here and defend her free, and all she could do was bring up the past and make him feel guilty.

''I...I don't want to quarrel with you,'' she assured him. ''Losing Elaine the way you did was more punishment than I would ever have wished on you. You don't need my snide remarks.''

He squeezed her hand. ''I need anything you want to give me,'' he said softly, then straightened. ''I also need to talk to you. Why don't we go into the living room where we can be comfortable.''

''Okay,'' she said, anxiously wondering what he wanted to talk about. ''Just let me stack the dishes in the dishwasher first.''

A few minutes later they seated themselves on the sofa in the living room, and Fergus got right to the point.

''Sharon, you haven't said anything, but I'm sure you're aware that I wasn't using condoms when we made love. That was reckless and inexcusable, but I honest to God didn't think of it. I wasn't thinking period. Just feeling.''

Sharon nodded. He was right; she had been aware. But at the time it hadn't mattered to her. ''Fergus, I—''

"No, let me finish," he interrupted. "If you're not on the pill, which seems likely since you say you haven't had a lover, then you were completely unprotected."

Again she tried to break in, and again he stopped her. "I swear that it was never my intention to deliberately get you pregnant so you'd feel you had to come back to me. I want you more than I've ever wanted anything, but not that way."

This time she reached over and put her finger to his lips before he could continue. "Will you please shut up and let me say something?" she asked softly. "You're right, I'm not on the pill...."

He groaned, but she went on. "But the fact that I wasn't protected was as much my fault as yours. The first time I didn't think of it, either, and the second time there was no need, but the last time I was aware of it before we actually, uh, coupled, only by then I was too involved to stop."

His anguished expression tore at her heart.

"Honey, I—"

Again she shushed him. "Now be quiet and listen. It's unlikely that I'll get pregnant. This should be a safe time of the month. I'll know for sure in just a couple of days. If I'm not, then there's nothing to worry about, and if I am, well, we'll have plenty of time to deal with it then."

He looked slightly relieved, but Sharon felt a rush of tenderness at the thought of bearing Fergus's baby. While they'd been married she'd been in college and he'd been busy establishing his career as a lawyer, so they'd postponed starting a family. With the blind confidence of youth, they'd been so sure that the years ahead of them would be happy and successful, that they'd stay married for the rest of their lives and that they'd live forever.

Only it hadn't worked out that way, and in the years since their divorce she'd frequently wished she'd had Fergus's child. A small replica of him to love, and raise, and fill her lonely hours. It had been a lovely dream, but in less fanciful times she was glad they hadn't had children to be put through the torment of a broken family.

As for now, she didn't dare dwell on even the remote possibility that she and Fergus might have conceived a small son or daughter during this wild and wonderful afternoon.

Chapter Eleven

Sharon shivered and struggled to put the thought of babies and prison out of her mind. The only way she could do that was to change the subject.

Before Fergus could comment further on their predicament she said the first thing that came to mind. "Were you and Elaine happy together, Fergus?"

She mentally cringed at her insensitivity. That was strictly none of her business, but he'd said they should discuss her continued animosity toward him. She didn't want to quarrel with him; she just wanted to try to understand why he kept insisting that he still loved her, when he'd left her for another woman.

Well, actually, she'd left him, but it was because he'd all but admitted that he was in love with Elaine.

"Happy?" he said hesitantly, but with no apparent resentment. "*Happy* is a subjective word. It means different things to different people. I'd say we were reasonably happy, but there was always a shadow between us, your shadow, dimming that happiness."

Sharon blinked. "Are you saying that was my fault?" Her tone betrayed both her surprise and her chagrin.

Fergus shook his head. "No, it was mine. I couldn't stop loving you."

Sharon wanted to scream at him. Throw something. Instead she jumped to her feet. "Dammit, Fergus, will you stop saying that! It's insulting that you'd think I'd believe such a blatant lie. Why are you doing this? What in God's name do you want of me?"

He sighed and dropped his head in his hands, and her exasperation evaporated. He was genuinely tormented—she was sure of it. He wasn't a good enough actor to be so convincing, so why didn't he just admit that he'd never really loved her?

He rubbed his hands over his face then straightened up and looked at her. "I'm not lying. I'm telling you the truth, but I can understand why you don't believe me. I wouldn't have believed it, either, if the situation were reversed and it was you trying to convince me."

Sharon sank back down on the couch beside him. "We always hurt each other when we try to talk about this," she said. "Maybe we'd better listen to music or watch television or something."

"No," he said. "We've got to talk about it. Otherwise you'll never be able to forgive me. I'll tell you anything you want to know as long as it doesn't compromise Elaine's dignity or right to privacy."

She knew he was right, but she found prying into his relationship with his second wife distasteful and vowed to be more sensitive and considerate.

"You still miss her and grieve for her, don't you?"

"Yes."

Well, of course he did. That was a stupid question.

She tried again. "Was there any difficulty at the law firm when we were divorced and you married her?"

He hesitated. "There were no ethical problems, but the atmosphere was pretty sticky for a while. For months there was a lot of gossip and speculation behind our backs, and everyone seemed to feel embarrassed or awkward around us. The whole staff adored you, and although Elaine wouldn't admit it, I know some of the more self-righteous considered her a home wrecker and snubbed her."

His expression hardened. "The bastards. I just wish I'd caught them at it, but they weren't brave enough to confront me."

Sharon was startled by the surge of sympathy for Elaine that welled up inside her. She'd never wished the other woman harm, but neither had she expected to feel compassion for her.

"I'm sorry," she said gently. "If I'd known I'd never have condoned that type of thing."

His bleak expression softened. "No, I know you wouldn't. You're too kind and sweet to ever deliberately hurt anyone, no matter what they may have done to you."

She shook her head sadly. "Don't burden me with a halo and wings. I can be as vindictive as anyone. You of all people should know that. I've been scorching you regularly with caustic comments."

His mouth turned up at the corners in a small smile. "That's all right. It just reminds me that you're mortal, too."

She wanted to touch him, to curl up in his arms, but she couldn't do that when she still had questions about his marriage to Elaine. It didn't seem proper.

"Did you ever find out who sent those notes to me?" she asked. "The ones telling me you were involved with Elaine?"

"I wasn't involved with her…" he began, then paused and sighed. "Well, I suppose I was, emotionally, but not sexually. And no, I was never able to trace down who those notes came from. I even hired a private detective, but whoever did it covered his or her tracks like a professional.''

Sharon shuddered. "I hate the idea of someone spying on us like that and deliberately causing trouble. It makes me feel naked and exposed. I suspect it was someone in your firm, perhaps another attorney who was jealous because you were the fair-haired boy there.''

Fergus reached out and twisted a lock of her hair around his finger. "I wouldn't say I was the fair-haired boy," he said with a half smile, "but I agree that it was someone in the firm." His smile disappeared, although he continued to play with her hair. "If I ever find out who it was I'll see to it that he or she fries in hell." There was heavy menace in his tone.

Sharon had another question, but it was so personal that she hesitated. She'd been asked the same thing a number of times during their marriage and after the divorce, and it had always offended her.

Still, he'd said he'd tell her anything she wanted to know, and she really needed to know this. She couldn't look at him, but lowered her gaze and took a deep breath. "Fergus, you . . . you don't have to answer this if you don't want to, but I . . . I can't help wondering . . .''

Her voice trailed off and his filled the silent void. "Why don't you ask and let me decide whether or not I can answer?''

She glanced up and met his eyes. "All right. I'm wondering why you and Elaine didn't have children. I mean, when you and I were married I thought you were as eager as I to get to the point where we could start a family.''

His expression was impassive. "I was, but Elaine didn't want a child. I had no intention of forcing the issue. I've always felt that people who don't want children shouldn't have them. They seldom make good parents. Elaine was an excellent lawyer, and her career was vitally important to her."

Sharon had mixed feelings about that. What happens when one of a couple wants children and the other one doesn't? Is it always the woman's decision? Doesn't the man have any say in it?

She wasn't going to open that can of worms. "I see," she said, instead. "Then you were content to remain childless."

"I didn't say that!" Fergus exclaimed.

His tone told her he'd rather not pursue the subject further. She looked away again. "I'm sorry, I didn't mean to pry."

"I know," he said quietly. "Would it be prying if I asked you if you still want a houseful of babies?"

She brightened at the thought. A houseful of Fergus's babies would be heavenly. "Oh yes, I do. If I don't marry again I'll adopt. Single women can do that now, and there are so many unwanted children..."

Her bubble of dreams burst as reality punctured it, and she gasped at the sharp pain that swept through her. "That is, of course, if I don't have to go to prison."

He clenched his fists. "Don't say that," he grated. "It's not going to happen."

She knew that was wishful thinking rather than a statement of fact, but even so it was comforting.

Before she could reply he asked a question of his own. "If you should find that you are pregnant after our, um, carelessness today what will you do?"

She blinked. "Do? I'll have the child and raise it, of course. If I'm in prison I'll expect you to acknowledge it as yours and raise it."

Fergus's expression turned icy with shock. "You can't possibly think I wouldn't acknowledge a child of ours!"

"Of course I don't," she quickly explained. "The thought never occurred to me. That was just a bad choice of words."

His face twisted with emotion. "There are other options," he said shakily.

"Not for me." Her voice was firm. "But if I am pregnant I have no intention of having our baby in prison, so you'd better find out who really did kill Floyd."

Fergus stood and turned away from her so she wouldn't see how close he was to losing control.

Our baby! Two words he'd given up hope of ever hearing her say. They made him glow with anticipation inside, even as they broke his heart. How could he have been so careless? So reckless?

My God, she had enough to worry about without adding the possibility of an unplanned pregnancy!

"I will," he vowed, "but if you're not pregnant I strongly suggest that you start taking the pill again."

She didn't answer, and the ominous silence grew until finally he turned around to look at her. She was sitting sort of hunched over, with her head lowered.

"Sharon?"

She looked up slowly, and he saw the anguish in her expressive blue eyes. "That won't be necessary," she said sadly. "What happened this afternoon was wonderful. We both needed it, and I... I can't say I'm sorry it happened, but it won't happen again."

He caught his breath, but she hurried on. "We can never be casual lovers, Fergus, and I won't marry you again. But even more important, I'm going to be on trial for murder and you're my attorney. We can't be passionate lovers at night and still maintain a professional detachment in the courtroom."

He had to stifle the urge to put his hands over his ears. He didn't want to hear this! How could they not repeat such a mind-blowing experience? Especially when they were living in the same house. Their bedrooms were just a narrow hallway apart!

"Sharon, do you know what you're asking of me? Of us? You were as involved in our lovemaking as I. Are you telling me you can just shut off all that passion and pretend it never happened?" He knew he was overreacting, but my God, he was a human being, not a machine!

"No, that's not what I'm telling you," she said. "You found out today how strongly I'm still attracted to you, but lust isn't the same as love."

"The hell it's not!" he argued. "Passionate love is equal parts of unbridled lust and deeply committed caring. At least, that's the way I love you."

Sharon's expression hardened. "And is it also the way you loved Elaine?" she asked coldly.

All the indignation drained out of him, and he sank down onto the nearest chair. *It always came back to that. The curse of caring deeply for one woman and being passionately in love with another.*

His love for Sharon was intense. Passion, fireworks and ecstasy. His devotion to Elaine had been more mature. Calm, tranquil, a meeting of the minds. Although there'd been an instant attraction between them from the time they'd met, he'd always known that it was more cerebral than sexual.

Elaine had been his age, early thirties, with nine years of college and law school, plus four years of work experience, behind her. Her career was as important to her as his was to him, and they could discuss it intelligently and with full understanding. There was nothing frivolous about her.

Sharon, on the other hand, had been ten years younger and still in college. A schoolgirl, bright and ambitious, but so very young. Her interests had been college sports, rock concerts and saving the environment single-handedly.

In bed they'd been combustible, but outside the bedroom they'd had little to talk about. She'd known nothing about the law, and college sports had bored him almost as much as rock musicians had. He'd adored her, always would, but he'd gotten a little tired of waiting for her to grow up.

That had been a mistake, and he'd paid dearly for it.

He couldn't tell Sharon because it would be disrespectful to Elaine, but Elaine had never catapulted him to the glorious heights that Sharon always did. Sharon was fire. Elaine had been compliance.

"All right, Sharon," he said wearily. "If that's the way you want it I'll respect your wishes."

"Fergus, I . . . I didn't mean—"

Belatedly he noticed that her expression had softened again, and she sounded uncertain. "No, it's okay," he assured her. "Besides, you're right. It's not a good idea for an attorney to sleep with his client. It puts too much pressure on both of them—the lawyer to win at all costs and the client to keep him satisfied so he'll feel obligated."

"That's not what I meant," she protested.

He managed a tight smile. "I know, but it's the truth all the same. Don't worry, I won't seduce you against your will."

She uttered a little cry, and then she was kneeling on the floor in front of him. Immediately his knees parted and she moved between his legs.

"I never thought you would," she said brokenly as she put her arms around him and laid her face against his chest. "I'm sorry. I didn't mean to be so bitchy."

His willpower totally shot, he engulfed her in his hungry arms and held her against him. She was so soft and cuddly, and in spite of their marathon lovemaking earlier he could feel himself straining against his jeans again.

Obviously there was no limit to his virility where she was concerned. They were going to have to lay some ground rules in order to protect his sanity if he had to abide by her edict.

Reluctantly he put his hands on either side of her rib cage and moved her back away from him. "Sweetheart, I hate to tell you this, but if we're going to live together like brother and sister, then we're both going to have to exercise a little restraint." His voice sounded gritty. "No more touching, or hugging, or kissing...."

Damn! Just the thought of doing those things with her made his mouth water and his voice break.

Taking a deep breath, he continued, "I have limited control when it comes to you, and I can only guarantee it so far."

She looked stricken. "I'm sorry," she said, and got to her feet. "I wasn't thinking...."

"Neither was I," he confessed, "but that's the problem. I've never been able to think straight when I'm with you. From now on we're just attorney and client, okay?"

Like hell! his unruly conscience screamed. He was glad she couldn't hear it.

Two days later Sharon started her period, but instead of being relieved that she wasn't pregnant she felt a disappointment so sharp that, much to her dismay, she broke down and cried when she told Fergus. Fortunately he misunderstood and thought her tears were from relief.

"Don't cry, sweetheart," he said as he broke his own rule against touching and took her in his arms. "It's over now and you don't have to worry anymore. I'm so sorry that I put you through this added suspense. It was selfish and inexcusable of me."

She wanted to protest. To tell him the real reason she was so upset. But it would only confuse him even more. How could she explain that she'd welcome his baby, even though she wouldn't marry him and be a family?

Except for that episode, Fergus and Sharon spent the rest of the week striving to maintain a polite distance. A struggle that became more difficult every day as the magnetic tension between them continued to build.

Fergus and Ray spent most of the time going over police reports and tracking down leads that usually led nowhere. Sharon was able to help by supplying background on the employees of the hotel and providing tidbits of office gossip that might be useful. She also contacted her doctor and got a prescription for birth-control pills, just in case.

Then, on Monday, Fergus was summoned back to Chicago to take care of more of his neglected business there. The phone call came in midmorning and left him shaken and frustrated.

"I had no idea this trial date would be moved up," he said as he told Sharon about it, "and I have to appear. There's no way I can get out of it "

Sharon's heart sank, and the fear she'd managed to temporarily push back returned full force. He couldn't go to Chicago. She needed him here. How could he prove her innocent if he was off in another state defending someone else?

Before she could pull herself together and say something, he continued, "Come with me, honey. Under the circumstances I'm almost sure I can get the judge's permission to take you out of this court's jurisdiction. You're in my custody, and I have urgent business in Illinois."

For just a moment she let herself dream of going back to Chicago with him, living with him alone in his apartment....

That's where the fantasy stopped and reality set in.

"I—I'd like to," she stammered, "but that would be most unwise. Not only would it look bad, but before long we'd be playing house and making believe it could last forever."

Fergus scowled and shoved his hands in his pockets. "And what's so wrong about that? There's always the possibility that it *could* last forever if we'd only give it a chance."

She shook her head. "That's a gamble I'm not ready to take. Right now I've got all I can handle with my own trial coming up in less than two months."

His scowl disappeared. "I know. That's why I'd like to take you away from here for a while. We can always waive your request for an early trial, you know."

Sharon shivered. "No. I couldn't stand more than two months of this waiting, not being able to plan for the future. Not even knowing if I have a future."

In the end Fergus drove off alone, but not before he'd kissed her goodbye. A kiss that melted her bones, and, if it had lasted a second longer, would also have melted her resolve not to go with him. As she watched him leave it was all she could do not to run after him, beg him to take her along and damn the consequences.

With Fergus gone, Ray continued their investigation and reported to her each evening. After a couple of days he suggested that she come into his office and handle the paperwork and phone calls regarding her case, thus freeing his secretary to fulfill her duties for the fledgling law practice he was building.

Sharon was delighted. It gave her something to do instead of just sitting around going out of her mind with worry and loneliness. It also gave her the opportunity to be in on everything that was happening.

However, on the down side, she could see how little progress they were actually making. Whoever had come into Vancleave's office through the sliding-glass door and killed him while she was gone must have been invisible. They'd tracked down and talked to a number of guests who had been in the pool area at that time, but none of them had been paying attention to anything but their own pursuits, either in the water or lounging poolside.

In fact, only two of them had even noticed there was a door other than the main exit leading to the area.

The brightest spot of Sharon's days was Fergus's evening phone call. He never missed a day, and she eagerly looked forward to them. On Wednesday of the week after he'd left St. Louis, he told her that the prosecutor had rested his case and the defense would start presenting theirs the following day. "The D.A. didn't have anything we can't counter," he said optimistically. "I expect a verdict of innocence sometime next week."

That cheered her immensely. "Oh, I hope so. We're sort of at a standstill here, and I... That is we... Ray and I... We've missed you."

He lowered his voice to a husky murmur. "I miss you, too, love, and I don't mean you and Ray. Just you. The sweet image of you haunts me during the day and torments me at night."

Her whole body tingled with pleasure, even as she chided herself for not having more control over her feelings. How could she love him so completely, when she knew he was incapable of making a lifetime commitment to just one woman? She was letting him sweet-talk her into getting her heart broken again.

Sharon slept badly that night, and the next morning she decided not to go to Ray's office as she usually did. He was scheduled to be in court all day, and the inaction of sitting behind a desk, reading reports and taking and making phone calls, was getting to her. Going over the same material day after day was not only frustrating and boring, but it was turning her mind to mush.

It was the first week in July, and she needed to get out in the warm sunshine and fresh air to release some of her pent-up energy. She also needed to take an active part in tracking down Floyd Vancleave's killer instead of just following up on leads someone else had provided.

With this in mind she decided to drive over to the neighborhood where the Vancleaves lived. She'd been in their home a couple of times when they'd hosted barbecues in their big backyard for the people Floyd worked with. It wouldn't hurt to scout around, maybe talk to some of the neighbors and try to find out how they felt about Floyd and Helen.

It was midmorning when Sharon parked her car at the curb a block away from the Vancleaves' house. She'd brought Anna's golden retriever, Viking, along for the exercise, and they got out and started walking. She had him on a leash, and he bounded happily ahead of her.

It was a beautiful day, pleasantly warm, but with a promise of uncomfortable heat later. She was wearing shorts and a sleeveless blouse, and walked on the sunny side of the street in the hope of improving her tan. The air was redolent with the scent of flowers and newly cut grass, and a slight breeze fanned her bare arms and legs and gently tousled her hair.

The homes and lawns were all well kept, and from the people she observed coming and going it was evident that the neighborhood included a mixture of young families and senior citizens. Bringing the dog was a stroke of genius. He served as a conversation piece, and people stopped her to comment on him. An elderly gentleman in one yard abandoned his lawn mower to pet the dog, and farther along she stopped to chat with a mother whose two little girls wanted to play with him.

She learned from them that the Vancleaves seldom socialized with their neighbors except to wave or nod in passing.

As she neared the Vancleaves' place she noticed an older woman crouched on the grass, weeding her flower bed right next door. Great. Sharon was especially eager to query the close neighbors, and it would be far better if it could be a casual meeting rather than having to knock on the door and ask if the occupant would answer questions.

She crossed the street, then sauntered along as if she had nothing on her mind but giving her dog an outing. When they drew near, the woman looked up and smiled.

"My, what a beautiful dog," she said. "Frisky, too."

Sharon chuckled. "Oh yes, he's frisky all right. Nearly yanks my arm out of the socket when he sees a squirrel."

Sharon surreptitiously lengthened her hold on the leash so Viking could romp farther afield, and he headed for the woman, his tail wagging furiously with excitement. She reached out and petted him, while Sharon restrained him far enough away so he couldn't jump on her and knock her over.

"My late husband used to have a retriever just like this one," she said as she got to her feet. "He was a great hunting dog, but frisky, like yours. The man next door—" she nodded toward the Vancleave home "—put up such a fuss about his barking that we finally had to sell him to keep the peace." Her expression hardened. "Floyd Vancleave was an offensive man," she muttered, more to herself than to Sharon. "I'm not surprised that someone killed him."

Sharon's heart raced. So he wasn't liked by the neighbors closest to him. That information could open up a whole new line of inquiry, but she'd have to be careful not to seem too nosy.

"Oh, are you talking about the man who was murdered recently in that hotel downtown?" she asked, striving for just the right tone of casual interest.

"Yes." The woman rolled her eyes. "My, that really stirred things up around here. This is usually a very quiet neighborhood, but for a few days there it was overrun with reporters and police. It's calmed down again now, though."

That figured, Sharon thought. The police were so sure she was guilty that they didn't bother looking for any other suspects.

"His poor wife must be grief-stricken by the loss of her husband," Sharon said sympathetically, hoping it would encourage the woman to open up and gossip.

"I doubt it." The neighbor's tone was cryptic. "He slapped her around a lot."

Sharon's eyes widened with surprise and excitement. This could be a real breakthrough. "No! Really? Did she report it to the police?"

The other woman shook her head. "No, but I did a couple of times. I was afraid he'd kill her. I could hear him clear over here, yelling and throwing things. He was a real bully."

Sharon could hardly contain herself. "Was he arrested?" She'd worked with Floyd for several years, and although he was a jerk, she'd never had any indication that he was a wife beater.

Again the neighbor shook her head, this time with a great deal of agitation. "That silly woman wouldn't press charges. She always said she'd fallen or run into something. I gave up after the second time. He told me to mind my own business, and truth to tell, I was afraid of him."

As soon as she could without arousing suspicion, Sharon excused herself and hurried back to her car. She was eager to tell Ray what she'd learned. She'd call Fergus, too. At the least this information put a new slant on the mystery.

Although she hadn't known Helen Vancleave well she had noticed that Floyd's wife was unusually withdrawn and quiet, not at all outgoing. On the other hand, Floyd was brash, loud and always hogging the spotlight. She remembered thinking that Helen and Floyd were such different personalities that she wondered what they could possibly have in common.

As soon as Sharon got home she gave Viking a couple of the special doggie biscuits Anna kept on hand to reward him when he'd done something especially clever. He'd certainly earned it today. Then she called Ray's office, but he was still in court. Since it was almost time to adjourn for lunch, she left a message with his secretary, asking him to meet her as soon as possible at a popular restaurant near the courthouse that had both good food and fast service.

As she put the phone back in its cradle she noticed that her hands were shaking with elation. She didn't know how this new information could be used, but she was sure it was important. Maybe even crucial!

Chapter Twelve

Sharon had only been seated in the restaurant a few minutes, when Ray arrived. A big grin lit his face when he spotted her. "Hey, it's not every day a beautiful woman invites me to lunch," he said cheerfully as he slid into the booth across the table from her. "Is it my boyish charm or my rugged good looks that makes me irresistible?"

Sharon laughed. "Both, but today it's your super P.I. skills that seduce me."

"You've come up with something important?" he said eagerly.

"Stumbled onto something is more accurate," she said, then told him about her talk with the Vancleaves' neighbor.

They were interrupted once when the waitress took their order, but by the time she brought their food Sharon had just finished recounting her undercover interview. "I have a feeling that this is really important, Ray," she said, as the waitress placed the seafood salad in front of her and the hot-roast-beef sandwich with mashed potatoes and gravy before him.

He picked up his knife and fork and dug in. "I'm sure it is, but I don't think we have a chance in hell of getting Mrs. Vancleave to admit that her husband abused her. If she wouldn't do it to protect herself when he was alive, she's not likely to do it now that he's dead. I have contacts in the police department, though. I'll see what I can find out, but it'll have to wait till tomorrow. This trial probably won't go to the jury until late this afternoon, and I can't get away until it does."

Some of Sharon's elation dimmed. She'd expected him to be more excited. Surely the fact that Floyd was a wife beater as well as a womanizer made him a target of the wrath of numerous individuals.

"Maybe I could find out something if I had a talk with Helen," she ventured.

"No, Sharon," Ray said firmly. "Don't do that. In the first place she probably wouldn't talk to you, and in the second place, if there is something important here you could blow the whole thing. As soon as we finish eating I'll call one of my buddies down at headquarters and ask him to dig into some of the files, but if no charges were ever filed against Vancleave it's doubtful there would be a record."

Sharon reluctantly agreed, but resolved to tell Fergus about it that evening when he called.

The call came at nine o'clock and Fergus sounded tired. "Everything's pretty much on schedule here, but I resent every minute of the time I'm away from you. I feel I should be there, doing something...."

"I wish you were here, too," she admitted. "I need your advice."

"Advice about what?" he asked anxiously. "Has something happened? Are you being harassed?"

"No, nothing like that, but I did find out something today that I think is important." She told him about her conversation with the Vancleaves' next-door neighbor. "I didn't even get the woman's name," she concluded. "I was too afraid she'd become suspicious and stop talking."

"Her name's not important," he said offhandedly. "We can always get it later. You said Ray's checked with the police?"

Her disappointment at his casual attitude was as painful as a blow. "Not personally—he's been tied up in court all day—but he said he'd call a friend in the department and ask him to go through the files. Darn it, Fergus." She couldn't keep from voicing her frustration. "You don't sound any more enthusiastic than Ray did. I thought you'd be happy—"

"I *am* happy, sweetheart," he interrupted. "This gives us a whole new area to explore, but it doesn't prove anything except that Vancleave was a real bastard, and we already knew that."

"But what about his wife?" Sharon's voice was strident with exasperation. "Doesn't that give her a strong motive for killing him? She might not have known he was bedding every woman who'd have him, but she sure knew he was beating her up."

"Sure it gave her a strong motive," Fergus agreed, "and it gives us a more persuasive case for reasonable doubt that you did it, but don't count on the prosecution or the jury to consider her a serious suspect. If she'd put up with the physical abuse without seeking protection and retribution, it's not likely she'd kill him, either. Besides, she wasn't at his office. You walked in without being announced, and she wasn't there with him, was she?"

"No, he was alone," Sharon admitted. "But that doesn't mean she couldn't have come in the back door after I walked out, the same as anyone else."

"That's true, and we'll look into it, but you didn't see her anywhere near the hotel when you left, did you?"

"No, but—"

"You'd almost certainly have run into her, since you were going to the hotel parking building and she would have been coming from it. There's no place else to park around there. Besides, unless she went there specifically to kill him, there was no reason for her to go in the back, when she could walk into his office through the reception area anytime she wanted to. Receptionists don't keep their boss's wives waiting."

"What makes you so sure she didn't go there to kill him?"

"I'm not sure," Fergus explained, "but it seems unlikely. If she left home with the intention of killing him it would mean that she'd planned to do it, but she didn't bring a weapon. He was stabbed with the letter opener from his desk.

"Also, it's unlikely that she'd go to his office, a very public place, to do the deed, when it could so easily have been accomplished at home or in a more private area."

He hesitated a moment. "As I remember it she had a good alibi," he continued. "When the police went to her house that day to notify her of her husband's death they found her sick in bed. I mean violently ill, not just the sniffles or a headache. They called her doctor and he examined her. He said it was a type of intestinal flu that was going around, and gave her a prescription for medication."

Sharon was reluctantly forced to admit that Fergus and Ray were right, Helen Vancleave had nothing to do with her husband's murder. But if it wasn't her, then who?

Fergus must have sensed her disappointment, because his voice coming over the phone was soft and compassionate. "I'm sorry, my darling. I hate to have to deflate your balloon, but I don't want you to get your hopes up too high, only to have them come crashing down again. I'd much prefer to be there with you, but there's a lot I can do on the phone. I'll keep in close touch with Ray, and I want you to call me anytime you have a question or feel the need to talk. Okay?''

Sharon sighed. "Okay. I guess it was unreasonable of me to think that all we'd have to do was ask a few questions and the guilty person would be revealed. I remember when you and I were married you'd sometimes get exasperated and tell me to grow up and start thinking like an adult. Obviously I still haven't gotten the knack of it.''

She heard him groan at the other end of the line.

"Sharon, sweetheart, that's not at all what I'm saying. I can't imagine why I ever thought I wanted to change you. I loved you then and I love you now, and I can't bear the thought of you being hurt any more than is necessary by this messy business.''

They talked for a few more minutes, but when they hung up she still couldn't shake the feeling that this new turn of events was vitally important. Granted, she was a rank amateur, whereas Fergus and Ray were trained to sort out important facts, but she had a gut feeling that she was on the right track, and she wasn't going to give up.

Early the next morning, which was Friday, Ray phoned. "Just wanted to let you know that my contact at the police department couldn't find any record of Floyd Vancleave's being questioned on suspicion of spousal abuse, but that doesn't mean he wasn't. The jury's out on my trial now, so I'm going over there and see what I can turn up.''

Sharon's excitement started to build again. "That's great, Ray. I want to go with you.''

Ray hesitated. "Oh, I don't think that's such a good idea,'' he said thoughtfully. "Fergus wouldn't want you poking around the station.''

She wasn't going to be put off so easily. "Would it compromise my case?''

"Well, no," he admitted, "but it's a pretty rough place, and you know how protective Fergus is—"

"Fergus Lachlan is my lawyer, not my husband," she interrupted impatiently. "He has no business being protective of me. Now, are you going to stop by and pick me up, or do I have to drive down on my own?"

Ray chuckled. "Okay, babe, if you're not scared of him, neither am I. If you're determined to go along I'll pick you up. Half an hour all right?"

Sharon agreed that it was, and was dressed in jeans, a pullover shirt and sneakers when he arrived.

At the station Ray was greeted by good-natured slaps on the back and banter. He introduced Sharon and explained what they were after, but none of the officers could remember being called out to a disturbance at the Vancleaves' address.

"That's a pretty high-toned neighborhood," one of them explained. "Those people seldom call the police with a complaint about spousal abuse. They call their psychiatrist, instead, and we never hear about it."

"But these complaints were turned in by a neighbor," Ray explained. "She said she was afraid the husband was going to kill his wife in one of his rages."

"The call would have been handled by this precinct," another officer commented, "but police officers do get shifted around some. Why don't you go to headquarters and find out which of our officers have retired or been reassigned in the past five years or so? It could be that one of them will remember."

Ray and Sharon thanked them all for their help and headed for central. It took some persuasion, but they finally got the names they wanted. There were only four, three men and a woman. Two of them had retired, and the other two had been reassigned. They took the names, addresses and phone numbers and, after picking up sandwiches at a deli for lunch, went to Ray's office to make their calls.

The first two they contacted were unable to help, but on the third try they connected. Officer Kathryn Underwood remembered the Vancleaves because it had frustrated her so when the woman had refused to press charges.

"Usually in marital disputes the two parties are furious with each other," she said. "They both yell and swear and each blames the other, so that you can't tell which one started it. In those cases we're relieved when they don't press charges, but the Vancleave complaint was nothing like that."

Her voice turned hard. "That arrogant son of a bitch had given his wife a black eye, a split lip and God only knows how much more damage that didn't show unless she could be examined without her clothes on. She winced every time she was touched, and you could see she was afraid of him, but she wouldn't admit it. Instead, she stuck to her story that she'd fallen down the stairs. I really hated to leave her there with him, but there was nothing we could do when she wouldn't cooperate."

Officer Underwood agreed to testify if she was needed, and Sharon was jubilant. Grabbing Ray, she gave him a big hug, and he laughed and swung her around, but when they calmed down he warned her again that this evidence alone didn't prove anything, since Mrs. Vancleave had refused to admit that she'd been abused.

"I agree," Sharon said, "but I'm going over to the Vancleaves' home first thing in the morning and speak to her—"

"No, Sharon, don't do that!" Ray warned. "At least not until you talk it over with Fergus. There are legal ramifications that you can't possibly be aware of."

"But all I want to do is speak to her," Sharon insisted. "There can't be anything wrong with that."

"The hell there can't," Ray insisted. "Use your head, woman. You've got one of the best defense attorneys in the country, and he's taken your case at great professional and financial sacrifice. For heaven's sake, let him defend you.

Don't try to second-guess him and make it just that much harder."

Sharon felt thoroughly chastised. He was right, of course. Fergus had dropped everything and come running when he'd heard she was in trouble. He'd stayed with her and neglected all his important, high-paying cases, even though he knew she couldn't possibly pay his usual fee. The very least she could do was take his advice and not go running off half-cocked on her own.

She dropped into one of Ray's office chairs and sighed. "I'm sorry," she said. "I guess I let my enthusiasm get out of hand. I'll talk to Fergus tonight and tell him what I want to do, but don't forget, I'm trained in the art of getting along with people and mediating disputes. It's part of my job at the hotel."

"I know," he said, "and I understand you're very good at your job, but you've been charged with murder. You're not a lawyer—you're not even a paralegal—so let Fergus handle this. Promise?"

He was so intense that she couldn't help but smile. "I promise," she said, and meant it.

Fergus's call came while Sharon and Anna were eating dinner, and Sharon excused herself to take it in her bedroom. She started to tell him about finding an officer to corroborate the Vancleaves' neighbor's story, but he interrupted. "I know all about it, honey. I just talked to Ray. He says you're determined to talk to Helen Vancleave."

Sharon was surprised and even a little disappointed. She'd wanted to tell him. "Yes. She knows me," Sharon said, trying not to let her disappointment sound in her voice. "Not well, but at least I'm not a stranger or, worse yet, a police officer. I'm sure she could give us important information."

"I'm sure she could, too," he agreed, "but don't forget, you're the woman accused of killing her husband. She won't even let you in the door, let alone talk to you. Don't even try it, Sharon. You'll scare her off and we'll never get any co-operation from her."

"I'm not inexperienced at this type of thing, Fergus," she snapped, now more irritated than disappointed. "Don't forget, I minored in psychology in college, and I mediate personnel disputes all the time at work."

"I know, and I respect your ability," he said in what she recognized as his best conciliatory manner, "but you can't ignore the fact that in this case *you* are the problem. She undoubtedly believes that you stabbed her husband in the heart."

"Then I'll have to convince her that I didn't, or she won't talk to you or Ray, either, since you're both defending me."

Fergus sighed. "Sweetheart, let me handle this. I have to be here Monday to give my closing statement, but I'll leave for St. Louis as soon as the jury goes out. Just wait for me, please!"

Monday. Impossible! She couldn't sit around and do nothing for three more days. She'd go out of her mind!

She lowered her voice to a sexy pitch and hoped it would still work as well with her ex-husband as it had when they were married. "I'm sorry, darling. I'd do almost anything else for you, but please try to understand. I *need* to talk to Helen. I need to tell her that I didn't kill her husband, and to offer my sympathy for her loss. I'd do as much for any close acquaintance, and she was my boss's wife. If, in the course of the conversation, she says something that will help us, what harm could it do?"

For a long time there was silence at the other end of the line, then she heard Fergus draw a deep breath. "I'll make arrangements to fly down there in the company plane first thing in the morning." He sounded both gruff and exasperated. "Promise you won't do anything until I get there. I need your word on that, Sharon."

"I promise," she whispered, and she didn't have to work at making it sound sexy. She couldn't have sounded any other way. If he'd been in the room with her they'd be making quick, hot, passionate love on the floor again. Why did she even try to resist him?

Fergus arrived in a taxi at nine o'clock the following morning. It was Saturday, Anna's busiest day in real estate, so she had already left for work. Sharon had dressed for her visit to Helen in a turquoise flowered silk slacks suit, with a buff-colored scarf accenting the V neck of the jacket.

She opened the door for him and he stepped inside; without saying a word, he put his arms around her and kissed her. Her lips parted hungrily to admit his probing tongue, and for a few minutes she lost track of everything but the heat of his long, slender body pressed against hers, and the scent of him that was part shaving lotion and part male.

She felt whole again, and secure. Fergus would love her, take care of her, slay all her dragons. That feeling of tranquillity lasted until they finally broke apart, then all her doubts and insecurities came rushing back to haunt her.

She shivered as the voice of reason intruded into her fantasies: *You've got no one to depend on but yourself, dummy, so shape up and stop looking to Fergus to solve your problems. He let you down once. You can't be sure he won't do it again. There are no knights in shining armor to come to the rescue anymore. You have to fight your own battles.*

"Is there any chance that you missed me even a third as much as I missed you?" Fergus asked as he put his arm around Sharon's waist and started walking them toward the kitchen.

"I probably missed you every bit as much or more," she admitted, "and I'm sorry I'm being such a pest...."

He squeezed her and chuckled. "Don't be sorry. If you weren't such a pain in the a—that is, in the *neck*—I wouldn't be able to justify the time involved and the use of the plane to come back just for the weekend. Is there any coffee?''

Sharon laughed and felt happy again. "Sure is. Have you had breakfast?''

He looked momentarily uncertain. "I'm not sure. I don't think so. I've been up since four-thirty, catching up on some work I had to finish before I could leave, and now I don't remember whether I ate or not."

She felt a fresh wave of guilt. "Oh, Fergus, I'm sorry. I not only messed up your weekend, but I interfered with your sleep."

He sat down on one of the kitchen chairs and pulled her down on his lap. "You always interfere with my sleep," he murmured as he burrowed his face in the valley between her breasts. "Every time I go to bed and close my eyes I think of you lying beside me, but when I reach for you, you're not there."

She cradled his head in her arms as he nuzzled her breasts through her clothes. It felt so good. So right.

But it wasn't right. It could only end up one place, in bed, and in a few more minutes she wouldn't have either the willpower or the desire to stop him.

She kissed the top of his head, then pulled away from him and stood up. "I'll... I'll fix you some breakfast," she stammered and hurried across the room to the refrigerator.

"Coward," he said from behind her, and his voice wasn't very steady, either.

"Damn right," she admitted. "I told you how much I missed you, and you have a way of sapping all my resistance."

"God, how I wish that were true," he murmured. "What do I have to do or say to get you to trust me again? I've never lied to you, Sharon."

She stood in front of the open refrigerator door and contemplated. "No, You probably didn't lie to me about Elaine," she conceded. "You just didn't tell me about her at all, and while that may not be lying, it is deception. I don't see that there's much difference."

"I suppose there's not," he said wearily as she picked up a box of eggs and a package of bacon and closed the door. "I don't want to quarrel with you, so let's change the subject. Why are you so all fired intent on talking to Helen Vancleave?"

For the next hour they talked about that while Sharon fixed and served breakfast. By the time they'd finished eating they'd come to an agreement of sorts. They would both go to the Vancleave house, but Sharon insisted that she be allowed to talk to the woman alone. Fergus balked at that, but Sharon was adamant.

"Helen is a very private person," she argued. "The shy, quiet type who lived in her husband's shadow. I've seldom heard her express an idea of her own, and she never voiced an objection to anything he said or did. It will be difficult to get her to talk to me about her marriage, but she'd never do so with a man present. I feel strongly about this, Fergus. At least let me try. If I don't get anywhere, then you can do it your way."

He reluctantly agreed to stay in the car and let her handle the interview, but only if she promised to leave the house immediately should she feel threatened in any way. "These quiet, submissive victims can be human time bombs when they finally reach the end of their tolerance."

According to the clock in Sharon's car it was ten-twenty when Fergus pulled it over to the curb in front of the Vancleave home. Sharon's excitement had mounted with every turn of the wheels on the way over, but there was also an undercurrent of apprehension. They hadn't called to ask if they could come because they were both certain the answer would be no. Sharon had rationalized that if she just appeared on the doorstep it would be easier for her to talk her way in.

Now she wasn't quite so sure. She knew the Vancleaves had never had children, but she wasn't sure whether there were other family members in the area. She was confident she could get Helen to talk to her, but what if there was a sister or brother or some other relative with her? They probably wouldn't be as timid about throwing an uninvited visitor out as Helen might be. Also, there was the possibility that she had a security guard to turn away curious strangers.

Sharon hadn't voiced any of these concerns to Fergus, and she didn't intend to. Instead, she turned to him with her most confident smile. "This may take a while. You don't need to wait. I can call a cab when I get ready to go home."

He glowered at her. "I'm not leaving, and if I see or hear anything suspicious I'm going in to get you. Remember that, and please—" he leaned over and kissed her, a warm lingering kiss "—be careful, love."

She cupped his face with her hands and kissed him again. "I will," she said softly, and quickly got out of the car.

She could feel his gaze on her back as she walked up to the house and rang the bell. There was no response and she rang again, longer this time. Still she heard nothing. But just as she moved to press it again a muffled voice called through the door, "Who's there?"

Sharon recognized Helen's voice, even though it was barely audible. She took a deep breath. "It's Sharon Sawyer, Mrs. Vancleave. I'd like to talk to you."

For a moment there was no answer, then Helen said, "I can't see you now. Go away."

Sharon thought she'd heard a note of panic in the woman's tone. She tried again. "Helen, I didn't kill Floyd. He was alive when I left by the sliding-glass door. Please let me in. I think you may be able to help me prove I didn't do it."

Another pause. "My neighbor's husband is a lawyer and he says I don't have to talk to anybody. Just go away and leave me alone."

This time Sharon was sure she'd heard panic. "Your neighbor is right," she assured the woman. "You don't have to talk with me, but I'm allowed to talk to you, and I don't want to shout my questions through the closed door for all the neighbors to hear."

"If you don't stop threatening me and go away I'll call the police," Helen said, her tone strident.

This wasn't going at all the way Sharon had planned. She didn't want to scare the poor soul—she just wanted to talk to her. "Helen, I'm very sorry if I'm frightening you. I don't mean to. If you'd feel more comfortable with a police officer present, then by all means call and ask for one. My attorney is waiting for me in the car. If you wish I'll ask him to join us, too, but all I really want is a quiet conversation with you to see if you have any information that might help me prove my innocence. Surely you wouldn't want me to spend the rest of my life in prison for a crime I didn't commit."

Sharon waited anxiously, wondering what would happen if Mrs. Vancleave did call the police and tell them she was being harassed by Sharon. She was almost sure they could revoke her bail and make her spend the rest of the time until the trial in jail. She should have listened to Fergus and Ray and let them handle this. Was her stubbornness in insisting on doing it herself going to put her in even more jeopardy?

Fergus would be livid, and she couldn't blame him if he refused to continue to defend her!

She was getting more desperate by the moment, when she heard the lock turn and the door slowly opened. Her relief was so sharp that she felt light-headed and had to steady herself against the door frame to keep from stumbling.

When she regained her ability to focus she got another shock. Helen Vancleave, who had always been dowdy but nevertheless immaculately groomed, looked as if she hadn't slept or changed her clothes and combed her hair in days.

She'd lost weight, too. Although she'd always been slender, she was now gaunt and pale. Her expensive silk dress was wrinkled and stained and drooped loosely on her bony frame, and her hair hung in limp strings around her haggard face.

When Sharon spoke she said the first thing that came to mind. "My God, Helen, have you been ill?"

The other woman stepped back to let Sharon enter. "My husband is dead" was her bleak reply.

Sharon shut the door and followed her into the living room. The interior of the house was dark and gloomy, and Sharon noticed that all the drapes were drawn. The rooms weren't exactly cluttered, but there were dirty dishes, mainly cups and glasses, scattered on the dusty tabletops. It was evident that the place hadn't been cleaned lately.

A chill of alarm crept through her. This woman bore no resemblance to the Helen Vancleave she'd known. "Helen, are you living all alone here?"

"Yes, Floyd died you know," she repeated in a dull monotone as she walked to the nearest chair and seated herself. "You can sit down if you want to."

Sharon's alarm escalated. There was something dreadfully wrong here. "I know your husband is dead," she said carefully, "but don't you have a relative or a friend who could come and be with you? You don't look well."

"Oh no, we never had a family." She looked straight ahead and spoke without a trace of emotion. "I was going to have a baby once years ago, but Floyd didn't want children. They upset him. He made me have an abortion."

Dear God, the poor woman was totally spaced out! How long had she been this way, and why hadn't somebody noticed?

Sharon tried again to establish contact and get a rational answer. "I'm sorry," she said gently. "That must have been very sad for you, but now tell me about yourself. Don't you have friends who could come and stay with you for a while?"

Helen shook her head. "No, Floyd didn't like for me to have friends. He said they were a bad influence. That I didn't need anyone but him."

That man had been a psychotic bastard. It was no wonder his long-suffering wife had finally snapped, but did she kill him? If so, how did she get in and out of his office without being seen?

"Well, you need someone now," Sharon said. "Have you eaten anything lately?"

It was obvious that she hadn't, but Sharon was trying to lead her, step by step, back from the shell she'd retreated into.

Helen blinked and frowned. "Eaten? I don't remember. I have coffee if you're hungry."

"Look, why don't we go into the kitchen and I'll fix you a nice hot breakfast?" Sharon suggested, and reached down to help the woman stand.

Helen ignored the extended hand and shook her head. "I don't want any food. It makes me sick."

Sharon remembered Fergus telling her that according to the police report Vancleave's wife had been sick in bed the day they'd come to the house to tell her about the death of her husband. But that had been over three weeks ago. Had she been ill all this time? Had her doctor seen her since that day?

She leaned down and took Helen by the arms to half lift her out of the chair and onto her feet. "I'll cook you some hot cereal," she said, and prayed that there was something in the kitchen to cook. "That shouldn't upset your stomach."

Helen allowed herself to be led through the living room and dining room into the kitchen. There were no blinds to pull in there, and it was light and sunny. A large room, it had all the usual appliances plus a small breakfast table and two chairs at one end. There were also dirty dishes in the sink, and scraps of food covered with ants scattered around.

Sharon seated Helen in one of the chairs and started rummaging through the cupboards until she found a box of oatmeal. It only took a couple of minutes to cook it in the microwave, but unfortunately the milk in the refrigerator was sour. She poured it down the sink and added brown sugar to the cereal to give it a caramel flavor.

It took some coaxing to get Helen to take the first bite, and it was only then, when she clumsily picked up the spoon, that Sharon noticed her hands were red and swollen.

"Helen, what happened to your hands?" she asked.

The other woman examined them for a moment before she answered. "It's eczema. I'm allergic to soap and detergents. Sometimes it gets really bad, like now. It itches," she said as she rubbed the top of one with the palm of the other. "I guess I forgot to put the salve on them."

She dipped the spoon in the oatmeal and took a bite, then ate it all, along with a piece of dry toast made from bread Sharon had found in the freezer. The loaf in the bread box was moldy.

"Now you feel better, don't you?" Sharon said as she wiped Helen's mouth and hands as she would for a child. "You mustn't ever forget to eat. Your body needs the nourishment."

"I won't," Helen said, still with no animation or real understanding. "I'd like to go to bed now."

Sharon knew she had to get help. This woman was ill, both physically and mentally. But she didn't want to frighten her. She felt sure Helen was very fragile, and almost anything could push her so deep into the trancelike state that she would never come out.

Chapter Thirteen

"You can go to bed in a little while," Sharon told Helen softly as she again helped her to stand, "but let's go back into the parlor and talk for a few minutes first. Okay?"

Helen didn't respond, but allowed Sharon to lead her out of the kitchen and settle her on the couch in the living room. "Now, you sit right here and don't move," she told the woman. "I have to get something out of my car. I'll only be gone a minute."

Helen nodded with childlike trust, and Sharon hurried outside. Fergus scrambled out of the car when he saw her coming, and met her halfway.

"What's the matter," he asked in alarm as he cupped her shoulders with his hands.

"Nothing," she assured him. "That is, I'm in no danger, but Mrs. Vancleave seems to be in some sort of a trance. Something's awfully wrong with her, and I want you there as a witness when I question her. Come back in with me, but stay out of sight. I'm sure she won't speak at all if she knows you're there.''

"I'll come," he said, "but I have to warn you that since I'm an officer of the court there might be legal repercussions if I don't read her her rights and she says something to incriminate herself while I'm listening. The information probably couldn't be used in court unless she'd be willing to repeat it to a police officer."

Sharon hadn't thought of that, but there wasn't time to do anything about it now. They'd just have to take their chances that it could be straightened out later.

"That is a complication," she agreed, "but she's too emotionally unstable to risk upsetting her by introducing a strange man into the discussion at this point. She doesn't seem to be aware of much of anything except that her husband is dead. When we get inside I'll go to her in the living room, and you stay back out of sight."

Fergus agreed and they returned to the house. He stayed in the entryway, while Sharon sat down beside Helen on the couch. As before, Helen was staring blankly at nothing and didn't acknowledge Sharon's reappearance.

She touched the other woman's loosely clasped swollen hands in an effort to establish contact with her again. "Helen, has your doctor examined you lately?" she asked carefully.

Helen blinked, then managed to focus her gaze on Sharon. "My doctor? I don't need a doctor anymore. My husband is dead."

She was really hung up on the fact that Floyd was dead. Under the circumstances that wouldn't be unusual, except that she didn't seem to be able to focus on anything else.

"Yes, dear, I know," Sharon said again, as she had several times since she'd arrived, "but—"

She stopped in midsentence as she realized that what Helen had said could easily be interpreted as meaning that

she didn't need a doctor now because her husband was dead
and couldn't beat her up any more.

Sharon hesitated a moment to gather her thoughts and
put them together before continuing. She had to proceed
with a great deal of caution. Otherwise she could botch the
whole thing.

She took one of Helen's limp hands and held it. "Your
husband sometimes hit you, didn't he?" She said it calmly,
as a statement of fact, not a question that could be easily
denied.

In the silence that followed she held her breath, afraid
Helen would take offense and order her to leave, but she
merely nodded and spoke in that emotionless monotone.

"Yes, but I deserved it. He worked so hard, and was so
stressed when he got home. I tried not to upset him, I really
tried—but I usually managed to do something stupid,
and ... well ... sometimes he'd punish me."

For the first time she seemed to actually see Sharon when
she looked at her. "But he didn't mean it," she said urgently. "He was always sorry."

Sharon was appalled, but she managed to keep her voice
even as she assured the poor battered woman that it wasn't
her fault. That her husband had had no right to abuse her.

Helen merely shook her head sadly and looked off into
space.

Sharon pondered her next move. She had the perfect
opening for exploring the premise that kept niggling at her,
but did she dare attempt it? Was this confused woman
strong enough to face, and either admit or deny, the accusation Sharon desperately needed to voice? Or would it drive
her over the edge of reason into the bottomless pit of madness?

She wished she could talk it over with Fergus, but knew
she couldn't risk losing Helen's tenuous attention, which
she'd so painstakingly gained. It was doubtful that she'd
ever regain it.

Taking a deep breath, she offered up a quick, silent prayer. "Helen, it's unlikely that a jury would convict you for killing your husband," she said as calmly as she could manage. "Your neighbor and the police will both testify that he beat you on several occasions."

Sharon heard a muffled exclamation from the entryway, and knew Fergus was shocked and probably furious with her.

However, Helen's only reaction was one of relief. "Do you really think so?" she asked, and for the first time there was a touch of expression in her tone. "I didn't plan to do it, you know, but when I heard you quarreling with him and learned that he not only abused me but was unfaithful...I...I had no idea he was...was doing that. S-something just burst inside me...."

A sob shook her, then the tears came. She bent over, put her head in her hands and wept.

Sharon moved quickly to put her arms around the distraught woman. "That's all right. Go ahead and cry," she murmured. "Get it all out of your system. You were driven to do what you did. It's not your fault."

Although there was no noise other than Helen's massive sobs, something caused Sharon to look up. She saw Fergus standing in front of them. The past few minutes had been so stressful that she'd forgotten he was in the house.

His expression mirrored her own feelings, a mixture of deep compassion and profound relief. Her eyes filled with tears as he, too, knelt down and comforted both women with gentle strokes and softly spoken words.

Sharon felt as if a heavy suffocating darkness had been lifted and the brightness of sunshine had once more returned to her world. In an effort to protect her sanity she hadn't allowed herself to dwell on just how terrified she was of the charges that had been filed against her, and how impossible it would have been to defend herself against them.

Now, for the first time since she'd returned to Floyd
Vancleave's office and found him lying on the floor with a
letter opener protruding from his chest, she felt free. Free to
get on with her life, to hope, and plan, and dream of a future. A future with wings instead of bars.

It took quite a while before Helen managed to pull herself together and stop crying. When she finally straightened up and looked around she saw Fergus for the first time,
and blinked. "Who...who are you?" she sniffed.

He reached into his pocket and handed her a large white
handkerchief. "I'm Fergus Lachlan, Ms. Sawyer's attorney," he said. "Are you all right? Would you like me to call
your doctor?"

She blew her nose and shook her head. "No. He can't
help me. I...I guess I need a good lawyer."

Hope expanded even more in Sharon's heart. Apparently Helen intended to confess to the police. That would
make everything much easier for Sharon.

Fergus, ever the realist, didn't just wonder, he asked.
"Are you willing to tell your story to the police, Mrs. Vancleave?" His tone was kind and understanding.

Helen drew her arms tightly against her and hunched her
shoulders in anguish. "I... Yes, I will. I can't go on living
like this. Feeling so *guilty*. I never dreamed I was capable of
taking another person's life—"

"Anyone is capable of killing, given enough provoca-
tion," Fergus interrupted, "and you had plenty of it. If
you'll give me your attorney's number I'll call him for you."

She shook her head sadly. "I don't have one. Oh, I believe Floyd had a man who did our income tax, but—"

"That would be an accountant," Fergus explained.
"Look, I'm not trying to solicit business, but if you want me
to I'll represent you."

Sharon gasped. She knew he had more difficult, high
profile cases than he could comfortably handle without
volunteering for one any competent lawyer could defend

He'd taken hers because he'd felt obligated to, but he was offering to defend Helen because he was a compassionate and caring man.

Helen relaxed against the back of the chair and closed her eyes wearily. "I'd be most grateful if you would," she said.

Fergus stood up. "Fine. The first thing we're going to do is have you examined by your physician. Then, if he says you're strong enough, we'll go to the police station, and you can give your statement to them."

Helen groaned and opened her eyes. They were filled with fear. "Do I have to?"

"Yes, you do," he said gently, "but don't be afraid. I won't let them question you. All you have to do is voluntarily admit that you killed your husband and tell them how and why. When the judge sees how frail you are there won't be any trouble arranging for bail."

An hour later Sharon and Fergus were sitting in the waiting room of Dr. Jonas Hardy while the doctor examined Helen Vancleave. Fergus had called the office and arranged for an emergency visit, and she'd been taken back to the examining rooms as soon as they arrived.

Before leaving the house, Sharon had offered to help Helen shower and make herself more presentable, but Fergus had said no. "I want the doctor and the police to see her just the way we found her," he'd said. "Her appearance is bound to strengthen a plea of diminished capacity, or temporary insanity, as well as self-defense."

It wasn't long before they were told the doctor wanted to talk to them and were escorted to his office. Fergus had already given him a sketchy outline of what this was all about, so he got right to the point.

"I'm having Mrs. Vancleave admitted to the hospital. I understand that you were going to take her to the police station so she could confess to killing her husband, but right now her physical and mental health are more important than her legal difficulties. She needs treatment right away, and I can't allow her to be badgered by the police in her present condition.''

Fergus nodded. "I'd expected that she might have to be hospitalized, and I have no intention of allowing the police to 'badger' her. They can't even question her without your permission, but she seems to be overly burdened with guilt. She confessed to Ms. Sawyer and me voluntarily, but we don't know any of the details, because we haven't questioned her, either. I realized that I needed medical advice about her condition first.''

"You're very perceptive," the doctor said.

Fergus smiled. "Thanks, but it didn't take much perception to see that she's close to the breaking point both physically and emotionally. That's why I'd like for you to give permission for a police officer to come to the hospital as soon as she gets settled in and take her statement. I'm sure she'll feel better once she gets that off her mind, and I'll be right there all the time to see to it that she's not hassled. You're welcome to sit in, too, or appoint a medical representative to do it.''

Dr. Hardy hesitated for a few moments before answering. "I guess we can give it a try, but I definitely do want to be there, and I'll need your word that I can stop the proceedings if she seems to be getting too upset.''

"Of course," Fergus agreed.

Sharon and Fergus took Helen to the hospital and stayed with her while she was being admitted. They explained to her the arrangement they'd made with the doctor for the police to interview her later when she was rested, and she assented to it.

After that Fergus took Sharon home, then went to the police station to make his report and set up an appointment for an officer to meet them at the hospital to take Helen's statement later in the evening when the doctor would be free to be there. Sharon wanted to go to the station with him, but he refused.

"This is strictly legal business," he said, "and you'd just be in the way. Now, please don't argue. I'll be back in time to take you to dinner, and afterward we'll go to the hospital together. Meanwhile, why don't you try to reach Ray and let him know what's going on?"

Sharon and Fergus had dinner at a restaurant in one of the renovated hundred-year-old warehouses facing the cobblestone streets at Maclede's Landing in the old section of downtown, and afterward they returned to the hospital. They arrived a few minutes before the appointed time and found homicide detective Zurcher already there, waiting in the small lounge on Helen's floor. They were joined a short time later by Dr. Hardy, and after a little preliminary planning they all walked down the hall to Helen Vancleave's room.

Dr. Hardy went in first to check her vital signs and reassure her, then he opened the door and motioned the rest of them to come in. Helen was reclining on the bed and had an IV in her arm. Her red raw hands had been medicated and were protected by loose-fitting cotton gloves, but she'd been cleaned up and looked considerably better than she had earlier.

After they'd all greeted her, Lieutenant Zurcher took a small object from his pocket and approached the side of the bed. "Mrs. Vancleave, I understand there's something you want to tell me," he said softly.

Helen nodded, but didn't speak.

"I have a tape recorder here," he continued, showing her the device. "Do you mind if I tape our conversation?"

Her eyes widened. "No, I don't mind," she said in a frightened whisper.

He turned the recorder on and spoke briefly into it, noting time, place and people present, then looked again at

Helen. "Don't be afraid, Mrs. Vancleave. You don't have to say anything you don't want to. But what you do say will be recorded and may be used against you. Do you understand?"

She looked even more frightened, and the doctor moved closer and put his fingers on the pulse at her wrist.

"Yes, I understand," she said shakily, "but I want to tell you anyway." Taking a deep breath she plunged ahead. "I killed my husband, Floyd."

"How?"

She swallowed. "I . . . I stabbed him with a letter opener and he died."

"Can you tell me why you did that?"

"He . . . He was mad and he was going to hit me again."

"How do you know he was going to hit you?"

Her face crinkled up as if she were going to cry, but she didn't. "He raised his arm and I saw his fist. I knew he was going to swing."

"Had he ever hit you with his fist before?"

She cringed. "Oh yes. With his open hand, too."

"Did you report those attacks to the police?"

She shook her head sadly. "No, he always said he was sorry, and I didn't want anyone to know. Our next-door neighbor reported him a couple of times, but I told the officers I'd fallen."

The lieutenant grunted, but made no comment. "Can you tell me in your own words just what happened? Start with why you went to your husband's office."

Helen leaned her head back against the pillow and closed her eyes. She looked like a emaciated old woman, but Sharon knew she was under fifty.

"I'd been to a meeting of the deaconesses at my church that morning," she began, "so when it was over I decided to drive on downtown and have lunch with my husband. I always use the valet parking at the hotel, but that morning I spotted a space on the street, so I parked there. It was on the pool side of the hotel, so I went in that way. Floyd was alone in his office and opened the sliding-glass door to let me in.''

Sharon was elated. So that's why no one in the reception room had known Floyd's wife was there.

Helen paused and Zurcher spoke. "Did you put your hands on the outside of the glass door?"

"No, I don't think so," she said uncertainly. "I knocked with my fist, but Floyd slid it open from the inside."

Zurcher's gaze concentrated on her medicated hands. "What's wrong with them?" he asked.

The doctor answered for her. "She has a severe dermatitis, an allergic reaction to detergents, among other things."

"May I examine them?" the detective asked.

This time it was Fergus who spoke. "You don't have to allow that, Helen."

"I don't mind," she answered, and pulled awkwardly at the gloves.

"Let me do that," Dr. Hardy said, and carefully removed them.

Lieutenant Zurcher had her turn her hands several times for his inspection, but didn't touch them. "Were they like this the day you killed your husband?"

"Yes," she said. "Not this bad, but they were broken out and itchy."

"Were they bandaged?" Sharon held her breath with anticipation as she waited for an answer. She could see what the lieutenant was getting at. If Helen's hands had been bandaged it would explain why her fingerprints weren't on the murder weapon.

"No, but I was wearing gloves. My hands look so awful when they're broken out that I always keep them covered when I go anywhere."

Sharon let her breath out with a swoosh. It was all coming together. Helen's confession seemed to be airtight so far.

Zurcher nodded. "Sorry I interrupted you earlier. Now, please tell us what happened after you entered your husband's office."

She thought for a minute. "Floyd said he had some paperwork to finish before we went to lunch, so I went into his private bathroom to freshen up. I...I was in there when Ms. Sawyer—uh, Sharon—came storming into the office."

The bathroom! Of course. For some reason it had never occurred to Sharon that someone might have been in Floyd's private bathroom while she and he were quarreling. And the police were so sure she was the killer that they didn't investigate.

"She was awfully mad," Helen continued. "She...she accused him of...of sabotaging her promotion because she wouldn't sleep with him."

Helen's face had turned beet red and she stammered as she reminisced. "She was shouting, and he...he kept telling her to lower her voice. She...she told him she knew about...about the other women employees he'd prop-propositioned. She said she was going to get statements from them and file har-harassment charges against him—"

Her voice broke on a sob, and the doctor put the box of tissues from the night table on the bed beside her, within easy reach. "That's enough, Lieutenant," he said crisply.

"No! No, please," Helen protested through her tears. "I want to finish this now."

Dr. Hardy looked at her. "Are you sure? You don't have to do this until you're stronger."

"I'll be all right," she assured him. "I just want to get it over with." She wiped her wet face and blew her nose, then turned to look at Zurcher. "By then Floyd had lost control of his vicious temper and was yelling, too. He told Sharon to shut up and get out. That those women wouldn't tattle on him if they wanted to keep their jobs. He said he—" Again she broke off on a sob. "That he had plenty of willing women to choose from, and he sure as hell didn't need her.

He...he threatened to fire her if she stirred up trouble, and said he'd make sure she didn't get another job anywhere in the hotel industry.''

Helen stopped and took a deep breath. ''They shouted at each other some more, but I was too shocked and upset to catch what they said. I didn't know she'd left until I realized that the noise had stopped and there was nothing but silence.''

She closed her eyes once more, but it didn't stop the tears that ran unchecked down her pale, sunken cheeks. Sharon's own eyes filled as she absorbed some of the other woman's pain. She knew only too well what Helen was going through. Being accused falsely, as Sharon had been, was bad enough, but having to confess that you'd killed your philandering husband would be sheer hell.

Fergus, who was standing beside Sharon, reached out and took her hand. The gesture shattered her tenuous control, and she turned into his arms, buried her face in his shoulder and sobbed. He held her close and rubbed his cheek in her hair. ''Go ahead and cry, sweetheart,'' he murmured in her ear. ''You're entitled.''

Aloud he said, ''I think we'd better postpone the rest of Mrs. Vancleave's statement until tomorrow. She's been put through enough for one day.''

''I agree—'' the doctor began, but Helen cut him off.

''No, Mr. Lachlan. I really need to get this over with.'' She sounded exhausted, but determined. ''It won't take much longer. After Sharon left I confronted Floyd. He was furious, and was especially enraged that I'd stand up to him and dare to question his actions. I told him I was going to file for divorce.''

She stopped and shuddered. ''He looked at me with pure hatred and swung back his arm, his fist clenched to hit me. I was honestly afraid that he'd kill me, and I reached out for something to protect myself with. My hand closed on the letter opener that was lying on his desk, and I swung wildly with it. It plunged into his chest."

Another sob shook her. "I didn't want to kill him. I only wanted to keep him from beating me up again."

Dr. Hardy poured a glass of water and held it for Helen while she sipped it through a straw. "Don't put yourself through any more of this," he said softly. "If there's anything else they need to know they can question you later." He glared at Lieutenant Zurcher. *"Much later."*

She pushed the glass away. "There's just one more thing," she insisted. "Floyd didn't say anything, just looked stunned and stumbled against the desk. Then he fell and scattered things as he went down. I didn't know how badly he was hurt, but I panicked and ran out the way I'd come in, got to my car and drove home. When I got there I was violently sick." She sighed and relaxed against her pillow. "I guess you know the rest."

By the time Sharon and Fergus arrived home Sharon was exhausted. For the first time she fully understood what her grandmother had meant when she used to say, "I feel like I've been put through the wringer."

Sharon had seen pictures of those old-style washing machines with a contraption built on the side that ran clothes between two cylinders, one on top of the other, to wring out all the water from them. That's exactly the way she felt, as if she'd been wrung dry of all emotion.

This day had been a marathon of highs and lows. She knew she should be exuberant, and she was. The mystery of Floyd Vancleave's death had been cleared up and she'd been exonerated. Fergus assured her that getting the charges against her dropped was only a formality now that they had a confession from Floyd's wife that she'd been the culprit.

But "culprit" wasn't the word for Helen Vancleave. Actually, she was the victim and Floyd was the culprit. He'd been a mean, selfish egomaniac, with no redeeming qualities as far as Sharon could see. Helen had had a right to strike out in self-defense, and Sharon's heart bled for the poor, troubled woman.

Fergus seemed confident that the case would never go to trial, but Floyd had made Helen's life a hell for so long that she now seemed past caring what happened to her.

Anna arrived home a short time later and, after happily greeting Fergus, wanted to hear all about their visit with Mrs. Vancleave. Sharon was too drained to go through it all again and excused herself to go to bed, leaving Fergus to bring Anna up to date on the events of the day.

Sharon slept soundly all night, and woke up feeling rested and invigorated with the knowledge that she no longer had to dread the start of a new day, but could face it with anticipation and confidence.

Then she remembered that it was Sunday. Fergus would be leaving in a few hours to return to his home and his law practice in Chicago. And not just temporarily, as before.

He was no longer needed there to defend her, and Helen hadn't been arrested. At least not yet. But he'd already arranged for Ray Quinlan to be co-council and handle her defense—under Fergus's long-distance supervision, of course—if she should be.

No, this time when he left to return to Chicago he wouldn't be coming back!

Chapter Fourteen

Sharon dressed quickly in red shorts and a red-and-white striped pullover shirt. After brushing her teeth, splashing water on her face and adding a touch of lipstick, she ran a comb through her hair and tripped barefoot downstairs to the kitchen.

Fergus was sitting at the table with a cup of coffee and the newspaper. He lowered the paper when she entered the room and smiled up at her.

"Well, hello there," he said huskily as his gaze roamed over her, taking special notice of her full breasts, rounded hips and long, slender legs. "God, Sharon, you're even more desirable now than you were when we were—" He stopped abruptly and drew in his breath, then motioned to the chair beside him. "Sit down. Can I get you a cup of coffee?"

She felt both pleased and disappointed. Apparently he wasn't going to pursue his thoughts on the subject of her desirability, but why would he? She'd told him emphatically that she wasn't going to make love with him again.

How woefully naive she'd been at that time, when she was still sated by their stunning night of passion. Had she really been immature enough to believe that ignoring the attraction between them would make it go away? Why hadn't she realized it would be like trying to stop the tides? They reappeared on a regular basis whether you allowed them to or not.

She smiled back at him. "Good morning, thank you and don't bother to get up. I can pour my own coffee."

She took a mug from the cupboard and filled it. "Would you like a refill?" she said as she turned to look at him.

"No, thanks. Mine's nearly full," he answered.

She brought her cup and sat down in the chair he'd offered. "Is Anna still sleeping?"

"No, she left about an hour ago. She took the dog and drove down to spend the day with her parents in Arnold."

Sharon gazed past him out the window at the bright sunshine and cloudless sky. "Isn't it a beautiful day? You should have wakened me earlier. I haven't slept so soundly since I was arrested and charged with Floyd's murder."

"I'm glad you rested so well," Fergus said, "and I'm not masochistic enough to go into your bedroom while you're in bed asleep. When you've finished your breakfast we have to talk."

Her appetite disappeared along with her feeling of wellbeing. He was going to tell her he was returning to Chicago. That it was nice seeing her again, but now he had to get back to work, so goodbye and please try to stay out of trouble from now on.

"I . . . I'm ready anytime you are," she said, trying for a light tone and failing miserably.

He folded the paper and laid it aside. "Then let's take our coffee and go into the other room, where we can be more comfortable."

She agreed and followed him into the living room, where he headed for the sofa and she started toward a chair.

"No, sit here with me," he said, and patted the cushion beside him.

She knew that wasn't a good idea. Talk about desirable! That subject was definitely not one-sided. Fergus was wearing hip-hugging blue denim shorts that exposed his strong, muscular legs, and a snug-fitting, multicolored striped pullover shirt that outlined the equally powerful muscles in his chest. Just the sight of him made her mouth water!

No, sitting beside him wasn't a smart move, but it was an invitation she couldn't resist, and she obeyed. He reached over and cupped his palm around her bare knee.

"I'd better warn you, I'm going to do my damnedest to seduce you," he said huskily. "Please, give me a fighting chance and listen to what I have to say."

The muscles under his hand clenched and unclenched, and the coffee in her mug splashed back and forth as she fought to retain some semblance of resistance to his over-whelming nearness and appeal. This handsome Scotsman could charm the plaid out of her kilt! "Fergus, I—"

He squeezed her knee. "No, don't say anything until you've heard me out. There's a flight to Chicago later this afternoon and I'm going to be on it. I want you to come with me."

That wasn't what she'd expected him to say, and her coffee not only sloshed, but spilled a few drops on her thigh. She took a large swallow, then leaned forward and set the mug on the low table in front of them. In the process she managed to free her knee from Fergus's disturbing caress.

He didn't protest, but put his own mug down and sighed. "I love you, sweetheart, and I can't let you slip away from me again."

Her eyes widened and she opened her mouth, but he put a finger across it. "I'm not trying to seduce you for an afternoon, or a weekend, or even for a few months. I'm asking you to marry me, Sharon."

"We already did that!" The bitter words slipped out before she could stop them.

An expression of deep sadness settled over Fergus's face. "I know. What can I say? I'm sorry? I am, deeply so. I made a mistake? I did. I handled the situation badly, but I never wanted to lose you. I should have contested the divorce, but you were so insistent and I felt so guilty. I'd already hurt you so badly...."

He ran his fingers through his hair in a gesture of frustration. "How can I make you believe me?"

It was a cry of desperation that nearly broke Sharon's heart. If only...if only... But there were too many "if onlys" that weighed too heavily on her.

She turned to him, and this time she wouldn't be hushed. "I do believe you, Fergus," she said timidly, then hurried on when she saw both surprise and hope in his expression. "That is,.I believe you love me as much as you are capable of loving, but it always comes back to the same dilemma. How can I trust that love, when it wasn't strong enough before to keep you from being attracted to another woman?"

He winced, but she had to make him understand. "I know we've had this conversation many times lately, but it always comes back to that one insurmountable stumbling block.

"It's not that I don't love you—I do. It's not even that I can't forgive you. The problem is that I can no longer trust your love. I know pride is a lonely bedfellow, and I've certainly had enough experience with loneliness these past five years, but I just can't come to terms with being second best with you. I'd always know that you'd rather have Elaine—"

"Dammit to hell, Sharon, that's not true!" Fergus thundered. "I told you then and I'm telling you now, I never wanted our marriage to break up."

He stood and turned away from her. "In spite of my unwanted and unwelcome feelings for Elaine, I never wanted
a divorce. Elaine knew that. I told her so, and she was in the
process of moving to the West Coast, when you...when
you..."

"When I caught you together," Sharon said for him.

Fergus sighed wearily. "You didn't *catch us together*. I
was kissing her goodbye before taking her to the airport. I
was never unfaithful to you, I swear it."

"I believe you," Sharon said. "At least, I believe you
never slept with her, but you were unfaithful in your heart.
You were infatuated with her. And if you and I had stayed
together you'd always have wanted her. She's the one you
would have missed, the one you'd have wanted in your
bed—"

"Sharon!" His tone was a mixture of outrage and disbelief as he whirled around to face her. "My God, you don't
really know me at all, do you?"

She felt the hot flush of shame, but didn't know why. She
truly believed what she'd said, but she hadn't meant it as an
accusation of some unforgivable sin, just a regrettable fact
of human frailty that could happen to anybody under the
same circumstances.

"I... I'm sorry," she said, anxious to make him understand. "I didn't mean to imply that...that you'd deliberately be, well, lusting after her."

"Than just what in hell were you implying?" he demanded.

"I wasn't implying anything. I was just trying to explain
why I can't be content to be second best with you."

His expression softened, and he sat back down beside her
and rubbed his face with his hands. "You were never second best with me. Look, honey, let me try to explain to you
how I felt about Elaine. She and I came into the law firm at
about the same time. We were the same age, similar back-
grounds, and both brand-new law school graduates and

members of the bar. We worked well together and after a while we started dating.''

He cleared his throat. ''We had a lot in common, and enjoyed each other's company. There was no formal commitment. It was a comfortable arrangement, but I suppose you could say we were drifting toward marriage.''

Sharon blinked. He'd never told her he'd been involved with Elaine before they met. In fact, he'd never discussed any of the women in his past. That wasn't his style. He was a very private person.

He turned to look at her. ''Then I met you.''

He paused as though trying to gather his thoughts. ''You caught me off guard and changed the whole course of my life. You were so cute, and so sexy, and so... so persistent.''

Sharon felt the warm blush and lowered her head. ''I know I chased after you shamelessly—''

He put his hand under her chin and lifted her face. ''No, don't apologize,'' he said softly. ''You were a delight. I was perilously close to becoming a pompous ass, taking myself too seriously and forgetting how to just enjoy life. You changed all that. You made me laugh, and eventually you made me cry, but the emotions you aroused in me were strong and sharp. They forced me to feel joy in just being alive and in control of my destiny.''

He ran his fingers through her hair. ''The only reason you had to chase me instead of the other way around was because I was so conscious of the ten years' difference in our ages. You were so very young and carefree, and we had almost nothing in common.''

He dropped his hand and turned to face forward again. ''It seems I was right to worry about that. It's what finally came between us,'' he said sadly.

Sharon was startled. ''Don't blame that on the age difference,'' she snapped. ''You just discovered after it was too late that it was Elaine you wanted instead of me.''

"I know you've always believed that, but it's not true. From the first time we met until now I've never stopped wanting you, but living together wasn't easy for either of us. I was totally immersed in my law practice, and the subject bored you."

She opened her mouth to object, but he stopped her. "Your main interests were rock bands and the college activities you were involved in. I'd outgrown that sort of thing years before. Mostly we spent our time quarreling and making love."

She scowled at him. "I thought you enjoyed making love with me. You were the one who usually initiated it."

"Damn right I did. All I had to do to get turned on was come home and find you there. Even quarreling with you aroused me, but it takes more than just good sex to make a marriage. We didn't have anything to talk about once we got out of bed."

Sharon opened her mouth to protest, then closed it again when she realized he was right. She'd been in college most of the time they were married, and her interests had all been shallow ones: the football games, the rock concerts and the myriad of campus activities she was involved in.

She must have bored Fergus to death with all her inconsequential chatter, just as she'd been easily bored when he'd tried to discuss his problems and concerns with her.

She hung her head. "I'm sorry if I wasn't the kind of wife you wanted. You should have told me—"

"You *were* the wife I wanted," he interrupted, "but neither of us was perfect. We were too close to our problems to see them clearly. I started discussing my work with Elaine because she was interested and understood all the intricacies of the law. We were able to help each other, and we sort of got in the habit of having lunch together. That progressed to sometimes staying late at the office, or stopping off for a drink after work to talk. I swear I didn't realize how much I was depending on her until we were more emotion-ally involved than we should have been.''

Sharon's mind was in turmoil. If he'd been so dissatis-fied with their marriage, why hadn't he told her? Why hadn't he made her listen?

But on the other hand, why had she been so blind to his discontent? If he'd really been unhappy she should have known without being told.

"You lied to me on those nights when you said you had to work late," she said. "Didn't that bother you at all?"

He shook his head. "Not at first because we were dis-cussing our cases, but as time went on and our conversa-tions became more personal I knew you'd be angry. I knew I'd be mad as hell if you were doing the same thing with an-other man, so yes, I did lie about it, and it bothered the hell out of me. That's when I told Elaine we had to stop meet-ing."

He hesitated. "She confessed that she was in love with me, and the next day she applied for the position in Cali-fornia. There was never anything physical between us while I was married to you except a few kisses."

Sharon winced. The very thought of him kissing Elaine was agony. She understood more clearly now that she had been equally to blame for the breakup of her marriage, but she couldn't escape the certainty that he could have made her see the problem and change her ways if he'd really wanted to. She may have been immature back then, but she hadn't been stupid.

"I'm sorry, Fergus," she said reluctantly, "but it still boils down to the simple fact that you just didn't love me enough to fight for our happiness, to *cleave unto me, forsaking all others,* when we were married."

He shook his head and started to say something, but she continued on. "I no longer blamed you. You didn't go looking for another woman, but nevertheless it happened and I have no assurance that it wouldn't happen again if we got back together. I've never been much of a gambler, and this time the stakes are too high. I'd make us both miserable by always wondering if you were seeing another woman when you said you had to work late, or attend a weekend conference..."

Her voice broke, and she stood up before she could seek the comfort of his arms, his lips, his hands.

Fergus felt leaden with sorrow and disappointment. In his gut he'd known she wouldn't give him another chance. She was right, he had betrayed her trust, even though he hadn't meant to.

Still, in his heart he'd nursed the hope that he could somehow make her understand that she'd always been the most important person in his life. He'd said and done all he could to persuade her that his love for her was strong enough to last a lifetime and beyond.

He knew that to be true, but he'd failed miserably in his effort to convince her, and now all he could do was give up and try to learn to live without her. If she couldn't take him on faith then there was no hope for them.

He rose slowly, painfully, from the couch, like an old man burdened with the weight of years. Was this what life was going to be like for him from now on?

"I'm sorry, love," he murmured. "Sorrier than you can ever know. I'd hoped we could work something out, but I can see that I was wrong. I'll pack up my things, and then I have to go down to the police station. You can come with me if you'd like."

In spite of her total rejection of Fergus's proposal of marriage, Sharon felt a wave of disappointment at his nonresisting acceptance. She'd expected him to argue, try to change her mind, maybe even plead with her...

Quickly she wrenched her thoughts away from that quagmire. Dear Lord, was she still trying to punish Fergus? Or was she punishing herself? Was it possible that she was trying to wring an admission out of him that would allow her to go back to him and still keep her pride intact?

But what could he confess to that would do that? He wouldn't lie, not even to get something he badly wanted, and Sharon knew she wouldn't be the woman he wanted if she was playing brutal and deceptive games with his feelings for her.

Fergus's voice brought her out of her reverie. "Sharon? Do you want to go to police headquarters with me or not?"

She blinked and shoved her dismaying thoughts aside. "Yes, please. May I help you pack?"

Fergus and Sharon spent the rest of the morning and early afternoon straightening out the legal morass surrounding Sharon and Helen Vancleave. Fergus arranged to have the charges against Sharon dropped while at the same time delaying the filing of any against Helen.

"I'm hoping the police will agree that she was acting in self-defense and not indict her," he told Sharon. "Ray's not available today, but I'll be in touch with him by phone from Chicago. He's an excellent attorney. He'll know how to proceed."

When they arrived back home Fergus looked at his watch. "I'm going to have to hurry," he said as he unlocked the door and let them in. "I have to be at the airport early enough to turn in my rental car and pick up my ticket before flight time."

He headed toward the stairway, but Sharon stood immobilized. This was it. Fergus was leaving and this time he wasn't coming back! She'd probably never see him again.

Would he take her to the airport with him?

Probably not. He'd be busy checking in once he got there, and she'd just be a distraction.

Would he kiss her goodbye? That was doubtful. She hadn't given him any encouragement lately. He'd think she didn't want him to.

If he didn't initiate a kiss should she?

The very idea of it made her heart speed up and her stomach flutter, but the cold, accusing voice of her conscience nipped that tempting thought: *There's a name for women like you who tease their men but don't put out, and it's not a pretty one. If you don't want him to think that's what you're doing, then don't make any moves on him.*

She'd like to strangle the damned voice, but she knew it was right. If she wanted him in spite of her doubts and her stupid pride, then she'd better tell him so. She was well acquainted with his stubborn Scottish nature, and she knew he'd never again approach her about a reconciliation.

A noise on the stairs alerted her, and she looked up to see him coming down carrying a garment bag, a large suitcase and a briefcase. He'd also changed into navy slacks and a blue plaid sport coat and once again looked like the idealized picture of a successful young attorney, aloof and professional.

He set his luggage on the floor beside the door and turned to her. His face was an expressionless mask, but his eyes were dark with pain and regret.

"You have both my office and apartment addresses and phone numbers." His tone was impersonal, but his voice shook slightly. "Promise you'll call if you ever want or need me."

If I ever want or need him? She devoutly hoped she'd never want or need him any more than she did right now, but still she couldn't bring herself to tell him that. He'd fooled her so easily before. How could she trust him not to do it again?

"Fergus, I . . . I don't know how I can ever thank you—"

"Gratitude is not what I want from you, Sharon," he said tartly. "All I ask is that you keep in touch and let me know if you ever need anything. Will you promise me that?"

She swallowed the sobs rising in her throat and nodded. "Yes, I promise."

He moved closer and put his hands on her shoulders. "And will you kiss me goodbye?"

He couldn't have stopped her. She couldn't even stop herself as she nodded and clasped her arms around his neck.

He responded immediately by wrapping his arms around her waist and pulling her against him. Slowly he lowered his head to her upturned face and captured her mouth with his own. His lips were warm and his breath was sweet as she melted against him with a little cry of surrender.

His arms tightened, but he didn't try to deepen the kiss. Instead, he kept it sweet, tender and lingering, and it was more binding and deeply loving than unleashed passion at its most explosive.

So much so that when he finally raised his head she moaned and tried to recapture the magic of his mouth with her own, but he put her away from him, gently but firmly.

"Goodbye, my darling," he said huskily. "Have a happy and fulfilling life."

Before she could catch her breath and respond he was gone.

Chapter Fifteen

In Sharon's world the weeks dragged by. July became August and then September. St. Louis in midsummer was hot and muggy, but it really didn't matter, because all she did was go to work, come home, watch television and go to bed, all in the comfort of air conditioning.

She seldom went anyplace else, although other summers had been filled with fun on the river, going boating and water-skiing or on dinner cruises with compatible men she liked and dated.

Not this year, even though she'd been absolved of all charges in Floyd Vancleave's death.

So had Helen. The district attorney had ruled it a case of self-defense, and she was never charged. Fergus and Ray arranged for her to be admitted to a private psychiatric facility for treatment and therapy. Sharon went back to her position at the hotel, and both management and employees had welcomed her wholeheartedly.

Still she was miserable, although she managed to hide it from everyone except Anna. Her roommate tried to get her to seek counseling, but Sharon refused. She knew what was wrong with her. She also knew that she wouldn't be able to shake the melancholy that ravaged her until she came to terms with the cause of it—her ambivalent feelings about her ex-husband.

She tried not to think of Fergus, but he was never really out of her mind. The nights were the worst. That's when she had to face herself, take responsibility for her own decisions and admit that she had no one else to blame for the anguish she was going through.

She'd thought she was doing the right thing when she'd sent Fergus away without her. Surely nothing could be worse than living with him and always being afraid that someday he'd again meet another woman he wanted more than he wanted her.

But now, after ten weeks to the day, she was forced to admit that she'd been wrong. That life without him was worse now than it had been before he'd come back into her life. At least when she'd sent him away the first time she'd had a good reason: he'd admitted to being emotionally involved with another woman.

This time . . . this time was it just her stubborn pride that was keeping them apart?

Was she making a horrendous mistake? So what if he didn't love her as much as she loved him? Where was it written that love had to be weighed in equal measures? Was she really willing to spend the rest of her life alone and miserable without him, rather than settle for a little less than perfection?

And what had happened to forgiveness? He'd told her in every way he could how sorry he was for hurting her. She'd assured him that she'd forgiven him, but had she really? Wasn't she letting her wounded pride interfere with her good judgment?

One thing she knew for sure. Fergus hadn't set out to seduce Elaine, and if Sharon hadn't found out about it he would have sent her away and stayed with his wife.

Come to think of it, what more could she ask of him?

Ah, but that was the heart of the matter. She was asking for his deep, abiding, undivided love, all of it, as long as they both shall live. It was no more than she was willing to give him. Was it so unreasonable to expect the same commitment in return?

Maybe it was. Life wasn't always fair. No one was given a guarantee of happiness, and most people never got a second chance at it. Wasn't it better to grab it when it did come around and then work hard to make it last?

It took two more days of tortured indecision before Sharon finally came to the realization that she had no intention of living the rest of her years in quiet desperation. She'd never been much of a gambler, but neither was she a quitter.

She was going to embrace life and fight for a future filled with love and contentment, and that wouldn't be possible without Fergus Lachlan!

The only question now was, did he still want her? He hadn't contacted her again since leaving St. Louis, although she knew he'd been back once for a brief time to wrap up Helen's legal entanglements. Ray had told Sharon about it when he'd called to tell her that Helen wouldn't be charged for killing her husband.

Sharon grimaced as she wondered if Fergus was thoroughly disgusted with her by now. He wasn't the type to beg for anything, not even forgiveness. He'd acknowledged that their breakup was his fault, and he'd said he was sorry, but still she'd refused his proposal of marriage. She knew without doubt that the next move was up to her.

Had she been too unyielding? Had she waited too long? Had he become tired of banging his head against the stone wall of her abstinence and turned to someone else for warmth and love?

She hoped the answer to those questions was a resounding *no*, but she wasn't going to wait any longer to find out. She needed to go to him, talk to him face-to-face. But maybe he wasn't in Chicago right now. He was a nationally known attorney and much in demand. He defended people all over the country who were accused of crimes.

He'd spent a lot of time in St. Louis when he was defending her, and he traveled all over the country to represent other clients, as well. It made no sense to drive to Chicago to see him if he wasn't there. On the other hand, she didn't want to call and make an appointment. That was too cold and impersonal.

Then it occurred to her that she didn't have to talk to him if she called. His secretary would answer the phone. Sharon could ask her if Fergus was in town. Unfortunately it was Sunday, September 17, and the office would be closed, but she'd call the first thing in the morning.

That night Sharon slept peacefully and awoke feeling ready to fight if necessary for her second chance at happiness. It was too early to place her call before she left for work, but shortly after she arrived at the hotel she picked up her phone and dialed.

"Fergus Lachlan's office," said the voice at the other end. "How may I help you?"

"I'd like to know if Mr. Lachlan will be in his office late today or anytime tomorrow," Sharon answered.

"He'll be here part of both days, but he has no appointment times available until later this month. I can possibly schedule you then, if you'll give me your name and—"

Sharon hung up and went to the office of the front-desk manager, her immediate supervisor. The man who had been brought in from the Dallas Starlight to fill Floyd Vancleave's position, the one that should have been hers. She told him she had a family emergency in Chicago and asked for the rest of the week off starting the following day, Tuesday.

The leave was granted, and she spent the rest of Monday tying up all the loose ends she could before delegating her responsibilities to the woman who would be filling in for her. That evening she had her car serviced and packed a suitcase, and early the following morning she left for Chicago.

Autumn in Illinois was as colorful as spring had been, but for different reasons. The blossoms were now chrysanthemums and gladiolus in deep shades of gold, orange and lavender, and the leaves on the trees were turning to yellow and red.

As Sharon neared Chicago her stomach started doing flipflops. Flipping with excitement, flopping with trepidation. She'd lived all her life in this city, until the breakup of her marriage had shattered her illusions and broken her heart. Then she hadn't been able to get away fast enough. Away from Fergus and everything that reminded her of him.

Away from their mutual friends and the humiliation of knowing that they all knew she hadn't been loving enough, or pretty enough, or whatever it was she'd failed to have enough of, to keep him becoming attracted to another woman.

Now, after almost six long years she was going home, and her excitement mounted.

But going home to what? To memories that haunted her? To friends who had forgotten her? To a man who might not even want her anymore? It was the uncertainty of these questions that dampened her enthusiasm and caused her stomach to clench.

It was midafternoon when Sharon drove into the public parking lot nearest the building that housed the offices of Everingham, Jessup and Lachlan. The name of the firm had changed since she'd left town. Fergus had told her that Orrin Newberry had retired and he, Fergus, had been made a full partner.

At the thirtieth floor, high above the sprawling city, Sharon strode out of the elevator and down familiar hallways to the suite. At the door she paused to savor the thrill of seeing Fergus's name on it. During the time they were married that had been his ultimate goal, to see his name on the door in discreet gold letters that announced to all who saw it that he was a full partner in the old and prestigious firm.

When she stepped inside the thrill was replaced by misgivings. This was madness! What had she been thinking of just to appear and expect to see an attorney as well-known and respected, to say nothing of *busy,* as Fergus. The young blond receptionist sitting at her desk a few feet away, who was new since Sharon had last been there, would throw her out unless Sharon told her she was Fergus's ex-wife, and she didn't want to do that. The receptionist and most of the other junior employees would have known Elaine as Mrs. Lachlan, and Sharon didn't want to cause a commotion.

"May I help you?" the woman asked as she looked up.

Sharon managed a small smile in spite of the fact that her knees were shaking. "Yes, I'd like to see Mr. Lachlan, please."

"Your name?"

Sharon swallowed. "Sharon Sawyer."

The girl glanced at an open notebook. "Do you have an appointment, Ms. Sawyer?"

"Uh, no," she admitted, "but I'm sure he'll see me if you just tell him—"

"I'm sorry," the receptionist interrupted briskly, "but Mr. Lachlan is booked up for the next several weeks. Would you like to see his secretary and make an appointment?"

"But I... I'm from out of town. I've come all the way to Chicago to see him. If you'll just tell him I'm here..."

"I can't do that," the other woman insisted. "He's not in his office right now. If you'd like to leave your name and a number where you can be reached I'll tell him you asked to see him, but frankly, Ms. Sawyer, he's a very busy man and he seldom sees a new client without an appointment."

Obviously the receptionist didn't recognize her name as that of the client he'd so recently rescued from the horrors of prosecution.

"I'm not a new client," Sharon told her. "I'm the woman he defended a couple of months ago in St. Louis."

The receptionist looked taken aback. "Oh, I'm sorry. Is there a problem? If you had called ahead I could have tried to work you in, but—"

"No, there's no problem," Sharon assured her. "This is a personal visit."

The woman sighed. "I see." She sounded disgusted. "Then I suggest that if you have his home number you contact him there."

Sharon was rapidly losing her timidity. "Is that where he is?" she asked testily.

"The itinerary of our attorneys is confidential," the woman snapped. "I can't give you any information as to his whereabouts."

She turned her attention back to the papers on her desk, coolly conveying the message that this conversation was over.

Angrily Sharon turned and started toward the door, just as it opened and Fergus walked in. They collided in the middle of the room, and threw their arms around each other to balance themselves, hers at his neck and his at her waist.

They looked at each other, surprise in her expression, shock in his.

"Sharon! What are you doing here?"

His arms tightened around her, pulling her close against him.

"I . . . I came to see you, but you weren't here." That was a stupid remark, she silently berated herself. He could see that without her telling him.

"Well, I'm here now!" he exclaimed. "Come with me."

With one arm still around her he walked her past the desk where the receptionist sat looking both embarrassed and dismayed, then down the short hall and into a large, richly furnished office with a big picture window overlooking Lake Michigan.

"You have a new office," she said breathlessly, remembering the smaller, cell-like one he used to have.

He grinned. "Yeah, I took over Newberry's when he retired. Pretty impressive, huh?"

It was more than impressive. Luxurious would be a better description. For the first time Sharon realized that Fergus was a wealthy man. Not just comfortable, as they had been when they were married, but rich, as in having more money and property and even influence than he would ever need!

How could she have overlooked such an obvious fact? She knew lawyers made a lot of money, and Fergus was recognized as one of the top attorneys in the country. That should have clued her, but when he'd come back into her life she'd been so happy to see him, and so frightened and upset about the charges filed against her, that she hadn't even thought about his financial situation.

What was she getting herself into? Would he think she only wanted to come back to him because of his wealth? It would be such a natural conclusion to draw—

"Sharon, answer me!"

Fergus's raised voice broke into her thoughts, and she realized he'd been talking to her.

"What are you doing here? Why didn't you let me know you were coming? Is something the matter?"

She also noted that he no longer had his arm around her, but had released her and put some space between them. He looked and sounded worried and impatient.

"Oh no, nothing's the matter." she quickly assured him. "I just wanted to talk to you. But the receptionist says you're too busy—"

"I'm never too busy to talk to you," he snapped. "If you don't know that you should. What is it you want to talk about?"

Now she'd made him angry as well as taken up his valuable time. Couldn't she ever do anything right?

"Fergus, I'm sorry. I should have made an appointment—"

"Appointment, hell!" he grumbled. "You don't need an appointment to see me. All you need to do is tell me what you want. I'll give it to you."

"What will you give me, Fergus?" she asked softly.

With a groan he closed the space between them and again took her in his arms. "I'll give you anything you ask for," he said huskily, and rubbed his cheek in her hair.

"I want to go home with you?"

"Home?" He blinked with surprise. "You mean you want me to take you to my apartment?"

She nodded. "If that's where your home is."

Without another word he took her arm and led her out of the office. As they passed the reception desk he paused. "Cancel the rest of my appointments for today," he told the woman.

Her eyes widened. "All of them?"

"Yes, all of them," he answered as he ushered Sharon out.

It was only a short distance up Lake Shore Drive between the skyscraper that housed the firm and the one where Fergus lived. Sharon followed his car with her own, and in fifteen minutes they'd reached their destination.

Fergus unlocked his door and stood back to let her enter. One glance around convinced her that he must pay as much rent in a month as he'd earned in that amount of time when they were together. The living room was huge, and opened to include a dining area and a sunken recreation section that contained a giant-screen television, a book-lined wall, a state-of-the-art stereo system and a desk.

"I see you've moved up into the high-rent district," she said in an attempt at lightness that didn't come off. Her tone was filled with awe.

"I guess you could say that," he replied, "except that I don't rent, I own it. Can I fix you a drink?"

"I . . . I guess maybe you'd better," she stammered.

He walked over to the black leather bar that took up one corner. "White wine?"

As she absorbed the high-priced luxury of his living quarters her determination began to ebb. "I need something stronger this time. How about whiskey on the rocks?"

Fergus looked doubtful, but reached for a bottle of bourbon. He poured a generous amount into two crystal glasses and added ice, then carried them both over to the black leather sofa that backed up to the glass wall overlooking the lake.

Sharon followed him and stood looking out. "The view is magnificent!" she exclaimed breathlessly.

"Yes, it is," he agreed, and nodded toward the sofa. "Sit down."

She did, and only seconds before her knees would have buckled.

He handed her one of the glasses, then sat down beside her. "Now, if you've run out of excuses for not telling me, I'd like to know why you came all the way to Chicago to see me. You're not still being hassled by the police, are you?"

He sounded more annoyed than glad to see her. She never should have come. She'd suspected it would be a mistake, and apparently she'd been right.

"Nobody is hassling me," she assured him, and took a sip of her drink. It was smooth and didn't even burn when it went down. "It's just that I . . . I have something I want to talk to you about, and I didn't want to discuss it on the phone. I'm sorry that I've inconvenienced you."

Fergus took a healthy swallow of his whiskey, then set it on the coffee table and turned to her. "Honey, I'm the one who's sorry," he said contritely. "I don't mean to growl at you, but you shocked the bejesus out of me when I walked into the office and you practically fell into my arms. It was like an answer to an impossible dream, so just tell me why you're here and end the suspense."

She took another sip of her drink, then put it down, too. It was now or never, and no matter how painful and embarrassing it might be if he said he no longer wanted her, she had to try.

She took a deep breath and exhaled slowly. "First I need to ask you a question, and I want you to answer it truthfully. Don't try to spare my feelings or feel guilty if the answer is no."

He frowned and glared at her. "I always tell you the truth, Sharon. What is it you want to know?"

His green eyes bore into her blue ones, and she looked down, unwilling to let him see her fear and uncertainty. "Do you... that is, do you still want to marry me?"

She held her breath in the silence that followed. Why didn't he answer? Or at least breathe? She was looking at his chest, and there was no in-and-out movement.

Slowly her glance moved upward. The blood had drained from his face, and there was a tightness in his expression, as though the skin had been stretched over his cheekbones. Their gazes met again and his eyes were cold and expressionless.

"Are you playing games with me, Sharon?" When he spoke his tone was as cold as his eyes.

"Oh no," she moaned, and shook her head from side to side. "I've never played games with you, darling. I love you."

His expression didn't change. "I find that hard to believe."

She reached out and put her hand on his cheek. His skin even felt cold. "You shouldn't," she said gently. "I've always loved you. Right from that very first day when you gave that lecture on civil rights at the rally on campus at the university. I don't remember a word you said—I was too busy falling in love."

His expression softened. "You were just a kid. Still young enough to believe in love at first sight."

She stroked his cheek with her fingers. "I was nineteen," she reminded him. "Old enough to fall in love, but too young to be discreet about it. I pursued you shamelessly. That's where I made my first mistake."

He reached for her hand and kissed her palm. "Oh no, you weren't mistaken," he said huskily. "You lit my fire the first time you approached me. It was right after I'd finished that lecture. You were so beautiful and bouncy and filled with the sheer joy of living. You came up to me, introduced yourself and put out your hand."

He squeezed the hand he was holding and held it against his chest. "I took it and it was small and soft, but with a firm grip that tugged at my heart. At that moment something connected and sparked. Something I tried my damnedest to ignore, but then you asked if I'd have lunch with you. I looked into those deep blue eyes of yours and my resistance crumbled. I had an extremely important lunch date with a client that day, but I didn't even take the time to cancel it. I followed you into that cafeteria like an eager puppy itching to be petted."

She smiled. "And *were* you itching to be petted?"

He smiled back. "Damn right I was, and I still am. It's an itch only you can scratch, and it never goes away."

Sharon relaxed somewhat and slowly moved her hand caressingly over his chest. Maybe he did still want to marry her again after all. It was time to quit stalling and find out.

She leaned toward him and he took her in his arms and cuddled her against him. He was wearing a gray suit with a white dress shirt and a conservative blue patterned tie. The jacket was scratchy against her cheek and she unbuttoned it.

"Wouldn't you like to take off some of these clothes and get comfortable?" Her voice sounded shaky.

He tightened his arms around her. "How many clothes do you want me to take off?" he asked, and he sounded shaky, too.

"As . . . as many as it takes," she said.

He put her away from him, then removed his jacket and loosened his tie before reaching for her again. "Will that do?"

She snuggled close and liked the feel of his crisply ironed shirt against her skin. "For now," she said, and raised her hand to finger his buttons.

She could feel his heart thumping and his rib cage rising and falling rapidly. Her own heart and ribs were doing the same thing, and she had to concentrate to unfasten the tiny buttons on his shirt. When it was open halfway down he caught her hand in his.

"Why are you doing this, Sharon?" he said gruffly.

She looked up at him, puzzled. He sounded as if he didn't like it. "I want to make love with you," she answered simply.

"Why?"

She blinked, and a cold dread enveloped her. He'd never objected before when she'd started to seduce him. "What do you mean, why?" It was more of a squeak than a question.

"I mean why do you want to make love with me? You were the one who insisted that having sex again would just be frustrating and upsetting, since there was no chance of a permanent relationship between us. Do you get your kicks out of tormenting me? Are you just trying to find out if you can still arouse me? If so, I'll show you."

He moved her hand from his chest to his crotch, then held it there. He was swollen and hard.

Shocked by his accusation, she pulled away from him and stood up. "I'm sorry," she said. "I've never proposed marriage to a man before. I'm so afraid you'll say no, that you don't want me anymore. Oh damn, I'm making such a mess of it—"

Fergus jumped up and caught her by the arm. He looked stunned. "You came here to ask me to marry you?"

Sharon nodded. "Yes. I knew you wouldn't ask me again, and I couldn't face all the rest of my life without you, but I . . . I'm afraid I've waited too long."

He caught her other arm and turned her to face him. "Why do you want to marry me now, Sharon? You were most emphatic about turning me down when I left St. Louis."

"I was an idiot." She could taste the bitterness of her words. "I was looking for perfection in an imperfect world. I've been holding you up to an impossible standard—"

"No, that's not true," he insisted. "I'm the one who was flawed. You had every right to expect me to be faithful to our vows."

"But you were faithful, weren't you?" Had he lied to her after all?

"Physically, yes, but I did get emotionally involved with Elaine, although I never stopped loving you."

Relief washed over her. "I know you didn't," she said, and she did know. "I think I'm also beginning to understand your feelings for Elaine. It was an unfortunate situation, but we all could have handled it better. The best thing we can do now is leave it behind and get on with our lives, and I'd like the rest of my life to be spent with you." She paused and looked away. "That is, if you're willing."

"Willing?" he said huskily, and put his arms around her. "Willing doesn't even began to cover it. I love you—I need you—I want you for my wife, the mother of my children."

Sharon felt light-headed with pure joy as she flung her arms around his neck and buried her face in his shoulder. "Oh, sweetheart, I was so afraid I'd lost you."

He pulled her closer and nuzzled her neck. "I never stopped loving you, my darling, and I never will. I hope someday you'll be able to believe that, but—"

"I do believe it," she assured him as she stroked his nape, "and that's all that's important. We can't dwell on the past—we've got a future to build." She rubbed her groin into his and they both shivered with desire. "You said something about babies?"

His hands on her buttocks held her intimately against him. "Yes, I did," he murmured, "but only if it's what you want, too."

"You know it is," she said shakily. "I told you so, and since we're not either one of us getting any younger, could I interest you in getting started on that project?"

He raised his head and looked at her. "Right now?"

She smiled and kissed him. "I'm ready if you are."

With a big grin, he swept her up into his arms and started across the room. "I've been ready ever since I walked into the office and bumped into you."

She giggled. "Are you bragging or complaining?"

"Just telling it like it is," he said, and walked through an open doorway into a big, luxurious bedroom.

He lowered her to the bed and followed to lay partially on top of her. Capturing her mouth with his own, he inched his hand up her thigh under the full skirt of her dress, sending tiny shock waves to the target he was aiming for.

She writhed and clutched at his back as his fingers brushed back and forth across the crotch of her panties and his tongue explored her mouth. "You're wet and ready, too," he whispered contentedly.

"You sound surprised," she murmured as her tongue played with his ear. "You shouldn't be. I never could resist you."

His fingers probed under the narrow strip of material, eliciting a moan of pure ecstasy from deep in her throat. "Then we'd better get rid of some of these clothes," he said, and rolled off her.

She turned on her side and finished unbuttoning his shirt while he nearly sent her into orbit by caressing her bare thigh and buttocks. She was glad that her legs were tanned and smooth enough that she hadn't felt the need to wear panty hose.

When she finished with his shirt she unbuckled his belt and unbuttoned the waistband of his trousers. Now he was the one doing the writhing, as she skimmed her hand over the bulge beneath his fly, then pulled down the zipper.

She reached for him again, but he clutched her hand and held it as he sat up. "Enough, you little devil," he groaned as he stood and started to remove his clothes. "My self-control with you isn't as strong as it used to be."

"It never was very strong," she said with a grin as she, also, stood and undressed herself.

They flung articles of clothing aimlessly and left them where they fell as they crawled back into bed. Unable to tolerate more foreplay, they joined their bodies in the rapture of a profound and enduring love, earthshaking in its intensity and infinite in its durability.

When it was over and they lay entwined in each other's arms, Sharon silently vowed that never again would anything shake her faith in the depth of Fergus's love for her. He'd demonstrated that love in so many ways, and she finally understood what he'd been trying to tell her.

All people were flawed and capable of hurting those they loved most, but the ones who were truly blessed could forgive, and then forget the transgression and work toward a better life.

* * * * *

Silhouette®

SPECIAL EDITION™

COMING NEXT MONTH

#961 RILEY'S SLEEPING BEAUTY—Sherryl Woods
That Special Woman!
Abby Dennison's last adventure before settling down had landed
her in trouble that was seemingly inescapable. Only Riley Walker
could call her back from a terrible fate—but would his love be
enough to save her?

#962 A FATHER'S WISH—Christine Flynn
Man, Woman and Child
When she had Alexander Burke's baby, Kelly Shaw gave it
up for adoption, thinking he didn't want her or the child. Now
she was back in his life, and old flames had begun to ignite
once again....

#963 BROODING ANGEL—Marie Ferrarella
Blue blood had met blue collar when Mary Elizabeth Clancy and
"Mitch" Mitchell loved and lost years ago. Now a tragic twist of
fate had brought them together, and only Mitch's determination
could prevent them from losing each other again.

#964 CHILD OF HER HEART—Arlene James
Gail Terry had finally found the daughter she'd thought lost to
her. She never expected to fall for the child's guardian, rancher
Rand Hartesite, whose sexy charm—and dad potential—were
hard to resist.

#965 THE GIRL NEXT DOOR—Trisha Alexander
Simon Christopher was Jenny Randall's best pal—but her secret
feelings for him had long ago gone beyond friendship. Now
opportunity knocked at Jenny's door—along with Simon, who
suddenly realized that just being friends could never be enough!

#966 A FAMILY FOR RONNIE—Julie Caille
Forced to share guardianship of her nephew with old flame
Luke Garrick didn't make things easier for Alicia Brant.
Especially when both wanted sole custody—and both still
desperately felt the love they'd once had....

Silhouette celebrates motherhood in May with...

Debbie Macomber
Jill Marie Landis
Gina Ferris Wilkins

in

Three Mothers & a Cradle

Join three award-winning authors in this
beautiful collection you'll treasure forever.
The same antique, hand-crafted cradle
connects these three heartwarming romances,
which celebrate the joys and excitement of
motherhood. Makes the perfect gift for yourself
or a loved one!

A special celebration of love,

Only from

V *Silhouette*®
™

—where passion lives.

ANNOUNCING THE

FLYAWAY VACATION SWEEPSTAKES!

This month's destination:

Beautiful SAN FRANCISCO!

This month, as a special surprise, we're offering an exciting FREE VACATION!

Think how much fun it would be to visit San Francisco "on us"! You could ride cable cars, visit Chinatown, see the Golden Gate Bridge and dine in some of the finest restaurants in America!

The facing page contains two Entry Coupons (as does every book you received this shipment). Complete and return *all* the entry coupons; **the more times you enter, the better your chances of winning!**

Then keep your fingers crossed, because you'll find out by June 15, 1995 if you're the winner! If you are, here's what you'll get:

- Round-trip airfare for two to beautiful San Francisco!
- 4 days/3 nights at a first-class hotel!
- $500.00 pocket money for meals and sightseeing!

Remember: The more times you enter, the better your chances of winning!*

*NO PURCHASE OR OBLIGATION TO CONTINUE BEING A SUBSCRIBER NECESSARY TO ENTER. SEE REVERSE SIDE OR ANY ENTRY COUPON FOR ALTERNATIVE MEANS OF ENTRY.

VSF KAL